D0555217

A CHANGE OF HEART

Will Ridd stood in profile at the foot of the bed, facing away from the doorway. Ursula watched as he drew off his coat, and then untied his cravat. Her eyes widened as he tugged a clean shirt over his head. The upward motion caused the sloping muscles of his arms to flex dramatically, while his sleek ribcape swelled and the rippling planes of his abdomen tightened.

Ursula nearly groaned aloud at the sight, yearning suddenly for the lost, early intimacies of her long-dead marriage. She was not proof against this potent reminder of what it had once felt like to caress a man's warm, lean body. She craved that heat now, like a traveler seeking refuge from an ice storm. But certainly not from this man, this bailiff . . . even if his physical beauty was more than mortal woman should have to bear. . . .

SIGNET

REGENCY ROMANCE

COMING IN SEPTEMBER

Cupid's Choice
by Gayle Buck
Guineveve's mother plans to have her daughter married off soon—with or without love. But shy Guin fears she's doomed, until while at a dance she meets Sir Frederick, who is determined to draw her out of her shell—and into his arms...

0-451-20694-0

Lord Nick's Folly
by Emily Hendrickson
Fate forced Nympha to share a coach with Lord Nicholas, the most irritating man in England. But *nothing* could force her to love him.

0-451-20696-7

A Scandalous Journey
by Susannah Carleton
Few people know that George Winterbrook is a hopeless romantic who will only marry for love. His plans are thwarted when a crazy widow kidnaps him, but fate sends him a breathtaking savior...

0-451-20712-2

To order call: 1-800-788-6262

The Discarded Duke

Nancy Butler

A SIGNET BOOK

SIGNET
Published by New American Library, a division of
Penguin Putnam Inc., 375 Hudson Street,
New York, New York 10014, U.S.A.
Penguin Books Ltd, 80 Strand,
London WC2R 0RL, England
Penguin Books Australia Ltd, Ringwood,
Victoria, Australia
Penguin Books Canada Ltd, 10 Alcorn Avenue,
Toronto, Ontario, Canada M4V 3B2
Penguin Books (N.Z.) Ltd, 182–190 Wairau Road,
Auckland 10, New Zealand

Penguin Books Ltd, Registered Offices:
Harmondsworth, Middlesex, England

First published by Signet, an imprint of New American Library,
a division of Penguin Putnam Inc.

First Printing, August 2002
10 9 8 7 6 5 4 3 2 1

Copyright © Nancy Hajeski, 2002
All rights reserved

REGISTERED TRADEMARK—MARCA REGISTRADA

Printed in the United States of America

Without limiting the rights under copyright reserved above, no part of this
publication may be reproduced, stored in or introduced into a retrieval
system, or transmitted, in any form, or by any means (electronic, mechanical,
photocopying, recording, or otherwise), without the prior written
permission of both the copyright owner and the above publisher of this book.

PUBLISHER'S NOTE
This is a work of fiction. Names, characters, places, and incidents either are
the product of the author's imagination or are used fictitiously, and any
resemblance to actual persons, living or dead, business establishments, events,
or locales is entirely coincidental.

BOOKS ARE AVAILABLE AT QUANTITY DISCOUNTS WHEN USED TO PROMOTE
PRODUCTS OR SERVICES. FOR INFORMATION PLEASE WRITE TO PREMIUM
MARKETING DIVISION, PENGUIN PUTNAM INC., 375 HUDSON STREET, NEW YORK,
NEW YORK 10014.

If you purchased this book without a cover you should be aware that this
book is stolen property. It was reported as "unsold and destroyed" to
the publisher and neither the author nor the publisher has received any
payment for this "stripped book."

Dedicated to my nephews, Benjamin and Jonathan—brothers and friends

Most mighty duke,
behold a man much wrong'd.

—Shakespeare
The Comedy of Errors

And did those feet in ancient time
Walk upon England's mountains green?
And was the holy Lamb of God
On England's pleasant pastures seen?

And did the Countenance Divine
Shine forth upon our clouded hills?
And was Jerusalem builded here
Among these dark Satanic mills?

Bring me my bow of burning gold:
Bring me my arrows of desire:
Bring me my spear: O clouds unfold!
Bring me my chariot of fire.

I will not cease from mental fight,
Nor shall my sword sleep in my hand
Till we have built Jerusalem
In England's green and pleasant land.

—William Blake
Jerusalem

Chapter One

*W*illiam Ridd sat on an outcropping of rock and sur-
veyed his kingdom. His subjects were peaceful this
morning, grazing on the moor grass in small, relaxed hud-
dles. Unlike other men, Will did not count sheep at night;
he counted them by daylight. Each new addition to his
flock was a blessing, and this spring had brought forth a
bounty of lambs.

A black-and-white dog crouched beside him, eyes alert
as he too watched the sheep. He whined fretfully as a lone
ewe wandered off from one group to nibble the weedy
tidbits that grew along the hedgerow. Will smoothed one
hand over his companion's head. "Whist, lad. She'll come
to no harm."

The dog was young, less than a year old, but the need
to keep order among the flock was bred into him; it ran
through blood and bone and obsessed the small but canny
brain that lay between his silky ears.

Having settled the dog, Will leaned back on his elbows,
relishing the warmth of the April sun on his face and his
bared forearms. His skin was tanned but not yet weathered,
save for a few graceful lines beside his wide-set eyes. The
slight breeze feathered his hair, which showed sparks of
gold among the sun-bleached strands that drifted above
his forehead.

It was just past sunrise and his work day had not yet
begun. He often allowed himself these morning interludes,
carrying his breakfast out to the fields that ranged below
his cottage. He reckoned a man could face whatever the
day might bring with tolerable humor if he began it with a
few moments of solitude in the open air. It was as close to a
religion as William Ridd professed, and it served him well.

He'd especially needed his interlude this morning. The

dreams had come again last night, plucking him from sleep
just as the first probing fingers of dawn lit the eastern sky.
It had been months since they'd troubled him, and with
each day that passed, he'd hoped they were gone for good.

He raised his head and breathed in a deep draught of
air. The rich elixir, a combination of moor grass, wildflowers, sea salt and the pungent, woolly odor of sheep, eased
his thoughts and sent the phantoms of last night fleeing
away. The darkness was all behind him, he reminded himself; it had been banished for going on fifteen years. Last
night's gut-clenching, sheet-tangling dreams now seemed as
insubstantial as the white billow of clouds that drifted
above his rocky perch.

He absently stroked the dog while he pondered what
might have caused the dreams to resurface. What could
disturb his tidy, orderly existence? The scene around him
appeared so timeless, so immune to change. But as he
watched the butcher's cart from the village make its way
along the narrow farm track toward the big house, he recalled that another vehicle would be driving up that lane
later today. The master was returning to the estate for the
first time in many years. As much as Will liked to think of
the farm as his personal domain, it belonged by law to the
Duke of Ardsley—a man he'd never met.

Perhaps that was where his wretched dreams had sprung
from. Change was on the wind, blowing in like a storm
from the Bristol Channel. Not all storms were destructive,
he knew; some came in softly, brought gentle rain and
cleared away the heat of summer. But others keened and
bellowed, pelting the leaves from the trees and flattening
the crops, leaving disaster in their wake.

Will was not one to borrow worry beforetime. By night-
fall, he would have met the duke and taken his measure.

Ursula Roarke had chosen to wear white. It was not a
practical color for a coach journey, but she'd been hoping
to dazzle the Duke of Ardsley. Ursula knew the white cambric of her carriage gown brought out coppery undertones
in her brown hair and made her pale complexion appear
almost ethereal. "Queen Mab, loveliest of all the fairies,"
Barbara Falkirk had called her that morning as she'd
helped Ursula dress in her room at the Bishop's Chair Inn.

Her strategy had worked. His Grace had barely taken his eyes off her since he'd handed her into his coach. He sat across from her now, pointing out sights of interest in his low, cultured voice as they made their way out of Minehead. Barbara, as befitted a proper companion, sat beside Ursula with her head bent over her knitting. Whenever the duke's conversation lapsed, however, Ursula saw the twist of amusement on her friend's prim mouth and could almost hear her thinking, "You've quite bewitched him, pet."

Blessed saints, she hoped that was the case.

Their meeting the previous winter had been pure happenstance. Ursula, only recently out of her widow's blacks, had chosen to reenter Dublin society at a Christmas party given by her friend, Lady Whitley. Ursula had just cleared the threshold of the Whitley ballroom when Estelle came bearing down on her, brimming with the news that the Duke of Ardsley had made an unexpected appearance.

"Whitley met him on the ship coming over from Liverpool," she announced breathlessly, "and mentioned our party in passing. Pity Whitley didn't mention to *me* in passing that His Grace might attend. Imagine my shock when Ardsley was announced. Husbands are such a trial, Sully."

Lady Whitley looked stricken for an instant—it was hardly a politic thing to say to a friend who'd lost her spouse a twelvemonth earlier.

Ursula patted her hand reassuringly. "That's certainly a social coup."

"Not to mention, he's practically an Adonis. You know there are barely a half-dozen dukes about in the *ton,* and most of them are in their dotage. Ardsley can't be above thirty. I don't recall exactly—you know I am hopeless with my Debrett's. I do recollect there was a great tragedy in the family years ago . . . the first son died of some hideous ailment. But Ardsley looks healthy enough." Estelle shot her a wicked look, then whispered, "Ah, here he comes now. You can form your own opinion."

Ursula watched from behind her fan as the duke approached them. He was above middle height and slender—in form and stature not unlike Roary, except that her late husband had been Gypsy dark and this man was fair. His light brown hair was combed back from a high forehead; it waved a bit where it brushed his collar.

He bowed graciously as Estelle introduced them, and Ursula at once saw the dawning interest in his amber eyes. Nine years earlier she'd been a toast in London, and she hadn't forgotten how to read that look. Her breathing hitched for an instant as she experienced a fleeting intuition that this meeting had been preordained. Her rational mind immediately dismissed the notion. Still, she knew what she'd felt, the room going a little fuzzy. A person couldn't live in Ireland for nearly a decade without absorbing some of the national mania for portents and signs.

Her instincts insisted that this meeting with Ardsley would alter her life for the better. And a very good thing, too, since she was not only widowed but also frighteningly in debt. Her chief remaining asset, her husband's bloodstock, was soon to fall under the auctioneer's hammer. Furthermore, the farm itself was entailed to Roary's cousin—who'd given Ursula notice that she must vacate by the spring.

Roary always said that Fate favored the bold, and so Ursula determined, even before a word had passed between them, that she was going to marry the Duke of Ardsley. The gentleman, unaware that his future had been settled without so much as a by-your-leave, played neatly into her hands by inquiring if she was the present owner of the famous Roarke Stud. It turned out he had a keen interest in race horses and had recently decided to set up his own breeding stable.

Estelle discreetly faded away with a satisfied smile as Ursula and the duke launched into an animated discussion of bloodlines. By the end of the evening, the duke had not only danced with her twice, he had also agreed to visit the Stud.

His intended three-day stay at her home had lengthened to a week, and when he left for England at last—his ailing grandmother required his attendance—it was with apparent regret. She'd been dancing on air until Barbara reminded her that the man had been as enamored of her bloodstock as he'd been of her.

"He wants your horses," Barbara observed tartly. "Don't know if he's angling for a wife."

The truth of this was borne out when she received a letter from Ardsley's man of business offering to buy her stallion and broodmares. She was blue-deviled for days that Ardsley had not himself written; she'd come to enjoy his company and had thought the sentiment returned. Although it was hard to tell; he was so high-bred that he rarely unbent, even in private. The only time he'd touched her during his stay had been to take her hand at parting. Not at all satisfactory.

She'd hoped to spend enough time with him to cement his interest, but then the grandmother had intervened. What she needed was to be in company with him again. A trip to London was the obvious answer, but it was far beyond her means. She doubted he could be lured back to Ireland; he'd seen the horses and made his decision. Still, there had to be a way.

It eventually occurred to her that if the horses had brought them together once, why couldn't they do so again? She penned a carefully worded response to the duke's man in London, agreeing to the sale, but with a few stipulations.

"These are Irish horses," she wrote, "bred in a climate of sea mist and warm sunlight. They are accustomed to rolling hills and lush grass. I also need an assurance that they will be in the care of an experienced stud manager—someone conversant with the needs of blooded horses. Although I realize it is not my place to insist, I would *prefer* that these considerations be met. The horses of the Roarke Stud were my late husband's greatest joy, and I would not part with them lightly or indiscriminately. And to this end, I ask that I be allowed to view their prospective home."

To her delight, Ardsley himself wrote back, saying he fully understood her concern. He had a small property in Devon, he told her, that perfectly fit her requirements. Furthermore, he would show her around the place himself during the coming spring.

Ursula was elated. For one thing, Roary's creditors had begun closing in, like wolves around a distressed lamb. If they thought she'd won the notice of a duke, however, it might buy her time. She'd scrimped and saved during the rest of the winter in order to afford a few new gowns. It was vital that she play the part of a prosperous widow, one who could meet Ardsley on his own terms. She'd led him to believe she was selling her bloodstock because the stud was too much for a woman to handle—even though she'd been managing it very nicely for close to eight years.

Barbara sniffed at her optimism. "Even a rich duke wants a woman with a dowry. It's the way of the world."

"I had a dowry once," Ursula reminded her forlornly.

She didn't have to add that Roary had gambled it away, as well as most of his private fortune. Barbara knew all of Roary's vices, and she knew, as well, how Ursula had fought to keep him from selling off the breeding stock—their only remaining source of income. And all so he could continue to sit night after night in some cursed gaming hell and lose at cards and dice and at any foolish wager that came his way.

Sir Connor Roarke had raised losing to the level of high art.

She now shifted on the padded seat and stole a glance at her host. Enough of bemoaning the past. Her future sat across from her, his boot-clad legs crossed at the ankle, his caped driving coat falling in graceful folds around him. He was handsome and wealthy, capable of intelligent conversation, and she suspected he was kind-natured.

Roary had been a kind man, in spite of his one besetting sin. He was generous with his blunt during the rare times he was flush and generous with his talents—schooling a neighbor's green colt or teaching the intricacies of fly casting to the squire's son—when he was pockets to let. She had few requirements of men in general, but it occurred to her now that she would always put a premium on kindness.

"You've gone rather quiet," Ardsley said gently. "I hope the trip from Ireland didn't tire you overmuch."

"It was an easy crossing. For us, at least." She grimaced slightly. "I am not so sure about Imperator."

Ardsley shifted to peer out the window. Beside the vehicle rode a groom leading a blood bay stallion. The bay capered beside the staid cob, his coat gleaming, his nostrils flared and showing a touch of scarlet. The duke's eyes lit up, and he sighed like Romeo beholding Juliet by moonlight. "He looks in fine fettle to me. I'd forgotten what a splendid creature he is."

"That is not exactly what the sailors were thinking while they were trying to load him on the ship. Spawn of Satan is probably more like it."

"Still, I'm very pleased that you brought him along. There is, of course, a small stable at Myrmion for the work horses. And I've had a few hacks sent over from the local livery in Stratton. I knew you'd want to ride out and examine the property."

"I've never been to Devon, though I have seen the moors in Yorkshire."

His Grace shook his head. "No comparison. Exmoor is sweeping and green . . . the grass grows over the cliffs like a carpet, right down to the Bristol Channel."

"Is Myrmion a derivation of the word moor?"

"No one knows what it means. The estate was part of my paternal grandmother's dowry, been in her family for centuries. We used to summer there when I was a boy."

He stopped abruptly, or at least that was her impression. Something in his face was now shuttered. She immediately took up the conversational flow. "I used to summer with an aunt in Ireland, in Kerry. It was so different from home."

"I recall that you were brought up in East Anglia. It boasts an unusual climate—"

She made a sour face. "Bleak, I believe is the word. And damp. Though one got used to squishing through the fields and drying one's slippers by the fire. But my soul craved a place like Ireland"—she leaned toward the window—"a place like this, full of bright sunlight."

He reached forward, as though to touch her hair, but drew his hand back at once. "Yes, Lady Roarke, I do believe you were meant for sunlight."

Don't rush your fences, lad.

Ardsley heard his old groom's words as if from a great distance. Rigger Gaines had never given him a sounder piece of advice. He'd nearly done the inexcusable and touched her hair. The lady was only months out of mourning, he reminded himself, mourning a husband, he'd heard it said, who had been a love match. A lucky man, Sir Connor Roarke . . . though not so lucky at the card tables. Or at evading an untimely death.

The duke had gone to Ireland to inspect breeding stock, having recently become fixed on the notion of starting up a stud farm—his friend, the Earl of Stoke, owned one near Newmarket, and Ardsley had spent part of the autumn there. What luck, then, that on his second day in Dublin he'd fallen into company with the woman who ran one of the premier studs in Ireland.

He looked across at her, still wanting to touch those copper tendrils that drifted below the brim of her ivory-colored bonnet. What a fanciful creature she was, dressed all in white like a beautiful wraith. It was fitting—her image had been haunting him since Christmas. She'd been wearing blue the night he met her . . . a deep, mysterious blue that made her pale eyes glow like moonstones. Even at her farm, where she'd worn clothing more suited to tramping across the countryside, he'd thought her lovely beyond words.

Unfortunately, he had given her little indication of his interest; they'd barely said three words to each other of a personal nature. Every conversation revolved around horses. For all his years in Society, the duke found he had no idea of how to court Ursula Roarke. His inbred reserve seemed an impenetrable barrier between them.

Bad cess to his grandmother, who had called him home before he'd been able to relax his guard. The dowager had pleaded some trumped-up ailment, but he was sure she'd outlive him, as she'd already outlived her husband, her son and one grandson.

Still, he'd made tracks to Ardsley House near Bath, where she'd received him propped up in an enormous bed set about with tapestry hangings. The butler had forewarned him that the old lady, who had a spy network worthy of the Foreign Office, had gotten wind of his visit to Roarke Stud and was not pleased.

Her small, glittering eyes impaled him the instant he set foot in the room. "I won't mince words, Ardsley. This horse-racing business is a parcel of nonsense."

"Not going to be racing them," he said reasonably. "Breeding is what interests me."

Her mouth tightened. "Breeding or racing, it makes no difference. It drains the purse with little hope of profit. But you will go your own way. Duty means nothing to you."

The arrant unfairness of this left him nearly speechless. He took a turn about the room to settle his thoughts, foremost reminding himself that he was the duke and not some hapless footman forced to suffer her tongue lashing.

Duty . . . he reflected sourly. After his brother Anthony died, he'd thought only of his duty to his parents. He'd been quite the dullest fellow at Eton, never, ever got up to mischief. And after his father died, he'd tried even harder to apply himself. Oxford was a trial, but he managed to graduate because family tradition demanded it.

"Duty has been my watchword since I was a child," he said at last. "Nonetheless, a man can't live a full life with only duty to console him; it becomes a millstone. I have sat in Lords, supported issues I do not even believe in . . . because the Danovers are Tories, and I am head of the Danovers."

"Please spare me. I have no wish to learn of it if you have Republican sympathies."

"No . . . it's not that exactly. But I am sick to death of doing things because I *ought* to. For once I'd like to do something because I *want* to. Undertake some venture where I could leave my mark. If I could just make you see, Grandmama . . . there is nothing so stirring as a race horse galloping full out. There is majesty and wonder in it. I want to be a part of that world, improve the bloodlines and contribute to the sport."

"Twaddle," she muttered. "They may call it the sport of kings . . . sport of paupers is more like it. And even if the royals are all agog over racing, well, look at them. A sorrier lot of scoundrels I have yet to see." She dismissed his dream with one bony hand. "Twaddle, I say."

Ardsley felt something rise up in him, not defiance or resentment exactly. It was more of a clear-headed resolve that he would not be thwarted, not this time.

"I am going to buy Lady Roarke's horses," he declared. "I have discovered that she is deep in debt, so there should be no impediment. And I will set up my stud in Devon, at Myrmion."

The old lady gasped. "That house is cursed. Both your brother and your father died there . . . and look what the place did to your mother. You yourself haven't been back to Devon since your father's death."

"Maybe it's time to lay the ghosts, Grandmama. Besides, Tony was ailing for weeks here at Ardsley House before we traveled to Myrmion. Papa came down with a congestion of the lungs after his sailboat capsized. Hardly the work of evil spirits." His voice lowered as he settled on the edge of the bed. "And Mama . . . I suppose she just couldn't face any more losses once Papa was gone. She is happier now, I believe."

Her face softened slightly. "I visit her every week at the Dower House. She still asks for you, Damien. But I understand why you keep away. Maybe it's for the best."

His own face hardened. "It's no use. She thinks I am Anthony . . . then at some point she recognizes me, realizes Tony is gone, and it breaks her heart all over again. I can't bear it."

"You cannot know what it's like for a woman to lose her first-born child."

Anger rose up inside him. "She had me to turn to, old woman. She *has* me, if she could but see it."

She reached out as if to touch his cheek, but her hand fell to the coverlet. "I see it, Damien. In spite of my ill humors, I see you. A resolute and dutiful duke when you need to be, but I often fear your heart is not in it."

This appraisal cut too close to the bone. He drawled carelessly, "I have no heart . . . or so the ladies of the *ton* would insist."

"I am beginning to think they're right. I have given up any thoughts of great grandchildren, since you appear immune to the members of fair sex. At least to the *respectable* ones."

"Sorry to say, there is no lady in the *ton* who intrigues me."

"But this horse-breeding notion intrigues you, does it?"

"More than you can know."

She sighed. "I suppose a gentleman needs his foolish pursuits. Heaven knows your father was besotted with his sailboats. Much good they did him. But very well. Buy your precious horses and settle them at Myrmion. You will recall that your old groom, Rigger Gaines, is caretaker there now. He hired that Ridd fellow as bailiff—a sheep man, from what I hear."

"He'll have to go," Ardsley said brusquely. "Lady Roarke's bloodstock will require an experienced stud manager. Ridd will need to find another position."

The duke left Ardsley House little disturbed by the lie he'd told his grandmother. There *was* a lady who had taken his fancy. But fancies faded, as he well knew, and so he'd waited for his infatuation with Lady Roarke to dissipate. It had not, and with each passing day, his desire to see her again grew. But she was in Ireland and he had obligations in London until the spring.

Meanwhile, he'd offered for her horses, hoping the business connection would allow them to meet again. Her subsequent request to view his property had been a godsend, and the thought of seeing her in the spring was a source of great anticipation. He hadn't needed his grandmother's reminder of what was owed the succession; he'd become enamored of her without any thoughts of family duty whatsoever.

Ardsley shook himself back to the present. He wouldn't blame the lady if she teased him over his own long silence, but she was engaged in a pleasant cose with her companion. He admired her profile a moment, then turned his gaze out the window. The coach was still on the high track that ran beside the Bristol Channel; he could see the wide expanse of water gleaming in the afternoon sunlight and the ghostly rise of Wales in the distance. Soon they would descend into the valley where Myrmion lay. Nearly twelve years had passed since he'd set foot on the estate. It had apparently prospered without his presence—the revenues from the place were always impressive.

It was unfortunate that he had to dismiss William Ridd. For ten years, like clockwork, the fellow sent in his monthly accounting, copied out in a blocky, childlike hand. At first, Ardsley recalled, several people at Myrmion, including the housekeeper, had written to tell him that the new bailiff appeared to be a simpleton. He rarely spoke, they said, and when he did it was in a halting, stammering manner.

But Ardsley had been attending Oxford at the time, more concerned with the fall of ancient Rome than the problems at a distant estate. Eventually, the complaints leveled off. Even Mrs. Hutchins seemed to warm to the fellow, calling him "dear Will" in one of her infrequent letters.

Dear or not, Will Ridd was not the man to make Lady Roarke happy. And that goal was paramount to the duke at this moment. If she requested stalls of gold and mangers of silver, he would happily order them.

He realized he was thinking like a besotted fool. Frustration did that to a man. If only he could tell her how he felt. If only he didn't find himself full of stilted commonplaces whenever they spoke of anything but horses.

He caught her eye and forced an easy smile.

Her mouth twitched up at the corners. "I apologize for neglecting you, Your Grace. Miss Falkirk and I have been discussing the merits of chamomile tea. We are inveterate tea drinkers and can rhapsodize over oolong and imperial gunpowder for hours."

"It no doubt comes from living in East Anglia," he said. "All those squishy fields and wet slippers."

"Precisely," she said.

"Are we near your estate, Your Grace?" Miss Falkirk asked, setting down her knitting. At his nod, she added, "The moor looks to be a perfect place for childhood adventuring. A bit wild and overgrown."

"It is that. One time in that very dell," he said, pointing to the side of the road, "my brother and I managed to elude our groom. We were out of his sight less than two minutes when we startled a bull who had escaped his pen. The beast took off after us, and we galloped away through the trees. It was the summer I turned six, and I fancied myself something of a horseman. My piebald pony thought otherwise. He scraped me off under a low branch, then pelted off home with a wicked expression of glee. Anthony—my older brother—turned around and came swooping back after me, drawing me up onto his pony's rump. At the time, I was pretending we were British cavalrymen engaged in a heated battle, and that Tony, fearless and loyal, had rescued me from a regiment of French soldiers."

Both women were gazing at him alertly. "Go on . . ." Lady Roarke said in a low voice.

He shrugged. "Just boyish roughhousing, you know. We whooped and hollered all the way back to Myrmion, scaring the geese and the goats and two maids who were hanging linens in the yard. They dropped a basket of wet sheets in the dirt and faced a scolding, so Tony made me rewash them. He said, 'Now, little badger, you can pretend you are a laundry maid.' But he helped me with them after all, and we ended up blowing soap bubbles up the chimney flue in the kitchen." He chuckled. "Gad, he was a brick."

Lady Roarke's eyes had narrowed in concern. "How very sad that you lost him."

"It was difficult at first, but painful memories fade." His voice softened. "Loss fades."

After a prolonged silence inside the coach, Barbara Falkirk said, "Was your brother fond of horses? I . . . I was thinking he might have approved of using your old haunt to breed race horses."

"Tony was mad for the beasts. My interest in them is of a more recent vintage, I'm afraid."

"Maybe your wicked pony had something to do with that," Lady Roarke remarked.

Ardsley's mouth curled up at one corner. "Indeed, ma'am."

He pointed out a few more landmarks, the saw mill and the smelting furnace, but each well-remembered place drew him inexorably back to the summer his brother died.

It had begun at Ardsley House, Tony suddenly ill with a violent fever, the doctor fetched in frantic haste in the middle of the night. The next day, Damien had been sent away to an aunt's home, and when he returned weeks later, Tony was . . . different somehow. When one was only seven, it was hard to pinpoint in what way. Damien had fretted, needing to know what was wrong, but he was rarely allowed inside the sickroom.

His parents consulted London physicians, who recommended the air of the coast, and so they had all packed up and gone to Myrmion. Only his parents attended his brother there; he'd been kept away. Grandmama came to stay, and the grimness of her face frightened Damien.

And then it was over . . . a simple pine casket that shone with the same honeyed light as Tony's hair was carried back to Ardsley House. Myrmion was shut up, the servants dismissed. Damien prayed for the house to be swallowed up by the moors. Although his parents returned there from time to time, he had never gone back to Devon until his father's final illness.

He now thrust away the image of his brother as he'd last seen him, but the vision came to him, unwanted and as sharp as the cutting edge of blade—Tony being carried into Myrmion on a litter. He'd been wrapped in sheeting, his upper limbs pinned against his body, with only his head free of restraint. His gaze had caught and held Damien's, and there was a plea in his eyes that did not need words to articulate it. *Free me, little badger,* it said.

Damien had turned and run away.

It was time to lay the ghosts, as he'd told his grandmother. He had once been happy in Devon, trekking staunchly after his brother, the two of them frolicking like terrier pups over moor and meadow. He now had another companion with whom to share the wild Devon countryside. She was beautiful and clever; she might be the perfect person to ease his loneliness and help him move beyond his loss. It was long overdue.

Chapter Two

*W*ill knew the pup had potential. He was a believer in the potential of all young things. It only required a steady voice and a firm, caring hand to coax any young creature to follow your lead, whether lamb or calf, colt or kid. And collie pups . . . why, they followed you from the instant they could climb out of their basket and wobble across the garden. This one in particular had chosen Will. The other whelps in old Snap's final litter had been given away, but Will had kept the rangy black-and-white puppy. He didn't have a name yet . . . Rigger said dogs and horses shouldn't be named till they were broken in.

Snap showed little interest in her son once he was weaned, but Will knew she would school him when the time came. There were other collies on the farm, but Snap was one of the best herders in Devon, and Will wanted the pup to benefit from his dam's experience. He liked the familial quality of that.

Crotchety and arthritic, Snap had nevertheless done her duty and worked with the pup for three months. She had then retired to a shady cranny under the stable and refused to come out if her master or her son were anywhere in the vicinity.

Will always maintained that sheep dogs were the smartest breed on the planet.

Today Will was working the pup hard, asking him to move a large group of sheep from one pasture to another, which involved crossing the farm track. Will stood by the open gate of the second pasture, whistling to the collie. "Bring 'em in, lad!" he called with a sweeping motion toward the field behind him. The dog ranged around the outside of the bunched flock, whining and fretful, but did not attempt to move them from the road.

After ten minutes, Will was deciding whether to call in one of the more experienced dogs, who were intently watching from the hillside, when he heard a vehicle approaching. He gauged it would crest the rise where he and the flock waited in less than a minute. The driver would not be expecting a hundredfold of sheep to be standing blank-faced in his path.

He was just about to whistle down the other dogs, when a blaze of black and white streaked past him. It was Snap, moving faster than he'd seen her move in years, heading in the direction of the approaching vehicle. He heard her loud warning yips, and as the elegant black coach came into view, there was Snap, crisscrossing the track in front of the team of horses. Ten feet from the flock, the coach came to a creaking halt, while a mounted groom leading a bay horse drew up behind. Will eyed the ducal crest on the door.

The master of Myrmion had arrived. And earlier than expected.

Will pushed his soft felt hat farther back on his head and attempted to wipe the grime from his face with his handkerchief. Then, skirting the horses, he went to the coach door.

A man's face appeared at the window. "Ho there, fellow, what seems to be the delay?"

Will touched his forelock. "Sheep, sir. I've been training a young collie to move the flock." He added with a wry chuckle, "Not so you would notice."

The door opened, Will let down the step, and the gentleman climbed out, a pinched expression on his pale, patrician features.

Will knew this was Ardsley; there was a painting of him from childhood up at the house. The boyishly rounded face had become lean, perhaps even a little severe, but there was no mistaking the tawny hair and the clear brown eyes. He was a ringer for the old duke, whose portrait hung in state above the parlor hearth.

The duke's gaze shifted to the flock, which was blocking the lane from hedgerow to hedgerow. His fine brows drew down. "You must clear them out at once. My companions are weary and—"

Someone else was descending from the coach now, a

woman. Will spared her a glance, then nearly laughed. Was the chit daft, to be coming to the moorland all dressed in white? Even her half-boots, which trod so delicately upon the coach step, were of a pearly shade.

But then Will looked at her face, and the urge to laugh vanished. White suits her, he thought, sets fire in her hair and a bloom of pale rose upon her cheek. Her eyes were surely Nimue's eyes, the clear silvery blue of a pagan spring. Just now her brow was fretful, her mouth pursed in concern over the delay. Still, he had a feeling he could gaze at that face in all its moods—any red-haired woman was sure to have a bounty of them—and never tire of the aspect.

"Sheep," Ardsley explained to the lady.

"So I see." She took a few steps away from the coach, peering into the lane ahead. "Rather a lot of them."

"And you appear to have made a conquest," the duke murmured. "Yon shepherd has been struck quite speechless."

Will fought down a blush. He felt the woman's gaze travel over him like a palpable touch. He met that gaze, returning it with a steady, challenging look until her eyes lowered. Then he grinned crookedly and drawled, "Mind the dung." He tipped his head toward the pile of sheep droppings at her feet.

"Not *quite* speechless," she said under her breath as she took a hasty step back. "Do you suppose we could get under way anytime soon?" she asked. "Perhaps you should call in someone more . . . experienced to help you."

"I'll have the lane cleared in a trice—my lady." He whistled for Snap, who was playing touch-nose with one of the coach horses.

But it was the pup who heeded his signal, springing eagerly to life on the far side of the packed sheep. With sharp barks and well-chosen nips, he sent the entire flock scattering in panic—directly toward the coach. The alarmed team jerked back several feet, shifting the rear wheels into the runoff ditch that edged the lane. There was a muffled cry from the interior.

A moving stream of sheep engulfed them now, jostling and buffeting the duke and his lady. Will stood firm, cursing the dog under his breath, and at the same time trying to

hide his amusement—the duke appeared comically flab-
bergasted, as if he'd found himself in a sort of woolly bed-
lam, while the lady was trying determinedly, but not very
successfully, to push the encroaching bodies away with both
hands, calling out, "Shoo! *Shoo!*"

Will had to admire her pluck, which was more than he
could say for the duke. He'd just started toward her, when
one of the more energetic ewes bounded into the air and
caromed solidly into the lady. Down she went.

The duke gave a cry of alarm and pushed forward, but
Will had already scooped her up, all flailing arms and tumbled bonnet. With a murmured apology, he lifted her high
in his arms. She squawked—there was really no other word
for the raucous sound she made—and demanded to be
set down.

"I dare not," he said. "They think you one of their own,
all dressed in white as you are."

He carried her to the coach and deposited her on the
driver's box beside the two coachmen, who were trying to
hide their grins. "You'll be safe up here," he said.

She was trembling—not with fear, he suspected, but with
vexation. "I doubt I could be safe anywhere around you.
This has been the most—" She stopped abruptly, grabbing
for her skirt, which a stray breeze had sent billowing. Her
eyes widened as she looked down at the fabric in her hand
and she gave a muted shriek.

Will saw why—one side of her pristine white gown was
now dappled with streaks of oily lanolin, smudges of field
grime and even bits of dung. He was about to apologize,
when the duke, who had plowed his way through the sheep,
came up beside him.

"This is . . . inexcusable!" he panted.

"I am sorry, Your Grace. The dog is young yet . . . and
excitable. But he's—"

There was a sharp outcry from the box. "Please! Someone help!" The lady was standing now and furiously motioning toward the lane behind the coach.

Will swung around. A half-dozen sheep were milling
around the legs of the bay stallion, who was rearing up and
snorting. The pup ran up to the agitated horse and began
barking at the ewes. This was too much for the stallion—

he lunged violently away from his outrider and went tearing
down the track back the way he had come.

"That tears it," the lady moaned as she sank down. "Oh,
my poor Imperator."

"Send your groom after the beast," Will offered sensibly.

Her eyes raked him. "Imperator was a champion race
horse, you dolt. Nothing on this planet can catch him. And,
look, the groom can barely control his own horse."

This was true; the groom's cob, having taken exception
to the melee, had tossed his rider half off. The poor man
was barely clinging to his mount's neck.

"Badly done," the duke muttered. "This was not the welcome I had intended for Lady Roarke."

"A country welcome, to be sure," Will said. "We'll catch
the beast, never fear. But first, let me get you out of the
ditch."

He went to the rear of the tilted coach and set both
shoulders against the wooden boot. "Hup!" he called out.
The driver sent his team forward slowly, until the back
wheels cleared the gully. As the coach straightened out,
Will saw a woman's face at the window. She was perhaps
two score years and ten, with deep brown hair showing
under a straw bonnet. And, wonder of wonders, she was
smiling at him. "I am from Scotland," she said pleasantly,
"so I know how troublesome sheep can be."

He touched his hat to her. "Yet never quite as troublesome as certain people, by my reckoning."

She motioned him closer. "If you want to avoid trouble,"
she said in an undertone, "then you'd better catch her
horse. He's the bait, you see."

Will did not see, not just yet, but he assured her that
everything was well in hand.

The duke was lifting Lady Roarke down from the box
when Will returned to the lane. He took a moment to envy
the man . . . he'd likely never get that close to her again.

"I'll send riders out to find Imperator," the duke was
saying. "I doubt he's strayed from the road." He shifted to
Will. "And I'm afraid I will need to speak to the bailiff
about this . . . this blunder."

"Consider it done," Will said. He sketched a bow. "William Ridd at your service, Your Grace." When the duke's

sour expression did not alter, he added quickly, "And don't fret over the lady's champion race horse. You see, I have a champion herd dog . . ."

Snap was lounging at the side of the road, having wisely remained apart from her son's catastrophe. She came at once to Will's command, nosing against his hand. He drew her to the middle of the track, then snapped his arm forward. "Bring him in, lass. Bring yon horse to me."

Snap bolted off, skirting the sheep, who were now standing idle and a bit confused in the lane.

"This is absurd," the lady grumbled. "The dog is what frightened my horse in the first place."

"Different dog," the duke muttered.

"Smarter dog," Will added, glowering at Snap's son, who was now sprawled under the coach, his tongue lolling out. He wondered if he'd been wrong about the pup's potential.

There was a sharp bark from beyond the turning in the lane. "Bring him in, Snap!" Will called through his cupped hands. He winked at the duke, who was still looking dubious. "Best dog in Devon . . . she's a wonder with sheep."

The duke's mouth tightened, and he shifted on his feet. "Well, yes, I will need to speak with you about that. About the sheep. Come up to the house tonight, Ridd. At nine."

Will again touched his hat, trying to ignore the feeling of disquiet shivering down his spine.

Snap came trotting over the rise then, the stallion's lead held firmly in her teeth. The bay was a bit wild-eyed, but seemed little worse for his adventure.

"Thank goodness," Lady Roarke said as she hurried to the horse and grasped his lead.

Will praised his dog with a word and then approached the stallion, settling him with his hands, stroking them over his chest and down his forelegs. He stood upright then and looked across the beast's nose at Lady Roarke. "No harm done."

"That remains to be seen. And you are hardly the person to judge."

He nearly reared back at the harshness in her tone. When he spoke, his own voice came out low pitched, and maybe a little harsh as well. "I don't wonder he ran off," he said, looking her straight in the eye. "I'd run too, from such an ugly scowl as you are wearing on that fine, fine face."

He pried the lead rope from her fist, and then easily boosted himself onto the stallion's back. She leapt forward, crying, "No . . . you can't . . . he won't be ridden. Imperator is a stud horse."

Will felt the animal tense, knew that the weight on his back, once so familiar, had become an odd sensation. He soothed him with a soft murmur of words. "He's just a horse, ma'am," he said evenly, his temper in control again. "For all his fancy name and long pedigree, just a horse. I'll see him to the stable."

Ursula watched in wordless chagrin as he rode off, moving easily in time with the bay's fluid gait. The dog, Snap, fell in behind him.

At that point, the younger dog scrambled out from beneath the coach and, to her amazement, gathered up every sheep in the lane and neatly herded them through the open gate into the pasture. The duke looked on in silence; he seemed a little awed by the timeless ritual.

Ursula latched the gate, and then stalked back to the duke. "I know it's not my place to judge," she said, unwittingly echoing her own words to Ridd. "But your bailiff, if he really *is* your bailiff, is possibly the rudest man I've ever met."

"I must apologize for him," the duke said stiffly. "He had no right to rough you about as he did. I fear he's had little traffic with the gentry—none of the family has been back here since he took over. I trust you are unharmed."

She muttered something and attempted to shake out her skirts. His eyes widened when he saw the splatterings of mud and worse that marked the white fabric.

"Oh, and they've ruined your gown," he said with what she heard as a mixture of dismay and distaste. "I'll make sure that it is replaced." He curled one hand around her arm. "Now, come along. We'll get you home where Mrs. Hutchins can look after you."

He swung open the coach door and settled Ursula on the seat, doubtless feeling a great sense of relief at having gotten her off the road before any more disasters could befall her.

Barbara Falkirk was wearing an amused expression. "This was certainly a memorable welcome, Your Grace. Very entertaining."

Ursula sniffed. "It was only entertaining because you remained in the coach."

"Ah, but then I know my sheep."

"The duke's bailiff is a braw, bonny man," Barbara declared as she laid out Ursula's dinner gown.

Ursula looked up from her dressing table with a frown. She had bathed off her grime in a copper tub and was now sipping a cup of strong tea. Her frayed nerves were mending nicely, but she was still not in the mood for Barbara's teasing.

"He's a blundering oaf," she said, "who was responsible for my arriving at the duke's home looking like a bedraggled camp follower."

"I always favored a lean man with broad shoulders," Barbara went on, impervious to Ursula's deepening frown. "Broad shoulders and the face of an archangel. And those eyes—put me in mind of tropical seas. A man who looks like that is more than mortal woman should have to bear."

Ursula set down her teacup with a sharp clack. "And the point of this conversation is exactly what?"

"Just musing, my pet. A pity, though, that the duke hasn't such a bonny look to him."

"I find the duke's appearance quite pleasing," she pronounced. "His features are classically formed and his expression is one of—"

"—a man who's smelled a week-old fish," Barbara finished for her.

Ursula had to restrain a chuckle. Instead, she lobbed a hairbrush at her companion. Barbara ducked away with a grin. "So you think so too. I knew it."

"Ardsley is so blasted . . . proper," she groaned, bunching her petticoats into her lap and burying her face in the pouf of muslin. She groaned again, and then looked up. "Except for that one time in the coach, when he spoke of his brother, he has shown little animation in either voice or manner."

"You do have your work cut out for you, pet. The man is a dry old stick."

"And the worst of it is, he makes me behave so unlike myself that I hardly know who I am any longer. I acted like a shrew out in the lane."

"So I observed."

"Can you blame me? I wanted to gain the duke's admiration, not end up trampled by sheep with my hair coming down and dung on my gown. And that bailiff person . . . he was amused by me, Barbara. I know he was . . . there was sly laughter in his eyes."

"Oh, so you did notice his eyes."

"That is not the point."

"The point is, Roary would have laughed. He would have been belly down on the road lost in laughter. And so would you have been, if His Noble Grace hadn't been there for you to impress. No one was in any danger, not even Impy. That horse has gotten loose more times than I can count, as you well know, and the worst that's occurred is he's eaten himself to bursting on apples from Father Padraic's orchard."

Ursula hung her head. "I hate this, Babs . . . playing at being a lady of quality. I'd much rather be tramping about in my old calico gown and Roary's hunting jacket. But you know this is our only chance of coming about. I must marry Ardsley—and soon. Most of what I'll make from selling the bloodstock will go to pay Roary's debts. The little that will be left won't keep us in coal, let alone put a roof over our heads."

Barbara crossed the room and laid her hand on Ursula's shoulder. "You could sell the Magpie."

Ursula's eyes darkened. "No, he is not for sale. Not ever. I made sure that Ardsley never saw him while he was at the Stud. The Magpie is my trump card, even if Roary only bought him for me as a joke, because no one else wanted a race horse who was lame."

"Lame but potent," Barbara said knowingly. "Best foals in three counties. If you don't marry the duke, you might be able to live off the Magpie's stud fees."

"No, he won't fetch the fees that Impy gets, not for a while yet."

"Roary was a fool not to see the horse's potential. Although it's well that he didn't, that he gave the beast to you. Your husband's creditors can't touch him."

"Of course, if I marry Ardsley, I will have to tell him about the horse. At least I can bring the Magpie to Devon then . . . it will be some consolation."

"I mislike the sound of that. I'd think marrying a duke would be consolation and plenty. Even such a dour duke. Don't you believe he will make you happy? You certainly deserve some happiness after what your husband put you through."

Ursula spun back to her mirror and began fussing with her hair. "The duke will make me feel secure. It's what I require right now. Happiness is for the young, and I am beginning to feel very old lately."

"Oh, pish! Of all the nonsense. Come, let me dress you for supper. That saucy maid the duke assigned to you appears to have vanished—more bosom than brains, if you ask me."

Rigger Gaines was sitting before the fire reading the Exeter paper, when Will strode into his parlor. He looked up, not at all surprised at the advent of his guest. Rumor had it the meeting of absentee duke and his stalwart bailiff had not gone well. He studied his friend as he settled on the ottoman, long legs sprawled out on either side. The tanned face wore only an expression of consternation. Rigger sighed; he'd hoped to read something more there.

"Tell me right out," Will said. "For what purpose has the duke come here? You've been edgy as a cat for weeks now, and I'd chalked it up to lambing season. But now I can't help thinking it's the duke's visit that's caused your odd mood."

"You knew as much as I did—that he was arriving with a houseguest. I did hear from one of his coachmen, however, that he's thinking of starting a breeding farm here . . . for race horses."

Will nearly gaped. "The devil he is! We've no stabling or turn-outs for race horses. He must have, what, half a dozen other properties? Why here, Rigger? Why Myrmion?"

He hitched one shoulder. "Not a good idea to question a duke, lad. 'As they will, so shall we do.' I learned that at my father's knee."

"I wager it's the doing of that woman he's come with, her with her high-bred horse."

Rigger sucked in one cheek. "I hear Lady Roarke's got a matrimonial gleam in her eye. My cousin in Dublin sometimes mentioned Connor Roarke in his letters—the lady's late husband was a notorious gamester who bet away everything he owned except his horses. Still, it looks like the widow's found herself a fine, fat pigeon to pluck."

"They are welcome to each other," Will muttered. "But they are not welcome to Myrmion. We've made something special here, Rigger. For us and for the whole district. My wool keeps food on the table of half the families in the valley."

"Then you must point that out to His Grace. Dukes know their responsibility to the locals. Has he asked to speak with you?"

"Tonight at nine."

Rigger eyed Will's homespun shirt and corded breeches. "Then you'd best wash up and don your best suit."

"I was planning to change . . . I am not so lost to the formalities. Though I doubt His Grace can think any worse of me after our first meeting."

"What did you think of *him,* Will?" he asked intently.

"We had little chance for conversation. There were all these sheep, you see."

Rigger grinned. "Yes, I heard about your pup's disgrace. So you had no distinct impression of Ardsley?"

Will rubbed the back of his head. "He looks very much like the old duke in the parlor portrait."

"He doesn't remind you of anyone yet living?"

"You think Ardsley's father has a byblow in the district?"

Rigger laughed. "No, the duke was a faithful husband. If he had any mistress, it was the sea. Don't mind me, lad. I am full of daft notions lately. You go off and get cleaned up. We'll talk again in the morning."

"But not too early," Will said as he headed for the door. "It's been a long day . . . and it's not over yet."

Rigger rattled his paper, trying to find where he'd left off reading. It was pointless; he was no longer interested in the price of wheat or the latest balloon ascension.

For fifteen years he had awaited—and maybe slightly dreaded—this day, when the boy he had taken as his ward would finally come face to face with the old duke's son. He'd hoped to be there himself to witness the meeting, but Ardsley had arrived earlier than expected, while Rigger was down at the home farm. Though there hadn't been much to witness, according to the coachman, save a hundred spooked sheep and one very wayward collie.

He'd be having his own interview with the duke just after supper—he was curious to hear Master Damien's reaction to the bailiff. Not that he expected anything enlightening. He'd given up on getting any answers ten years ago, when he'd first brought Will to Myrmion. Rigger's hopes that the old place would jog some hidden memory in Will had been confounded. The lad's past was a blank slate and likely to remain such.

Not that he minded any longer—William Ridd was the pride of his life, grown into as fine an example of young manhood as walked this or any other valley. Rigger decided to let things be. Will was happy here; Myrmion was his home and his sanctuary. As long as it remained that way, Rigger had no reason to stir things up.

He forced himself to return to his newspaper, pretending that the questions—and the guilt—didn't still gnaw at him like a foul canker.

The duke had been quiet during dinner. Ursula followed his lead and kept the conversation light. Afterward he excused himself, pleading some business with the staff. She sensed he was preoccupied and decided it was nothing to do with her. It must be difficult for him, she reasoned, being back in this place where he'd spent time with a beloved, lost brother.

Barbara had pleaded weariness and gone off to bed directly after supper. For her own part, Ursula wanted to explore. Earlier, Mrs. Hutchins had whisked her to her bedroom so quickly, she'd barely had a chance to see much of the house.

At least she'd gotten a good view of the exterior from the coach. The estate was pleasantly laid out, with the home farm set below the level of house and stable. The sprawling manor had not been built to awe, situated as it was at the base of a wooded hillside rather than higher up. Still, she'd been taken by the low, undulating roofline, the half-timbered, stucco facade with its shingled porte cochere and the low-walled garden, now rioting with spring blossoms. Myrmion reminded her of an Irish farmhouse, though built on a grander scale.

Most of the interior, she now discovered, was waincoted in a rich, honey-aged oak. The ceilings were low, though the fireplaces were constructed on generous lines. The furniture appeared shabby, yet everything was scrupulously clean. And while her bedroom had been fitted out with new hangings, it was clear that the rest of the house had not been refurbished in decades. Again, she did not mind—the house at Roarke Stud was certainly no showplace, offering simple country comfort rather than high style.

She wondered if this old house, equally comfortable, might stir the duke out of his perpetual reserve. She tried to picture him lounging carelessly on one of the faded sofas or taking his ease on the hammock she'd seen near the stable. The images wouldn't materialize. Silly of her to try—even in the relaxed atmosphere of Roarke Stud, His Grace had maintained his London hauteur.

As Barbara observed, she had her work cut out for her.

During her tour, Ursula came across several portraits of the Danover family. In the drawing room hung a painting of Ardsley as a child, holding the reins of a piebald pony. In the parlor she studied the portrait of a handsome, tawny-haired man who was, by his clothing, most likely the former duke. On a writing table in the library, she found a miniature of the duchess, a blue-eyed, brown-haired lady in a plumed bonnet. Ardsley had her smile, if not her coloring. It occurred to Ursula that there were no paintings of Anthony Danover. He'd died of a hideous ailment, Estelle had told her. Perhaps he'd been scarred or disfigured in some way.

Whatever it was, it hadn't blighted his younger brother's affection. She recalled Ardsley's vivid, animated expression when he'd reminisced about Anthony. "I want to make him look like that," she said with a sigh as she wandered the perimeter of the library.

He had shared so little of himself thus far. She knew nothing of his likes or dislikes, what sort of books he read or if indeed he read at all. Did he enjoy the theater or the delights of a country fair?

When she'd first met Sir Connor Roarke in London, they had talked endlessly. Driving in the park or strolling through the Royal Academy, they never ran out of things to discuss. It was as though they were old friends long parted, who had a world of catching up to do.

Within two weeks, she felt she knew everything about the dashing Irish baronet. He'd opened his soul to her, he swore. She had certainly opened her heart to him. There was one secret, however, he had not shared. It was a year into their marriage before she discovered his only vice. All gentlemen gamble, he told her patiently after he'd pawned the silver tea service to pay a gaming debt. She was naive to think otherwise, he said.

Her heart had broken slowly, her faith in the man chipped away in fragments as, one by one, their possessions disappeared. Roary would promise to keep away from the gaming hells, and he'd actually restrained himself for one six-month period. Then two of his mares lost their foals, and he was so distraught, he gambled nonstop for a fortnight.

Barbara had stood by her, but that was poor compensation as Ursula watched her husband's strength of will dwindle and then die. She had been so sure that what they had together could survive any challenge. But all she'd really had from him from the first were glib words and charming persuasions . . . his weakness, his flaw, had remained hidden.

Roary had swept her off her feet, she saw in hindsight. She vowed that with Ardsley her feet would stay firmly planted. And perhaps the duke's slow and studied manner of courtship—if indeed it was courtship—would allow her a true understanding of the man. That way there would be no unpleasant surprises or hidden vices to contend with after they were wed. She had no tolerance left for a man with secrets.

Chapter Three

*U*rsula was scanning the shelves in the library—and chuckling over some of the quaint titles—when the door creaked open. She looked up in startled surprise.

At first she'd thought it was the duke, but then realized the gentleman who stood watching her from the threshold was a stranger. He was not attired in the latest style, but his clothing had been well tailored. She wondered if this might be Ardsley's secretary; perhaps he had traveled here with the baggage coach.

"I didn't mean to disturb you, Lady Roarke," the man said.

Her head tilted. "I'm sorry . . . have we met?"

He leaned against the door frame and crossed his arms. "Come closer, madam, and you shall have your answer."

She did take a few steps toward him, curiosity overcoming her initial apprehension. He was taller than the duke and displayed a startling length of leanly muscled thigh beneath his twill breeches. Ursula dragged her gaze away from this highly improper perusal and focused instead on his face. Skin browned by the sun, eyes wide set and bright, hair the color of ripened wheat except above his brow, where it was nearly white-blond. The nose was hardly notable, except for its location—it lay between two well-defined cheekbones and above a mobile, beautifully shaped mouth. A mouth that was slowly curling into a wry twist of amusement.

She nearly gasped. It was that insufferable Ridd fellow!

He laughed softly, deep in his throat. "Ah, so you do recognize me. Took you long enough."

Her head went up. "If you are seeking the duke, he is closeted in his study."

He moved into the room, and she had to force herself

not to back up. "I'm early for my appointment," he said, "so I thought I'd occupy myself in here." He tipped his head down and peered at her through his brows. "If that's all right with you, Lady Roarke."

"It's none of my concern how you occupy yourself."

He did not move toward the shelves, but stayed where he was, still watching her with those bright eyes. She gave him an arch smile. "You seem at a loss. If I may make so bold, there is a book here that might interest you."

She returned to the shelf she'd been scanning, and her fingers went at once to the quaint volume she'd seen earlier. She tugged it out and handed it to him.

He read the title aloud. *"The Village Idiot and Other Rural Oddments."*

Something tightened his face for a heartbeat, a wince of mortification, perhaps, but it was gone before she could place it. Whatever reaction it was that he'd so quickly erased, she now regretted her prank. True, she'd wanted to bait him—she was still resentful over her undignified arrival—but she hadn't intended the cut to go so deep.

Her hands flew out. "I didn't mean—"

But he had already swung away from her.

Will carefully set the book on the table, then spread his hands over the polished surface. *She cannot know, lad,* he assured himself. *There is no way she can know of your wretched past.*

Rigger had taught him years ago that the best way to defuse the barbs of others was not with sarcasm or lashing out, but with laughter. At himself, for his own mistakes, or at the situation, when he had no control over it. It was how he had responded this afternoon, seeing the humor inherent in his misguided attempt to clear the lane.

And so he laughed now, a soft chuckle that rumbled up from his chest.

"You will discover," he said lightly, "that you've only scratched the surface of our rural oddments here at Myrmion. We've a witch and a diviner and fully three lads with extra digits." He turned back to her then, aiming his words a little above her head. "I am small fry compared to them. Though I will endeavor to be a source of amusement to you, withal."

He ventured a glance at her face; she looked deeply

abashed, her mouth formed into a straight line, her silvery
eyes now huge. Still, her chin was up. She reminded him
of a willful child caught out in some mischief. A willful,
beautiful child. It was impossible to keep from touching
her, from brushing his fingertips for an instant along her
cheek. "Don't fret yourself, lass. No harm done."

As Will's hand dropped away, the duke came through
the door and found them gazing at each other in strained
silence. He went directly to Lady Roarke, but his words
were addressed to Will. "You can go into my study now,
Ridd. I'll be with you shortly."

He gave a curt nod. "As Your Grace wishes."

"I'm sorry if he has been upsetting you," the duke said
as he took up Ursula's hand.

She nearly snatched it back. His gesture, meant to reassure her, only increased her confusion. Ardsley's fingers
were as cool and smooth as marble. Will Ridd's fingers,
when he'd stroked her face, had been warm, work-
hardened. She had nearly leaned into that rough touch.

"I promise he won't be a problem for long," he added.
"Once I've hired a stud manager and sold off those pesti-
lential sheep, Ridd will be dismissed."

She fought off a skittering pinprick of guilt. It was one
thing to influence the fate of a faceless stranger, and quite
another thing to be responsible for the dismissal of a man
she'd met. One who'd surprised her with his ability to answer humiliation with good humor.

"Perhaps you could find work for him elsewhere. The
farm appears well maintained."

"It's not his skills as bailiff I fault, it is his lack of experience with race horses. I understood that my hiring such a
man was one of your prime requirements."

"It was . . . it is. But Mr. Ridd seems to have a canny
way with animals. He managed to ride Imperator, who has
not been under saddle in five years. You might assign him
to assist the stud manager."

"No, I want a fresh start. A new stable, for one thing. I
have workmen standing by at Ardsley House. They will
come here to begin construction the instant you give your
approval. It only awaits your word."

"I don't mean to be an impediment, Your Grace. You

understand that before I can decide, I will need to go over the estate. If you would ride out with me tomorrow—"

"It would be my pleasure. Unfortunately, I haven't been here for over a decade, so I think we should take Ridd along to guide us. I'll have a word with him about minding his manners." He moved to the table. "Now, let me see what you have selected from my library." He raised the book, and his brows quirked. "An unusual choice."

"I . . . I was teasing Mr. Ridd. He played the buffoon so well this afternoon, I thought the book would . . . amuse him."

His eyes clouded. "You cannot know this, of course, but the bailiff had . . . some impairment when he first came to Myrmion. My old groom is caretaker here, and he vouched for the fellow. But early on, I heard complaints that the man was a simpleton, that he had trouble speaking coherently."

"He seems to have gotten over that last problem," Ursula said under her breath, and then added, "Oh, but I am sorry I baited him. It was badly done. Though he seemed to take it in stride." She overlooked that instant when mortification had suffused his face. "He laughed, actually."

"He does that a lot," the duke observed. "But I suspect he won't be so jocular after our interview. No, don't frown, my dear—he'll likely have no trouble finding other work. For all Ridd's past singularities, he seems to have no present ailments. And he cuts a decent figure in his Sunday suit . . . I nearly mistook him for a gentlemen when I entered just now."

"I know," she said softly. "So did I."

The duke had kept his interview with Rigger Gaines short. The man, firsthand witness to so much of what Ardsley wanted to forget, made him uncomfortable. Still, they had a shared history. Rigger had been more than just a groom in the old days, he'd been his father's right-hand man, traveling with the family from house to house. Ardsley recalled that Rigger had taken Tony's death particularly hard and had disappeared for a time afterward.

Rigger looked fit enough, still like a blasted pirate, which was what he and Tony had pretended whenever the groom growled at them for getting into mischief. His black hair had grayed only slightly, and he was as lean as a knife blade.

And now the duke sat across from the man's protégé, congratulating himself that this interview was also going well. Will Ridd had maintained a respectful silence as Ardsley explained his plans for the estate.

"So you see, I no longer have need of a bailiff. A stud manager is what I require. Even if Lady Roarke chooses not to sell me her bloodstock, I still intend to convert Myrmion to a stud."

Ridd leaned forward and said sharply, "And what of my sheep?"

"*Your* sheep?" the duke echoed. "You forget yourself, I think. They are my sheep, to the last lamb. And I intend to sell them off at the earliest opportunity. I believe there is a weekly fair in Barnstable . . . you can ride there and post a notice of the sale."

Ridd pushed up from his chair and loomed over the desk. "It took me five years to breed those sheep, from Cotswald, Icelandic and Merino strains. They are unique in the world, certainly the best wool-bearing sheep in England. Their fleece is ideal for hand weaving, soft, strong and lightweight."

The duke rose to face him, reminding himself of what Rigger had said earlier—that the bailiff had been running things here for nearly ten years, that he might chafe at the bit. "Yes, that is quite admirable. Wool is not my concern, however—"

"But you d-don't understand. There are people—"

"Stop!" The duke's hand flew up. "This is not open for discussion. I am aware that the revenues from Myrmion have been steady. You have my thanks for that . . . it will be noted in your references."

"And what about the herd dogs, the collies?" Will asked in a dull voice. "D-do you own them as well?"

He shrugged. "I assume they cannot be trained for hunting, and it is clear they are not trustworthy around horses. If I were a practical man, I would order them destroyed"— the bailiff gasped audibly—"but if you promise to keep them clear of the estate, I will give the dogs into your care. Be warned, though, once the horses are here, my men will have orders to shoot any collie that trespasses on my land."

Ridd muttered something as he slumped back into his chair.

"What did you say?" the duke asked sharply.

The man met his eyes. "I said, you don't belong here. And before you rail at me for my insolence, let me remind you that you have as good as dismissed me. As for your blasted references, well . . . my work here at Myrmion is known throughout Devon. That is all the reference I require."

Ardsley shook his head to clear it. He was certainly un-used to anyone speaking to him in such a plain manner, barring his grandmother. But she, at least, was family.

"All right, Mr. Ridd, I am a reasonable man. Tell me why you say I don't belong here? This is horse country, is it not? The moor ponies grow fat and fertile on the grass in these valleys. My horses will flourish in Devon, and Myrmion Stud will become a byword for strong bloodlines."

Ridd rubbed one hand over his face. "Myrmion is not an island, Your Grace. It does not stand isolated from the world. You are the master of many properties . . . how can you not know that?"

"I fail to see—"

"The estate supports the town of Stratton and the other villages in the district. Myrmion supplies the cottagers with wool for weaving, which they—"

"Enough about your demned wool. Those cottagers will have to buy their wool elsewhere."

"You spoke of a new stable . . . will you at least be employing local men to build it?"

The duke felt as though his neck cloth was slowly stran-gling him. "I will be using builders from Ardsley House."

"So the district is to benefit in no way from your new enterprise."

He snorted softly. "The district survived before you brought sheep to Myrmion. It will doubtless survive once they are gone."

Ridd got to his feet again. "Rigger Gaines told me you were a fair man and a good landlord. I wonder . . . has that red-haired shrew made you forget all your responsibility to your people?"

"How dare you!" the duke thundered, thrusting forward over the desk. "It's bad enough you question my decisions, but you will *not* criticize Lady Roarke. Now this matter is closed. I expect you to finish out the month here . . . to dispose of the sheep, for one thing, and to help me guide Lady Roarke around the property."

"And if I refuse to stay on?"

"In that case I might be forced to sell your precious sheep to the army. Mutton is always a favorite in the mess tent."

Ardsley saw anger and caution warring in Ridd's face, and he was aware of it the instant the anger was replaced by sullen resignation.

"I will st-stay on."

"And have I your promise that you will treat Lady Roarke as befits a guest in my home?"

"Yes."

"Very well. You may go." The duke began to sort through some papers on his desk.

The bailiff stopped at the door. "When I first came here, I used to look at your p-portrait in the drawing room and wonder what sort of man you had become. I imagined you'd be someone I could admire. It's sad, isn't it, how often we are d-disappointed in our expectations."

Will went directly to Rigger's suite of rooms in the kitchen wing. He swiftly told him of the duke's edict. Rigger didn't say anything at first, fiddling with his pipe while Will paced the carpet.

"Settle down," Rigger complained. "It's hard to think with you tramping about."

"I lost my head," Will muttered. "I let him rattle me. Jesus, my stammer even came back. But he wouldn't listen to reason from the first. I tried to tell him about the weavers, about my wool making the valley prosperous again. He forbade me to talk about the sheep."

"Well, you do go on, laddie."

Will glared at him, and Rigger laughed. "I was joking. Lord, you are agitated tonight. Though not without reason. The dukeling is flexing his muscles to be sure. And don't you ever dare call him that—it was what the senior boys at Oxford called him, and he hated it."

Will collapsed into a chair and fisted his hands over his eyes. "Why didn't you warn me about him, Rigger? You knew him as a boy, you must have seen the arrogance, the pigheadedness.''

"It appears he grew into those. He was a sweet-natured child, generous and well liked. But I'm sorry I never warned you about aristocrats in general. You have an easy manner and treat everyone as an equal. The nobs treat anyone who is not of their station as a hireling.''

"I *am* a hireling," Will stated. "I understand that. But I had this foolish notion that a hireling who did good work would not be dismissed out of hand. Not at a lady's idiotic whim.''

"I hope you didn't share that sentiment with Ardsley.''

He groaned. "I called her a red-haired shrew. I was not feeling very charitable—she and I met in the library earlier, and she made a cruel jest. Implied I was the village idiot.''

Rigger sighed. "You've heard worse in your time, William.''

"Aye, but not from such a fine lady. It was . . . mortifying. So little remains of who I was . . . and yet the instant someone jabs at me, it all comes roaring back.''

"You lost your footing, that's all. Both with the duke and the lady. Perhaps it's time to bring in an ally, a member of the gentry whose opinion the duke will respect.''

Will's face broke into a relieved grin. "I must be muddled that I didn't think of her. Do you suppose she would do it—stand up to His Grace?''

"You have only to ask. You know she takes her role as lady of the district very seriously. Send a message to her tonight. Then you can sleep a little sounder knowing you've taken some action.''

Chapter Four

*J*udith Coltrane could walk a line regiment into the ground. She liked to think while she walked, sorting out her various causes or practicing her weekly talks to the weavers' guild. To the men in the fields and the shepherds on the hillsides she was a familiar figure, moving briskly along the lanes with a mannish, long-legged stride. Miss Coltrane never dawdled, unless it was to pass the time with one of the farmwives or the shopkeepers in Stratton. In a more closely settled society, she would have been considered a busybody, but in this area of widely spaced farmhouses, she was often the only person to carry news from one place to another. Rigger Gaines was wont to say that Miss Coltrane was more reliable than the Mail—and twice as speedy.

She paid little attention to her appearance, dressing in gowns long out of fashion and frequently forgetting to wear a bonnet, so that she was browned and freckled by the late spring of every year. Her only accessory was a tattered carpetbag, which she kept full of tonics and nostrums for those who might be ailing. There were also packets of peppermints for her favorite children and cracked corn for any wild birds she wanted to coax from the trees.

In spite of all her eccentricities, however, there was no one who could deny that she was a lady to the bone. If she was a witch—as some people whispered—she was a very high-bred one. Although her father was a mere baronet, her mother had been the daughter of a marquess. Miss Coltrane could stare the symbols off a signpost if someone provoked the imperious side of her nature. Fortunately, few people did.

*   *   *

The duke looked up from his breakfast when Rigger came into the room.

"There is a lady here to see you, Your Grace."

"I have no time for visitors, old fellow. I am to ride out with Lady Roarke this morning. She has this minute gone upstairs to fetch her hat."

"It's Miss Coltrane." He added in an undertone, "Chief lady of the district, sir. It wouldn't do to ignore her . . . and she's walked all this way.

But the duke had already returned his attention to his plate. "Well, she can just walk all the way back. Or send her home in my coach if you—"

"Hello, Damien." A lady's head appeared at Rigger's shoulder. "Though I suppose it's Your Grace now. Oh . . . and you're having breakfast . . . how lovely. I came away from home with only a seed cake. I wanted to make an early start, you see."

She'd moved into the room as she spoke and now plunked her carpetbag on the table. The duke's eyes widened as he half stood. "Really, ma'am, this is most—"

She pulled out a chair and seated herself. "Most what? Annoying? Irritating? Are you too important now to share your breakfast with an old friend?" She leaned her chin on her hand and grinned up at him.

Her eyes danced as recognition dawned in his face.

"Judith?" he said raggedly. "Judith Coltrane? Good heavens . . . it's been, what, ten, twelve years?"

"Twelve," she answered. And then reached for the plate of kippers. "Those were dark days, I fear. But you are looking well, much better than when last I saw you."

"I could say the same for you," he said, all the while trying to hide his shock. The Judith Coltrane he'd known had been a slender girl with a creamy complexion, raven curls and a merry smile. The smile remained, but she had turned into a nut-brown maypole with a wild tangle of hair.

"You don't need to tell me I haven't aged well. My mirror doesn't lie, much as I wish it would."

"You appear quite robust," he said lamely.

She lowered her fork and winked at him. "Robust enough to take you on, Ardsley. But that can wait . . . I find I am famished. The moor air does that to a person."

He watched in stunned silence as she attacked a plate of poached eggs, kippers and fried tomatoes, washing it all down with hearty swallows from a mug of ale.

Rigger was still loitering in the doorway; he harumphed softly to get the duke's attention. "What shall I tell Lady Roarke when she comes down?"

"She can ride out with Ridd this morning. Miss Coltrane and I have some . . . some catching up to do."

"Very good, Your Grace."

Rigger left the room wearing a relieved expression, which the duke did not note. Mainly because Miss Coltrane was grinning at him again. "Just like the old days, hmm? You and me and Rigger, all together. Pity Anthony's not here."

The duke's eyes flashed. "Don't speak of him. Please. It's hard enough being at Myrmion . . . remembering."

She reached out and touched the back of his hand. "Those were wonderful times for you. Where's the harm in remembering? Though I was only six, I still recall how jolly we all were. I was sad that you never came back here after he died . . . at least not until your father took sick. And then it was not jolly, I grant you. But we still managed to find things to laugh over."

He sighed, and then said stiffly, "You helped me through a difficult time, Judith. I don't think I ever told you what it meant to me."

She waved away his gratitude. "Neighbors aid each other, Damien. It's the country way."

The truth was, she had more than aided him. Judith Coltrane had been his rock during the two weeks of his father's illness, coming to the house every day, nursing the old duke, sometimes right through the night. She'd been the one to pry him away from Myrmion, away from his mother's distraught, tear-streaked face and his grandmother's hollow-eyed expression. She had ridden out with him and shown him all her special places on the moor—the rookery in the rocks, the willow pool, the secluded valley that harbored the herd of moor ponies she'd nearly tamed. He'd felt swept back to happier days, when the three of them, he and Tony and Judith, had been impossibly young and untouched by grief.

Judith had even watched him cry once, when it came

clear that his father was failing. She'd held him in her arms and comforted him, a simple act of compassion his mother and grandmother had never thought to offer him.

He and Judith had both been seventeen that summer, neither of them out in society yet, and she was the first young woman he had ever spent time with alone. It was natural he should form a deep attachment to her—she was easy-natured, spirited and kind. Her lively companionship was such a relief from the grimness back at Myrmion. He'd longed to speak to her of his feelings, and vowed to do so the soonest it was decent. But he had left Devon the day after his father's passing, forced to accompany his mother and grandmother back to Ardsley House for the internment.

His grandmother had taken him aside after the funeral and lectured him about forming *tendres* for unsuitable young ladies. She'd hammered at him about his duty to marry well. Money and property, she'd said, were paramount. It had seemed to him at the time that he'd just inherited plenty of both.

His grandmother had gotten her way, however. He'd not yet learned the trick of agreeing with her to her face, and then going his own way in private. Even though he'd promised Miss Coltrane that he would write, he had not. The ardent letter he had composed inside his head during the tense journey back to Ardsley House remained unwritten. Instead, he had put her from his thoughts the same way he'd banished his memories of Tony.

When it became clear that his mother's grief had twisted her mind in some way, he found himself caught up in a daily round of anxiety, and Judith Coltrane, she of the night-dark hair and shimmering smile, was lost to him.

He'd gone back to his second year at Oxford feeling like an old, old man, burdened with responsibilities. Even though his grandmother would help to oversee his properties until he was out of university, he felt smothered by the weight of his obligations.

He still did, if truth be told.

And during all those intervening years, Judith had obviously remained here in Devon, unwed and, he ventured to guess, uncourted.

He looked across at her. There was still fire in her dark

eyes, and a semblance of beauty in the angular rise of her cheek. Surely some man should have seen the merit of the woman and claimed her.

"What?" she said, raising one black brow.

"I'd have thought you married by now."

She shrugged lightly. "Scared them all off, I expect. I've always gone my own way, as you know. Poor Papa has despaired of ever having a docile daughter."

"No," he said quietly, "you were never docile. I always admired that about you. Even at six, you were giving your nursemaid the megrims."

"Still am," she said. "Unlike my father, old Hannah has not yet written me off as a lost cause." She pushed her plate away. "Well, thank you for a lovely breakfast. I am primed now for a bit of sparring. You see I've come armed for battle—you've been mucking things up, Damien. And it won't do."

His cheeks narrowed as he said with quiet intent, "Don't trespass on an old friendship, ma'am."

She made a face of mock dismay. "Not at our best in the mornings, are we?" She stood up and began to dig around in her enormous bag. He watched in puzzlement as she drew a paper packet from its gaping maw.

"Here," she said holding it out to him, "have a peppermint. Wonderful for the digestion."

Ardsley also rose. "I don't want a peppermint, Miss Coltrane. What I do want is to be left in peace to run my estate the way I see fit. I gather you are here as Will Ridd's advocate. He didn't waste any time, I see."

"I'm here at his request, to be precise. Will doesn't need an advocate . . . he usually does just fine speaking for himself. It is the people of Stratton Valley who need me to speak for them. My father is magistrate here, as you will recall, so it's natural I would share his inclination to see justice done. Or injustice circumvented."

"Injustice?" he echoed. "I want to breed race horses. On my own land. Where in blazes is the crime in that?"

The lady's eyes widened. "I really think you could use a peppermint."

Ardsley tore the packet from her hand and flung it against the wall. A dozen white drops clattered against the wainscoting like miniature billiard balls.

He then sank down into his chair and set his hands over his face. "Please, Miss Coltrane," he groaned. "Have a little consideration. I am back here not twenty-four hours and have been informed by every servant in the place that Will Ridd is something akin to a saint. But saint or not, Ridd and his sheep are no longer necessary to Myrmion. I am sorry if they are necessary to the economy of the valley, but that is not my concern."

"No," she said softly, "but it is mine."

"Nevertheless, I don't care for sheep," he said. "I never have. Tony now, he had a fondness for them. More than once he showed up at the house with a lost lamb over his saddle. Mama always made him bring the mewling creature back to its shepherd. But you will recall, we never kept sheep here at Myrmion."

"Sheep are good business," she observed. "Wool and mutton are both profitable, though Will's sheep are strictly woolbearers."

The duke leaned forward, his forearms sliding along the table. "Do you have any idea how tired I am of hearing about this?"

"I know . . . sheep aren't nearly as grand as race horses."

He glared at her. "What is that supposed to mean?"

She twinkled back at him. "Why, only that if you are set on making an impression on someone, a blooded horse will always carry the day."

"I assure you, I have no need to make that sort of impression."

She tipped her head and studied him. "No," she said, "I don't suppose you do. The title sits gracefully on your shoulders. I always knew it would."

He heard the wistful, almost mournful, quality of her voice. He said gently, "Then trust me to do what is best for Myrmion. Can you do that, Miss Coltrane?"

She hesitated a moment; he guessed she was tempering her response so that he would not fly off the handle again and require a peppermint.

"I think," she said slowly, "that you might want to reacquaint yourself with Myrmion before you make any decisions. Once you understand the many progressive changes Will Ridd has instituted, you may decide that it would be imprudent to alter such a profitable, well-run concern."

"I *know* it's profitable."

"But do you know why it's profitable?"

"From selling the wool, I imagine."

"But sheep are shorn only once a year. How do you explain twelve months of steady profit?"

"Why do I have the feeling I am about to discover the answer."

She smiled and said, "Will does not sell the wool . . . he gives it away."

He was on his feet in an instant. *"He what?"*

"He gives it to the weavers in the valley." She tucked her carpetbag under one arm. "Would you ring for your carriage, please."

"You can't just walk out after fetching me a leveler like that. I demand an explanation."

"And you shall have one. Come with me and I will show you firsthand where your monthly profits come from."

"But Judith—I mean, Miss Coltrane—you misunderstand. I don't care about the profits. Myrmion is going to be a—"

"One day is all I ask," she said. "One day for you to see the magic your bailiff has worked. Now, get your hat, sir—and don't make me resort to the horehound drops." She rattled her bag ominously.

Ardsley stalked past her and out the dining parlor door, grumbling about high-handed women.

Will knew it was long past time for him to begin work. The sun had been up for hours, and still he dawdled on his rocky perch. His usual companion, Snap's son, had been banished to the stable. Will realized the pup needed a name, if only because it would make it easier to ring a peal over him. Unfortunately the ones that came immediately to mind—Hopeless, Witless, Chaos, Nemesis—did not reflect well on either dog or master.

His gaze ranged down over the pasture to the house beyond it. Fifteen minutes ago, he had seen Miss Coltrane stride up to the front door. He wondered what was transpiring inside at this moment. Good things, he hoped.

He looked toward the path when he heard a rider approaching. It was Lady Roarke, mounted on one of the hacks from Stratton—a rangy gray gelding. He admired her

graceful posture in the sidesaddle. Of course, her celestial
blue riding habit was totally out of place, as was the matching feathered Scotch bonnet. It did not even boast a brim
to keep the sun off her fair sin.

"Daft," he muttered. "And I am dafter still to be admiring her."

She pulled up below him, easily controlling the fretful
horse.

"You were to take me around the estate this morning,"
Lady Roarke called up. "Or had you forgotten?"

"I recall my orders. But it was the two of you I was
supposed to guide." He tipped his head toward the house.
"His Grace seems to be otherwise engaged."

"Yes," she said. "But he left instructions that we are not
to delay on his account. Your cob is waiting at the stable."

"Oh, you mean I am not to run behind your horse like
a faithful gillie?"

He saw the smile start, and then how she quickly restrained it. She had a bit of backbone somewhere under all
those layers of inappropriate clothing.

"That will not be necessary," she drawled. "An occasional grovel should suffice."

He rose, hiding his own smile now, and gave her an exag-
gerated bow. Then he made his way gingerly down the
granite outcropping. Once he was on the path, he touched
his hat brim to her. "Wait here—I'll be back directly. And
try not to get into any trouble."

Ursula watched as he vaulted the pasture fence and went
striding off across the field. She hated to side with Barbara
on the matter, but the duke's bailiff *was* an eyeful—tall,
leanly muscled, without the shambling gait of some long-
legged men. No, he moved purposefully, powerfully, like
one of the Titans striding over a new-made planet.

She compared Will Ridd's healthy vigor with Ardsley's
stately grace. The duke rarely moved with any urgency or
purpose. It made her wonder what he saw in horse racing.
Now she could understand it if the vital Mr. Ridd had professed a passion for the sport . . . for the unleashed power
as the horses leapt away at the start . . . for the heated,
driving fury of the race itself . . . for that breathtaking,
heartstopping moment at the finish—

She felt herself blush. Blessed saints, what had she been thinking?

It was a foolish question; she knew very well what her imagery had conjured up. A deal more heat than her encounters with the duke ever had. If she were wise, she would banish Will Ridd from her mind, if that was where thoughts of him led. For all she knew, he had a comely wife stashed in one of the estate cottages.

He soon rejoined her, mounted on his roan cob, and as they rode off she inquired where on the estate he lived. He pointed out a tile-roofed cottage on a nearby hillside.

She couldn't keep from asking, "And do you live there alone?"

"Aye . . . except for a sheep dog or two. They take shifts keeping me company."

"Where is the young dog that was with you yesterday? What was his name?"

"He's been banished for all time to the stable," he said with a sigh. "And as yet he has no name—unless it's Pernicious Trial to Mankind." He looked at her over his shoulder. "I don't suppose you'd like to name him?"

She thought for a moment. "How about Titan?"

"I think the irony of that will escape him."

"No, wait. Hold up a moment." He slowed his horse until she was abreast of him. "You can't know this, but after you rode off on Imperator yesterday, your pup cleared the lane—herded the entire flock into the pasture. It was . . . impressive."

He cocked his head. "God's truth?"

She nodded. "I think Ardsley nearly dropped his teeth."

"I might have done the same. So the scapegrace redeemed himself, did he?"

"With honors."

His crooked grin widened into a smile, a display of white teeth and deep dimples. She felt her stomach do a little jig inside her, and immediately convinced herself she had imagined it.

"Titan it is," he pronounced, then added softly, "Titan, son of Snap, grandson of Bobbin, great grandson of Old Whisky."

She gave a short laugh. "It sounds as though you're reciting a race horse's pedigree."

"Herd dogs have pedigrees . . . we might not write them down in a book, but we know them all the same. And we breed our dogs with the same care you use on your horses, finding traits that complement each other. A canny dog is bred to a fast one, a courageous dog to an agile one."

"I had no idea. It sounds as though you've studied the science of breeding."

"I've had to. My sheep are a crossed strain, long-haired and prolific. It took me nearly five years before I had the mix I wanted." He paused and the animation left his face. "Come along now." He'd started his horse forward. "I could ramble all day about my sheep, but where's the point? They'll be gone before the end of the month."

When she didn't move, he swiveled in his saddle and glared at her. "*I said come along*. My orders were to show you about, not waste your time with idle chatter."

She rode up beside him. "I'm sorry—"

"Don't be. You didn't twist the duke's arm into making this place over."

She had a nasty suspicion that it was exactly what she had done, insisting on rolling green hills and sea breezes for her bloodstock. She doubted any of the duke's other properties met those requirements as perfectly as this farm.

Will Ridd's whole manner changed after that. His easy banter disappeared and he pointed out the places he thought would interest her with a cool, distant voice that the duke could not have improved upon.

The countryside was impressive. The rolling moors were the upland, soaring above the distant Bristol Channel so that only the crowns of the trees that grew in the numerous dells could be seen. It was a topsy turvy perspective, trees below, undulating flatland above. And everywhere there were sheep, dotting the landscape like small clouds tumbled down from the sky.

She decided her horses would adore this place. If someone had set her, unknowing, in the center of the field where they now rode, she'd have sworn she was in Ireland.

"Ready to head back?" Will Ridd asked after they'd been out for an hour or so. "This stream we're riding along is the western boundary of the property."

"Who owns *that* land?" she asked, motioning to the wild stretch of moor beyond the stream.

He frowned full out. "Why? Isn't there enough acreage at Myrmion for your precious horses?"

She drew in a calming breath, recalling that he had the right to be a little testy. "I was thinking of your displaced sheep, Mr. Ridd. Perhaps the duke could buy this land . . . run both horses and sheep. I happen to raise goats at Roarke Stud—but several of my neighbors keep sheep along with their hunters."

"To answer your question, no one knows who-owns that land. It used to be part of Myrmion, but it passed out of the family decades ago. Nothing there now but birds and wild ponies."

She nibbled at her lip. The vista intrigued her—the rocky crumbles of stone rising up high in places and below them wide swathes of ungrazed grass dotted with islands of oak.

"I could ask Ardsley to look into it. Is there enough land here to support your flock?"

"It doesn't matter," he said. "It is not *my* flock, as the duke was quick to point out, and he shall dispose of it as he sees fit."

"I'd fight back," she muttered. "Or at least try to find a compromise."

"And you might succeed. Because you are of his station . . . and because I suspect there is little he can refuse you."

Her chin went up. "You are mistaken. The only connection His Grace and I share is a possible business arrangement."

She overlooked his skeptical expression and turned her horse away from the stream, but his problem continued to prod at her as they rode along. Maybe she *should* speak to Ardsley on the matter, especially if he was as smitten with her as Mr. Ridd seemed to think. She certainly understood the loss the bailiff faced—the pain and frustration of being forced to relinquish something you'd lovingly created. For eight years she'd invested her time and energy in building up Roarke Stud. Like Will Ridd, she had studied breeding practices and bloodlines; like him, she had taken great satisfaction in watching her endeavor flourish.

She had an unwitting bond with the man, she realized—they were both trying to preserve something that had given definition to their lives.

They were crossing an open meadow, when she heard a plaintive bleating rising from a nearby dell. Ridd told her to wait and quickly rode off in the direction of the sound. She sat there for a minute or two, then followed him.

He was on his knees examining a prostrate ewe, who was uttering deep, staccato cries. When he looked up at Ursula, she was struck by the pain in his eyes. "I thought the lambing was over," he said, "but there're always a few ewes who hold back."

"Why is she crying like that?"

"The lamb won't come . . ."

"Here, help me down."

"No," he barked as he rose to his feet. "Stay up there . . . ride over to those trees."

"But—"

"Go!"

She backed up her gelding a few feet, but did not move away. He glared at her. "Suit yourself then." He went to his horse and slid a wicked-looking knife from the saddlebag.

"No!" she cried as she clambered down from the saddle, landing in a tangle of skirts. She caught up her long train and struggled toward him. "Wait! Let me see her. Maybe I can help."

He turned to her, the knife tucked back along his wrist. "I fear she's beyond any help."

She hobbled past him and sank down beside the ewe. Tracing her fingers over the swollen abdomen, she felt the lamb down low, felt the oblong shape of head where rump should be.

"Come here," she called to him. "Hold her front end propped up." When he didn't move, she rolled her eyes. "Good God, sir, I run a breeding farm. You think I haven't helped a mare through a difficult foaling?"

Ridd knelt down and grasped the ewe under her front legs.

"I'm surprised you didn't try to turn the lamb rather than kill the mother," she remarked as she drew off her riding gloves.

"It's these curst big hands of mine," he said softly. "But yours might do, Lady Roarke."

The ewe was not happy about the human fingers probing inside her; she gave a series of pitiful bellows, while Ursula crooned to her. She managed to grasp a small cloven hoof, and then two. "The lamb is too tightly wedged to turn . . ." she said breathlessly. "I am rather more used to a horse's insides." She saw that he was regarding her with open amazement. "What should I do? I have hold of his rear legs."

"Pull with her contractions, Lady Roarke. Put your fine back into it and pull."

She tugged and grunted and was sure she sweated profusely, but a minute later the lamb lay, still partly sheathed and bloody, in her lap.

"Bully, ma'am," he said softly as he released the ewe.

The animal bolted upright, then staggered forward to nudge the tiny creature that Ursula had set upon the grass. The lamb did not move.

"What's wrong?" she cried hoarsely.

She was shocked when he swiftly peeled out of his coat, and then tugged his lawn shirt over his head. He crouched down, and after cleaning out the lamb's nose and mouth, he began to vigorously massage its limp body with his shirt.

"The ewe is supposed to do this," he explained. "Lick the baby to get it moving. But she's inexperienced . . . and exhausted."

Ursula said nothing. Her gaze was fastened on Will Ridd's back. Dreadful purplish marks crisscrossed it along his shoulders and down to his lean flanks. They were not whip marks—she'd seen those on a few of her stable hands, who had forsaken the King's navy for an easier life on land. No, these welts looked to be the result of severe canings. She nearly wept at the sight.

The lamb begin to bleat, and she heard Will's low cry of relief as he set the creature on its spindly legs. The ewe came over to nuzzle it and to nudge it toward her udder. Still he remained crouched in front of Ursula, watching his charges. She leaned down, quite without thinking, and traced her palm over his shoulder. "Who did this awful thing to you?" she asked raggedly.

He leapt up and away from her as though she had burned him with a torch.

"It's nothing," he muttered as he struggled into his coat.

"Surely no one in the duke's service did that to you."

"I don't want to d-discuss it." He motioned abruptly

across the clearing. "Bring your horse over here so I can get you mounted. We n-need to get back . . . His Grace will be expecting you."

It was clear she had stepped onto forbidden ground; he was angry and, she realized with a sinking feeling, embarrassed. Once again she had humiliated him, and it had been totally unintentional.

He handed her his balled-up shirt. "Here, wipe your hands clean. I'm afraid there's not much you can do about your skirt till we get home."

She looked down and gave a cry of dismay. There were ruddy streaks of drying blood all down the front of her pale blue habit.

"You do have a knack for getting grubby, Lady Roarke," he drawled.

She held the offending portion of the skirt away from her. "I can't return to Myrmion like this. Yesterday was bad enough, but today I look as though I was attacked by a gang of Mohocks. Whatever will Ardsley think?"

"I doubt he will even notice—he rarely takes his eyes from your face."

He crossed the clearing, caught up her horse's bridle and led the animal back to her. As his hands closed around her waist to help her mount, she winced. She didn't welcome that firm touch—she could still recall the feel of his bare skin under her palm when she'd stroked his shoulder. It had unaccountably stirred her. To shock and pity—and maybe something more.

He misread her reaction. "Sorry for the familiarity, my lady. There's nothing for you to use as a mounting block."

His grip tightened as he boosted her onto the saddle, but then he quickly drew his hands away, placing them behind him. There was now a cautious, edgy expression on his face. She felt she owed him some explanation, that it was not his touch she found disturbing, but rather her reaction to it. She fell back on good manners and merely said, "Thank you."

He had already moved away from her. He swung onto his own mount and rode off, chin up, back ramrod straight. She sighed and followed him, sparing a glance at the lamb, who was now hungrily nursing.

She fretted in silence the rest of the way home, over her

horror at his damaged back and over her own begrimed appearance.

"I have an idea," she said brightly. "If we stop at your cottage, I could get cleaned up there."

He did not acknowledge her suggestion.

"Surely you have soap and water."

He just kept riding without a word.

"It's the least you could do . . . I saved your ewe and the lamb."

He pulled up his horse. "No, I don't allow strangers in my cottage. If you are so . . . so mortified at the thought of meeting the duke in all your dirt, you can go in through the kitchen and up the servants' stairs."

"Aha!" she crowed. "You're pleased to see me mortified, aren't you? Go ahead, admit it."

"You're daft, ma'am."

"No—you believe you owe me payback for last night, and for just now, because I saw those marks on your shoulders. Well, I think it's wretched of you to serve me such a turn. All I ask is a half hour in your cottage . . . you need to go there anyway to change your shirt."

He sighed. "I don't wonder you've managed to wrap His Grace around your finger. You are the most single-minded woman I've ever had the misfortune to meet."

"A half hour," she repeated.

"Done, ma'am. But not a minute longer. I haven't time to waste playing laundry maid."

She had a fleeting recollection . . . something Ardsley had said yesterday. His brother making a similar comment in a playful moment. The duke had seemed so approachable then, reminiscing and laughing.

Ursula reminded herself that she was piqued with His Grace. He had spent little time with her thus far. She was beginning to fear that what she'd told the bailiff was really true—that Ardsley looked upon their relationship as strictly business.

Chapter Five

The duke had wanted to take the coach, but Miss Coltrane insisted the farm gig would do fine for their trip into Stratton. As a groom drove the vehicle into the stable yard, Ardsley took one look at the straw-littered seat and the cobweb-laced wheels and decided his morning was not going to get any better.

"Sorry, it hasn't been used in a while," the groom explained as he hopped down. "It would only take me a minute to give it a quick polish—"

"Nonsense," said Miss Coltrane. "I'm sure you have more important things to do, young man."

The duke reached out to help her into the seat, but she had already swung herself up. He changed course and paced around the front of the vehicle. At least the black draught horse looked sound. He was relieved the groom hadn't hitched up one of his high-bred coach horses—they'd have become permanently deflated by such a shabby conveyance. The duke didn't feel much better himself.

Miss Coltrane offered to handle the ribbons, but she did not press the issue after he shot her a very dark look. "I wonder folks hereabouts haven't backed you for a seat in Parliament," he said between his teeth as he guided the horse down the farm track. "Since you run everyone's business for them, you might as well take a stab at running the country."

She did not appear affronted by his sarcasm. "Don't think it hasn't crossed my mind. I wager I could do a better job than that lot of glad-handing idlers and pocket-lining poltroons who sit there now. But I expect it will be decades before women are allowed in Parliament."

"I was joking, Miss Coltrane."

"I wasn't," she said. "And I know I am bossy at times"—

she ignored his audible chuff—"however, I generally find my way is the most efficient way. Here we are, nearly halfway to Stratton, instead of standing around forever while your groom cleaned the gig."

"Efficient," he echoed, as he pried a large sticklebur from his sleeve and flicked it into the road.

He'd spent little time in Stratton during his earlier visits to Myrmion, but once the shops came into view, he realized he'd been dreaming about the place over the years and never realized it.

There was a shallow duck pond at the near end of the town, which was fed by a meandering, tree-lined stream. The village shops lay on either side of the stream, with three rustic footbridges connecting the two thoroughfares.

The town seemed larger than in his dreams, and more prosperous. He mentioned this impression to his companion.

"Stratton has grown, Your Grace. That shop block with the greengrocer and the chemist was built new only two years past, and the livery has expanded. We have a small inn now, the Severn Tides. And there is talk of starting up a newspaper . . . but I'm not sure I will have the time to—"

"Good Lord, ma'am, they surely don't expect *you* to oversee it. It isn't proper, for one thing."

"As if I ever cared for what was proper." She then stood up, leaning dangerously out of the gig, and began waving furiously to a group of men. They all waved back.

The duke had to squelch the urge to haul her back down beside him. Still, it was clearly long past time that *someone* had a hand in curbing Judith Coltrane.

"Members of the weavers' guild," she explained as she settled back on the seat. "I am their president."

"Why am I not surprised. So you've taken up weaving in your dotage?"

"I needed to know firsthand what my weavers would require, since I was responsible for ordering the looms. A woman at Stratton Meadow tutored me. Of course, when the looms got here, I hired professional weavers from Leeds to teach us."

"This isn't going to work, Miss Coltrane. I know what you're about—trying to make me feel guilty for depriving your weavers of their livelihood. However, if they are skilled and industrious, what matter if they have Ridd's wool or someone else's?" He coughed once. "Oh, yes, I had forgotten. Ridd's wool is free."

"Pull up over there," she said, pointing to a row of shops. "And I am not avoiding your question. The answer lies only a few footsteps away."

He drew up the gig before a dry-goods store called Gimble and Grimes. Again, she had climbed down before he'd made it around to her side. "You ought to let me help you," he said peevishly. "It doesn't look right, you clambering about like that when there is a gentleman present."

"But there so rarely is," she pointed out as she preceded him into the shop.

Inside, the walls were shelved to the ceiling, each shelf stacked with bolts of cloth, bed linens and rolls of ribbon. The proprietor, a lanky, balding man, at once called out a greeting from behind an oak counter.

She called back, "Come say hello to the Duke of Ardsley, Mr. Grimes."

The man crossed the floor like a shot, his eyes bright with anticipation. His bow was awkward, but the expression of awe in his eyes was a balm to the duke's rattled pride. Mr. Grimes had obviously not witnessed their arrival in the hay wagon.

"Pity Gimble isn't here," the man said with glee. "First time I've stolen a march on him in our twenty years together. It's honored I am, Your Grace."

"The duke is here to see the Pride of Stratton Valley," she explained.

"Ah," said the shopkeeper. "Come right this way."

Ardsley made his unhurried way to the back of the shop, taking time to assess the various yard goods displayed on the side counters. Myrmion was in dire need of new hangings, and he had a mind to bring Lady Roarke back here to choose some bright fabrics for the dark old house.

When he arrived at the rear counter, Mr. Grimes had already spread several items over the surface. One last item he held in his two hands, with apparent reverence. The duke felt annoyance well up. The Pride of Stratton Valley was, as he had all along suspected, just a pile of woolens.

"Yes, yes," he said absently. "Wool from Will Ridd's sheep.

I've seen it . . . now can we go, Miss Coltrane? I still might be able to catch up with Lady Roarke if we hurry back."

She sighed wearily. "You've missed the point as usual . . . Your Grace."

"The point is that I—"

"Touch it," she whispered.

He cocked his head. "What?"

"Touch it," Mr. Grimes echoed with a glint of mischief.

Heaving his own growling sigh, Ardsley stroked one hand over the nearest item, a rose-colored throw. His first, startled impression was that it was softer than swansdown, if such a thing were possible. He lifted up a fold. It appeared to be thickly knit and yet it was incredibly light.

He moved to a blanket, which had been dyed in muted shades of autumn, umbers and golds. It practically wafted through the air as he shook it open. He raised one edge and rubbed it over his face. Ah . . . softer than a woman's cheek and just as warming. He met Miss Coltrane's eyes over the fringed edge, and instead of the smug, superior expression he expected, he saw only delight.

"Remarkable," he said as he lowered the blanket. "Quite remarkable."

"I gather you never used the scarves we sent you for Christmas these last four years."

He winced. "I receive gifts from all my estates at the holidays—jars of honey, sides of beef, wheels of cheese. I never see most of them . . . my secretary donates them to a foundling home in London."

Mr. Grimes reached up to the shelf behind him and drew down a gentleman's scarf in a rich shade of blue. Ardsley was at once reminded of his brother's eyes.

"If you would accept this as my gift," the man said.

"Thank you," the duke said, now holding the scarf with the same reverence he had earlier mocked. He could barely wait for winter, when he could wrap his throat in this cloud of warmth.

"I'll take the autumn blanket, as well," he said. "On my estate account, of course. And the rose carriage rug"—he pointed to the shelf—"and that shawl in pale green." His gaze darted around the shop. "And do you carry skeins of wool? Lady Roarke's companion knits, you see."

"Over there," Mr. Grimes said. "In all the colors of the rainbow."

While the duke stood in front of the wooden rack, a thought occurred to him. "You should try to market these goods in London," he said over his shoulder.

Miss Coltrane snorted once, then quickly covered her mouth.

He turned to her. "What?"

"For four years we have been selling the Pride of Stratton Valley to shops in London and Leeds, Bath and Brighton. This year, we started shipments to Boston. Winters blow cold in New England, I hear tell."

"And is that where my estate revenues come from?"

"Precisely. Will Ridd gives the weavers' guild the raw wool. The apprentice weavers card it, spin it and dye it. Then it is passed to the master weavers. And when the finished product goes to market, Myrmion takes half. The guild portions out the rest to the workers."

"And this was your idea, Judith?"

"Oh, no. This was Will's dream. The clay mines were closing . . . men were returning from the war to find there was little work available. Stratton Valley was dying. Will had been selling outside the district, but he had a notion to keep the wool here, to let the whole area profit from it. Because, you see, he knew how special it was, how rare and fine."

"Was it a fluke, then, that the wool turned out so soft and light?" The duke was pondering the possibilities—if the pasturage at Myrmion could produce such a superior fleece, what would it do for the muscle and bone of race horses?

Miss Coltrane dashed his hopes. "The flock at Myrmion is the result of five years of cross-breeding various types of sheep. You should let Will give you the particulars."

Ardsley recalled that the man had tried to do that exact thing last night. And he'd waved away his explanation with a scowl.

"I need to think," he said brusquely. "Is there a tea house in Stratton? I am suddenly parched."

The duke followed Miss Coltrane from the shop; they went along the street to a cheerful establishment called The

Rosemary Tree. He managed to hold a chair for Miss Coltrane, which made him feel unaccountably gallant.

At first they spoke only commonplaces about their respective families. She never asked after his mother, which led him to believe she knew full well how the duchess went on.

Once their tea arrived, Miss Coltrane got down to business. "I know that what you saw in G & G surprised you. I know, further, that this throws a stick into the spokes for you . . . and I'm sorry about that. But I was horror-struck last night when I read Will's note—that you were going to sell off the Myrmion flock and dismiss him. Everyone depends on him. *I* depend on him, and that's saying something. You saw here only a small sampling of what he's done. I was going to take you around to some of the weavers' homes, but I see now that you are weary."

"Not weary, ma'am, merely muddled. And I don't enjoy the sensation. I am also irritated that Will Ridd never wrote to me about this. Rather took on more than was his right, I'm thinking. He should have informed me of his scheme."

"Oh, so you could have promptly scotched it?"

"I might have come down here myself . . . seen the hard times the district was going through. I am not without conscience."

"Damien," she whispered sharply, "you wouldn't have come back. We both know why you stayed away for the last twelve years."

He looked startled, and then his expression darkened. "If I take your meaning correctly, then I have to say you are placing far too much weight on what I believe was a childhood . . . infatuation."

She gave an abrupt laugh. "Oh, you thought I was referring to us, to that brief time when we lived in each other's pockets? Please . . . that was barely worth an entry in my diary. No, I was referring to your brother. I swear he haunted you while you were down here, you had such a spooky look in your eyes at times. And then that last night, as the duke lay dying . . ."

"I don't want to talk about that night."

But she kept on, though in a quiet, compassionate tone. "He kept calling out, 'Find Anthony, bring my lost son back to me,' and 'God forgive me, he is not dead.' "

"You weren't family," he said gruffly. "You shouldn't have had to witness that."

"Your mother needed all the help she could get . . . and I was glad to be there. But it was very upsetting. Your father really believed Tony was alive."

"It was the delirium, nothing more. And maybe I did stay away because the place spooked me. But I know now there are no ghosts at Myrmion." He added with a wistful smile, "Although if my brother was going to haunt any of the Ardsley properties, it is the place he would pick."

She set her hand over his. "I'm glad you've come back, Damien. Whatever course of action you decide on, it's good to have my old friend here."

"Even one not worthy of a diary entry?"

She amazed him by blushing.

He amazed himself by saying, "Pity I was so callow back then, Jude. A wiser fellow would not have ridden away."

She quickly composed herself; she folded her hands and met his eyes. "I was wiser than you, I suppose. I never expected that you wouldn't."

They left the tea house soon after, but Judith refused a ride to Stratton Meadow. She hefted up her carpetbag and started off down the street, then turned before she had gone many paces.

"One thing I want you to remember, Ardsley, when you make your decision. While the Pride of Stratton Valley comes from the sheep, Will Ridd is the true pride of Stratton Valley. If we lose him, I fear the heart might go right out of the place."

The duke muttered to himself all the way home. Was the woman in love with his bailiff, that she sang his praises . . . over and over? He didn't want to think about her being in love with Ridd, didn't want to think about her loving any man.

No, he mused, she was long past that sweet season. She had turned into the worst caricature of a spinster—bossy, opinionated, convinced that she knew what was best for everyone, while going about like a pure fright in old gowns and worn boots. Hailing men on the street like a common fishwife, leaping out of carriages like a hoyden. Well, that she'd always been, he recollected, a charming, free-spirited creature with the most infectious laugh.

Still, it was fortunate he hadn't come back to Devon and courted her. She would have made him the devil of a duchess, with all her eccentricities and odd starts.

Somewhere in a deep recess of his brain, a voice argued that perhaps she had evolved that way out of necessity. She'd always had more energy and drive than anyone he knew; it was logical that she should seek outlets for those qualities. As his duchess, she would have had broader, more traditional outlets—charitable societies to promote, estate workers to look after, members of the *ton* to entertain. Judith had had to limit herself to a smaller canvas, he saw. But her duties here were not so dissimilar—she ran a weaver's guild, looked after the townspeople and doubtless acted as hostess at the squire's dinner parties.

If some of those pursuits bordered on the improper, they should not make her less in his eyes. Judith Coltrane had bloomed where she'd been planted, which was more than he could say for himself.

It was pointless to think of what might have been, he decided. She no longer evoked any tender emotions in him, save a slight proprietary tug. It was the shock of seeing her again that had stirred up that possessiveness. Being with her had merely reminded him of his foolish, youthful conviction, which he'd hidden from his heart for over a decade, that she was the only woman with whom he could be truly comfortable. These errant feelings would crumble like a brittle old newspaper once they were exposed to the full light of day. He was certain of it.

He told himself, furthermore, that if he could be relaxed and natural with Miss Coltrane, there was no reason he could not replicate that behavior with Ursula Roarke.

Will Ridd's cottage lay partway up a wooded slope and was surrounded by rhododendrons, now blooming in a blaze of pink. The three front windows that looked out over the pasture were mullioned, like those at Myrmion, though Ursula suspected the cottage was of more recent construction.

They drew up their horses at the back, near a work shed, and Ursula let him lift her down from the saddle without a word of complaint.

"I'll fetch some water from the well," he said as he tethered their horses to a bush. "You go on inside."

The back steps led to a small, tidy kitchen. A wooden trestle table sat against one wall, stacked with books on husbandry and other farming topics. An opened journal lay there, the pages covered with blocky, uneven printing.

This puzzled her. It was the handwriting of a young child or of someone barely schooled. Yet Will Ridd spoke like an educated man. She leaned over the journal and read the most recent entry, which described a thunderstorm. The sentences in the passage were well formed, perhaps even lyrical.

She sensed Ridd behind her just as his hand reached around her and closed the book. "Poor stuff for a lady's entertainment," he said as she turned to face him.

"I didn't mean to pry," she said quickly. "Although you do have a nice turn of phrase."

He grimaced. "I write like a lackwit," he said as he set the pail on a high stool.

"I meant your prose, sir. Your penmanship needs some work."

He shrugged and pointed to a stack of folded flannels above the stone sink, then knelt at the hearth to stir up the fire. She fetched a flannel and doused it in the pail. As she began to dab at her skirt, she realized he had risen and was now gazing at her assessingly.

Ursula was used to looks of male admiration, but she could read nothing complimentary in his narrowed eyes. His expression, rather, was that of a man who had allowed a wild animal into his home and was now gauging how long it would be before it bit him.

She showed her teeth, and he surprised her by chuckling. "My dogs do that when they're vexed by something."

"I'm flattered," she drawled, "that you would compare me to your collies."

"You should be."

"I know," she said.

She returned her attention to her skirt, wetting the cloth and dabbing, until the ruddy marks were gone. Unfortunately, the whole front panel was now soaked through.

She shot him a look of entreaty and he said, "Come stand by the parlor hearth—it sheds more heat."

She followed him, gazing around the small room while he knelt and again built up the fire. It was a cozy nest Ridd had created for himself. As at the manor, the furnishings were worn but comfortable—a small, brocaded sofa with scarred legs, a worn velvet armchair, a thin-legged writing table missing some veneer, and beneath them all lay a faded Aubusson carpet. A tall bookcase towered beside the hearth, while a low one sat between the two windows.

Her attention was drawn to a series of paintings displayed above the smaller bookcase. They looked to be simple watercolors of farm animals, but as she stepped closer, she saw that the beasts' faces had been sketched with sly humor. There was a merry red cow, a self-important hog, a collection of frantic chickens and one very perplexed sheep.

"Miss Coltrane painted those," he said, coming up behind her. "She is the squire's daughter, lives over in Stratton Meadow."

"She is very talented."

"There are more in here." He'd moved to the tiny front hall, where light filtered in from a half-moon window above the door. She again followed him, and then wished that she hadn't. There was barely room for the two of them in the small space. He must have sensed her unease; he reached around her and pushed open the door at her back. "I'll just change my shirt—"

He disappeared into the room, but did not completely close the door. She shifted slightly, so that she was able to see inside. A dark wood bedstead covered with a featherbed took up most of the space; beyond it stood a pine armoire. On the far wall, on either side of a washstand, ranged a series of brass hooks where hats, vests and a canvas drover's coat hung.

Will Ridd stood in profile at the foot of the bed, facing away from the doorway; she watched as he drew off his coat, and then untied his cravat. Her eyes widened as he tugged a clean shirt over his head. The upward motion caused the sloping muscles of his arms to flex dramatically, while his sleek ribcage swelled and the rippling planes of his abdomen tightened.

Ursula nearly groaned aloud at the sight, yearning suddenly for the lost, early intimacies of her long-dead marriage. She was not proof against this potent reminder of what it had once felt like to caress a man's warm, lean body. She craved that heat now, like a traveler seeking refuge from an ice storm. But certainly not from this man, this bailiff . . . even if his physical beauty was, as Barbara Falkirk had so aptly noted, more than mortal woman should have to bear.

Ursula stumbled back from the doorway.

When Will Ridd emerged from the room, knotting his neckcloth, her attention was fixed on one of the paintings—a comically frustrated bear cub capering around a beehive.

"That's you," he said a bit sharply. At her questioning expression, he added, "Your given name is Ursula, isn't it? It means little bear?"

"It does," she said. "I often try to overlook it."

He stood back and made a production of examining the watercolor. "Yes, I'd say that's you to the life." His eyes were burning bright with some dark humor as he drawled, "The little bear dancing around the honey pot."

Her brows flew up. "Are you implying that I—that I—"

"That you've set your cap at a wealthy, titled husband? Is it not the truth? Though I do not judge you for it . . . I am merely making an observation."

"How dare you!"

He gave a shrug. "You are in my cottage, ma'am. I believe I may dare anything."

She swept up her train and fled from his sudden antagonism into the parlor, where she took her place before the hearth. Something had riled him, but she had no idea what.

"Stand a bit closer, madam," he ordered brusquely as he came into the room. "Or you'll never dry off. You don't want to come down with the grippe. It's hard to beguile a duke with your nose all red and runny."

"You are the rudest . . . most infuriating man," she uttered from between clenched teeth as she violently fanned her skirts before the fire. "I am trying very hard to make up for *my* initial rudeness to you, but you keep needling me. If you find my company so distasteful, just say so, and I will inform Ardsley. Because, I ought to warn you, he intends for you to assist me in planning the layout of the new paddocks."

"Yes, he told me. He also told me to mind my manners with you."

Her head craned around. "Well?"

He stalked over to her and spun her to faced him. "But

who is going to tell you to mind *your* manners, Lady Roarke?"

"I don't . . ." she sputtered. "What—?"

He leaned down so that his face was only inches from hers. "I will not be gawked at," he growled menacingly. "Not by you, not by anyone."

She thrust him away. "I have never gawked at you, you great imbecilic buffoon!"

"No?" He drew back from her a pace or two, his expression severe.

"I have far better things to occupy my time—"

"There is a mirror over my washstand. I saw your reflection . . . in the doorway." His voice rose. "You had to see them again, didn't you? Those marks on my back . . . you just had to gawk at them again."

"No!" she cried softly as the shock of being found out— and being so badly misread—swept over her. "I wasn't gawking. God's truth, Will. I wasn't even looking at your back."

"What then? Never seen the inside of a bailiff's bedroom . . . is that your excuse?"

How could she possibly explain the compulsion that had led her to spy on him? "I have no excuse," she murmured. "Except that you are . . . very fit. I suppose I was admiring your . . . your physicality."

He gave a low chortle. "My what?"

She put her chin up. "My companion, Miss Falkirk, calls you a braw, bonny man. I was just curious to see how bonny."

His mouth twisted into a sly grin. "And what is your opinion, Lady Roarke?"

"I believe I just used the word 'admiring,' Mr. Ridd. That should be answer enough for you."

He leaned toward her. "It is. And consider the compliment returned."

He left her then, disappearing into the kitchen. She wondered if he was as embarrassed as she was by that last exchange. She longed to be gone from there, but her dratted skirt was still wet through.

She looked around for something to distract her. An etching of Myrmion above the hearth caught her eye, and she tried to picture herself as mistress of the house. She saw her horses grazing in the surrounding fields with nary a sheep in sight. The thought saddened her somehow.

Her gaze moved to the tall bookcase. It appeared Mr. Ridd enjoyed the classics—Homer, Virgil, Shakespeare, Pope. Fairly ambitious reading for a man with such a child-like hand. Mayhap the squire's talented daughter came over of an evening and read to him. Her teeth grit at the thought, and she immediately chided herself.

What did she care how Will Ridd amused himself or with whom? It was true he possessed a compelling face and form, but the neighborhood around Roarke Stud was full of handsome rogues, and she'd never found herself mooning over any of them after Roary's death. In fact, she'd thought herself completely immune to the attractions of the male sex. Not even Ardsley—whom Estelle had labeled an Adonis—had been able to stir her imagination. Ardsley's bailiff seemed able to accomplish it without even trying.

She determined to give the man a wide berth. Let Ardsley design his own paddocks with Will Ridd. She would find other pursuits to keep her busy. Perhaps she would ask the duke if she could plan a small party, something to announce their presence in the neighborhood. Invite the squire and his talented daughter—she managed not to grit her teeth—and a few other landowners. It would be the perfect means for showing the duke that she was duchess material.

She focused on the possibilities. If she hired musicians, there could be dancing in the drawing room. She'd set up card tables in the back parlor and serve supper in the garden. The cook was not very talented, but Ursula knew she could come up with a menu that was not beyond the woman's ability.

Will Ridd interrupted her pleasant musing. "Tea," he said, thrusting a mug into her hands. "And I've ginger crisps if you are hungry."

She shook her head, and then looked at him assessingly. Did he dance? she wondered. It never hurt to have an extra gentleman at a party. And bailiffs fell into that same peculiar category as governesses—not quite servants, not quite one's social equal. Still, they were useful when it came to filling out the numbers at the dinner table.

"What are you plotting in that red head of yours?" he

asked as he settled back on the sofa, cradling his mug. "I fancy Lucretia Borgia wore that same look when she was cooking up some scheme to poison an enemy."

"It's nothing to do with you," she assured him.

"There's a relief."

"And I believe we can go any time now."

"Your gown still looks fairly damp."

"The air will dry it once we are outside."

He shook his head. "There's a brisk breeze come up from the Channel. You really don't want to chance it."

"I thought you wanted me gone from here. I thought you had things to do."

He touched one hand gracefully to his chest. "You see me being accommodating, Lady Roarke. As ordered."

She sniffed. "I see you being contrary, you mean."

"It's all in the interpretation." He lapsed into silence then, drinking his tea and—she was quite sure—staring at her while she faced the fire. Perhaps he was getting his own back, doing a bit of gawking at her expense.

She heard him set his mug down, and when he spoke, there was a note of seriousness in his tone. "So have you made up your mind then? About whether to sell your horses to the duke?"

"I would hardly tell you before I told him. But it doesn't matter—he seems determined to turn Myrmion into a stud with or without my bloodstock. So don't lay the blame for all his changes at my door."

"But I do," he said. "If he didn't want your horses, then why did he bring you here? And if you don't intend to sell them to him, then why did you come?"

"To inspect the property," she said simply.

She heard his chuckle. "The property being a fine-looking gentleman with an ancient title."

She chose not to respond.

"And how will you fare if he doesn't come across with a proposal? No, don't flare up at me, ma'am. I know you are deep in debt, for all your fine trappings. You see, Rigger Gaines has a cousin in Dublin. Sir Connor Roarke's profligacy was something of legend in that city."

"I still possess a few things of value," she said.

"No thanks to your late husband. And your land is entailed, is it not? So your days as a tenant must be numbered. I imagine your meeting with Ardsley was very timely—a wealthy young duke, unattached and eager to set up his own stud. Now if you could just convince him to set up his nursery—"

She twisted around and offered him her haughtiest sneer. "If what you believe about me *is* true, Mr. Ridd, then you had better tread warily. If I gain the duke's favor, as you think is my intent, then you'd be wiser to make of me an ally than an enemy."

"Then again, if I manage to send you packing, the duke might just forget about breeding race horses. He'll likely find other amusing pursuits away from Devon, and I can continue on as before."

She swung full around to him. "And just how do you propose to . . . to send me packing?"

His brows rose. "Did Wellington tell Napoleon his battle plans?"

She blew out a breath of exasperation. "I will make a bargain with you, sir. If you agree not to interfere with my . . . plans, I will speak to Ardsley on your behalf."

He shrugged. "Miss Coltrane has already done so. She was the duke's morning caller."

Ursula bit back her irritation. The lady seemed to have a great deal of interest in the men at Myrmion. "It couldn't hurt you to have two advocates," she pointed out. "And my pleas are sure to carry as much weight as those of . . . a squire's daughter."

He was chuckling when he rose and crossed over to her. "You haven't had the pleasure of Miss Coltrane's acquaintance. She could argue the bark off an oak, had she a mind to."

"There are better persuasions a lady might use," she said in a low, throaty voice.

"I am sure of that," he said. He'd leaned down to examine the front of her habit, and when he turned his head to look up at her, his face was so close to her breast that her breathing hitched. "Just don't try any of them on me."

She fell back a pace, away from that provoking gaze, but then recovered her poise almost at once. "You needn't worry, Mr. Ridd," she said in an airy voice. "All my persuasions are reserved for men of power. Else where's the point?"

She gave him an arch smile as she set her mug on the

mantel. With a swirl of skirts, she swept from the parlor, through the kitchen and down the back steps. Fortunately, there was a tree stump near the work shed. She maneuvered her gelding into place and managed to mount unassisted. She was dashed if she was going to let that man come anywhere near her.

She was already arranging her skirts when he came out of the cottage. He didn't comment on her accomplishment, merely caught up his own horse and mounted.

They rode toward the house in silence, Ridd in the lead. He had forgotten his hat, and the sun struck golden fire in the pale strands of his hair. She wanted to lob something at that gilded head.

When they got to the stable gate, she said stiffly, "Thank you for your . . . time."

He did not ride off, but leaned back in his saddle with a thoughtful expression. "Be my advocate with Ardsley, if you so choose," he said at last, "and I will try to undo the things I've set in motion to remove you from this place." His eyes met hers. "You see, I do have a tiny bit of power."

"I never thought otherwise," she said quietly. "I will do what I can."

"And here's a bit of friendly advice that might aid you with the duke. If you are determined to seek out a man in his bedroom, little bear, it doesn't pay to hover in the doorway."

He touched his forelock, then set his heels to the cob's side.

She watched him ride off, feeling fully vexed that he had gotten in the last shot.

Will didn't feel as though he'd gotten in the parting shot. In fact, he felt rather battle scarred as he rode away. Allowing her inside his cottage had been a mistake. Especially since he'd been picturing her there since yesterday afternoon. Of course, the reality was never like one's imaginings—wherein she'd been a deal more accommodating, if not downright compliant.

He was a damned fool for thinking anything was possible along those lines. She hadn't even liked having his hands on her for that instant when he'd helped her to mount. He could still see her expression of distaste.

Yet he doubted she found him completely repellent. After all, she'd watched him undress from the doorway, admiring his—what had she called it?—his physicality.

He supposed that was the paradox a man faced when dealing with a high-born woman . . . she could look, but he couldn't touch. A pity. He'd been itching to touch her again, to feel that fine, slender waist under his hands. To stroke the curve of her cheek where bone turned to blossom.

Enough of this, he told himself sternly. Ursula Roarke was not for him and never would be. She'd ended up shackled to the duke or to some other idle, arrogant nob, and he'd better get used to the idea.

Ursula saw Ardsley crossing the stable yard and reined her horse in his direction.

"I was about to ride out looking for you," he said, grasping her bridle. "I've been holding back luncheon, but the vicar's due to come by in less than an hour."

"Thank you for waiting. And I'm sorry for the delay. I had to help Mr. Ridd deliver a lamb."

He looked up in surprise. "Was that necessary?"

"The ewe seemed to think so."

"I meant did Ridd honestly expect that of you?"

"Not part of the usual tuppence tour, I'm sure. But he didn't charge me extra for the added excitement."

The duke's expression was still clouded. "You seem in an odd mood, my dear."

"Do I?" she said, a little miffed that the duke would not banter with her. His bailiff could give him a few lessons in that direction. "Perhaps it's just hunger." She held out her arms to him. "Help me down, please."

He hesitated, then placed his hands gingerly around her waist. As he lifted her from the saddle, she purposely grasped his shoulders, curling her fingers over the lean muscle there Once she was on her feet, she swayed into him a little.

"Oh, you are light-headed, ma'am," he cried. "Shall I fetch you some water?"

"No," she said quickly, letting her arms drop. "I am fine."

Fine, she repeated under her breath. Frustrated was more

like it. She'd been trying to kindle some physical response in the man and instead ended up alarming him. She wagered Will Ridd knew what to do with a woman who melted against him.

Don't hover in the doorway . . . No, that one wouldn't let a woman hover. Not for long.

Chapter Six

*J*udith Coltrane tried to distract herself in Stratton, stopping in at the greengrocer's and the bookseller's, but she could not ease her mind. She finally gave up and headed off toward Stratton Meadow.

There was a deep dell beside the road about a mile from her home, where she often went to be alone. A small pool lay beneath a gnarled willow, and she liked to lie on the mossy bank and watch the tiny fishes swim and play. It was her place of dreams and had been since she'd first shared it with a tawny-haired young man. Damien had lain there one July afternoon and wept in her arms. It had been over a decade since she had watered that mossy bank with her own tears, but she went there now to weep.

She'd thought herself long over him. When he'd ridden away and never written, she'd cried here nearly every day for a year. The next year the tears came less often, but she still found the need for her haven whenever someone mentioned the name of Ardsley.

And then something wonderful had occurred. Rigger Gaines had brought a new bailiff to Myrmion, another tall young man with fair hair. Though he looked nothing like Damien, who was slender and pale of complexion, Will Ridd had reminded her of the young duke. Maybe it was his wry, crooked grin or the restless energy both young men had possessed.

Though not any longer, she thought sadly. The Damien she had met today appeared languid, even staid. That boundless energy seemed to have been leached out of him over the years. Will Ridd, on the other hand, was still full of eager enthusiasm.

Dear Will had been the saving of her. He hadn't known the source of her grieving, but he had recognized it almost at once. He'd had his share of grieving, she knew—so mistreated in his youth that he had lost all memory of his childhood. Rigger Gaines had somehow found him at fifteen, a lad for hire placed on a farm, doing the work of two grown men. Rigger had taken him away and hired tutors to school him; Will had known how to read and write, but could barely stammer out his words. Judith often wondered why Rigger had put himself out for a stranger, even one in dire straits. Not that Will hadn't earned his kindness. He'd done well with his lessons, and in time he and Rigger became as close as was possible without a blood bond.

Will was twenty-one, or thereabouts, when he came to Myrmion. At first, his manner with people had been fumbling, and his stammer sometimes came back. There were those who claimed that he was addled, placed in a position of authority only through Rigger's influence with the dowager duchess. Judith knew those awkward moments were only traces of his old life resurfacing. As the years passed, Will Ridd became the linchpin that held all of Stratton Valley together. Its heart, as she had told the duke.

Will had befriended her from the first and made her a part of his grand scheme to improve Myrmion. She knew her father had hoped they'd make a match of it—he'd suspected her anguish over Damien and would have welcomed *any* man who lifted her spirits, bailiff or no.

But she and Will had fallen into an easy accord, not unlike sister and brother, and though she was sure she loved him, she had never been in love with him. No, she had not been in love with any man since the young duke rode away.

And now he was back . . . so changed that she barely knew him. She was sure he'd thought the same about her, but all her alterations were of the physical variety. Her character had not changed one whit. He, on the other hand, had undergone some tragic metamorphosis—all his humor and spirit and . . . uniqueness had been ground away.

She knew he had brought a lady to Myrmion, the widow of an Irish baronet. Was it she who had wrought such a change in him? Did he feel he had to posture and pose to impress her? No, his stiff manner seemed of longer standing than that.

The more she thought about it, the more she knew where

to lay the blame. It was the work of his grandmother, the fierce dowager duchess who placed such a premium on rank and protocol. *She* had turned the lively boy Judith loved into this dour travesty of a human being.

The bitter tears came then, for all she had lost twelve years ago, and for what she sadly had not found that morning—the pleasure of Damien's company. She lay facedown on the soft moss and sobbed as though her heart were breaking all over again.

After a time, she raised herself on one elbow and fished a man's handkerchief from her bag. Perhaps it was better this way, she reasoned as she blotted her face. How much more hurtful would it have been if he'd still been her laughing, teasing Damien, and she knowing all the while that he was paying court to another lady? Let the Irishman's widow have him, she thought. And then laughed at her own magnanimity.

She'd glimpsed Lady Roarke in the hall that morning, seen the lustrous hair, with its glints of fire, the striking silver-blue eyes and the alabaster skin. Judith knew she could bathe in chamomile for a year and not achieve such a complexion.

She crept forward until she was angled over the pond. A wavering reflection stared back at her—tangle-haired, gaunt-faced. She was unfashionably tanned and, worse yet, there was a sprinkling of chestnut freckles over the bridge of her nose.

She rolled onto her back and stared up through the canopy of branches to the bright sky above. The color made her think of Will's eyes. *He* never minded how she looked or how she dressed. He didn't think her bossy—well, not impossibly bossy—or improper. Then again, Will Ridd was not the man she had waited for for twelve long years.

It wouldn't hurt to neaten her appearance a bit, she decided. She'd have to meet with the duke again over the sheep issue, and it might make him more agreeable if she looked like a lady of fashion instead of a washerwoman.

She knew there was no chance of rekindling the feelings he'd once had for her. And truth to tell, she wasn't sure she even liked this new incarnation of Damien. But she would offer the duke her friendship, as Will had offered her his. Great things had come of that alliance . . . and perhaps even greater things could come of her association with Ardsley. Or at the very least, she could prevent bad things from coming to pass in the valley.

Ardsley spent an hour with the vicar, who made numerous pronouncements on Will Ridd's assured place in heaven for all he had done for the parish and "him not even a churchgoing soul, bless the boy." The duke wondered if there was one person in Stratton who did not echo his sentiments.

His initial irritation that Ridd had never once sought his approval, let alone his permission, for the changes he'd made was now compounded by a very human feeling of envy. Ardsley realized he had pictured *himself* becoming the savior of Myrmion—the relocation of a famous stud to the estate was bound to attract many notable people, perhaps even royals, to the neighborhood. He saw now that he was not only being denied the role of district champion—he was viewed by some as a usurper.

He had spent his early youth dogging the footsteps of his adored older brother, and after Anthony's death he'd often felt like a disappointment to his father. "Second son, second best," he would recite to himself during those difficult days. After his father died, he had dwelled in the hawklike shadow of his grandmother, battling always to break free of her stifling influence. And now, when he had at last stood up to her, savoring the chance to create something that was truly his own, he again felt overshadowed.

By a bailiff!

It was intolerable. He had to reinstate himself here, and in a manner that would leave no doubt as to his wisdom, benevolence and foresight. And he had a notion of just how to do it.

He smiled. Will Ridd might have brought the town back from the brink of ruin, but Ardsley vowed that if his plan worked, he would make Stratton the bright center of North Devon.

Before they went in to supper that night, Ursula asked the duke for a private interview. He seemed taken aback. "We have business to discuss," she reminded him.

"You certainly don't need to make an appointment, my lady."

She tactfully did not point out to him that, starting with last night, he had been closeted with his household staff, his majordomo, his bailiff, Miss Coltrane, the vicar, the farrier and his head dairyman. If these were the normal demands on a duke's time, she took leave to wonder where little dukes came from.

He agreed to see her in his study directly after supper and added that he had a few things of his own to discuss.

The meal seemed endless, and between courses Ursula fretted over what she'd decided to tell him. As a woman whose business was horses, bargaining came second nature to her. Still, she was not sure if dukes bargained or if they merely decreed.

Once she was seated opposite him in the study, her fears solidified. He seemed distracted, fidgeting with a length of blue cloth that lay bundled on his desk. This was not the behavior of an eager suitor, certainly. Ursula felt her currency dip drastically.

But then he put the blue cloth aside and smiled at her. It was a relaxed, if somewhat rueful smile. "I realize I have not been exactly attentive, my lady. I should have come here first and caught up on my estate business before you arrived. Now that those duties are out of the way, however, you have my full attention."

She thanked him graciously. "I have a request . . . or a favor, rather, to ask."

He steepled his fingers. "You need only to speak it, my dear. And if it's within my power to grant . . ."

"I do hope so. Today Mr. Ridd and I rode along the property that adjoins your own to the west. He told me it was sold away from Myrmion decades ago. There are no fences or pastures on this land; it appears wild and uncultivated."

"I know the area you mean. I vaguely recall that my father sold it to a fellow from London. He's apparently done nothing with it since."

"I want you to buy it for my horses." She paused. "That is the condition of sale."

The stiffness returned at once to his posture. "I don't understand. There are countless acres here at Myrmion . . . lush grass, good water . . . everything your bloodstock could require."

"This is a sheep farm, Your Grace. I believe it should remain as such."

She was surprised when his dark expression gave way to a crooked grin. "You haven't been talking to Miss Coltrane by any chance: No, you didn't need to. You spent the morning with my bailiff. They all talk nothing but sheep hereabouts."

She set her hands on the edge of his desk. "While you were in Ireland, you mentioned this place in passing, told me it was a . . . a shabby little estate that somehow managed to turn a profit. Now that I have seen it, I can say that there is nothing shabby about it."

"I may have been hasty in my judgment. After all, the last time I was here, it had pretty much been taken over by moor ponies. My father only ever came here because it was near the sea, and he loved to sail."

"You told me you wanted to make a fresh start. Knocking down sound barns to build a stable, tearing up existing fences to make paddocks . . . it's more like vandalism than a fresh start." She saw his brows rise, but kept on. "That western parcel would offer you a clean slate—fields that have not been overgrazed, open land on which to build."

He drew in a deep breath. "You know I want to please you, but I'm not sure this is within my power to perform. And what purpose would it serve? You have all of this estate at your disposal."

"I frankly don't like knowing that the sale of my horses means the removal of Will Ridd and his flock."

"Ah, I see it all comes back to my bailiff. I gather he has won you over."

"He is still very unmannerly, I'm afraid. But knowledgeable and skilled, for all that. I never turned off a good worker at Roarke Stud, not once in eight years."

To her surprise the duke rose from his chair and leaned forward to drape the blue cloth over the front of the desk. It was a woolen scarf, she saw, dense and finely knit.

"Touch it," he said as his eyes lit.

She stroked her fingers along its length. "Soft as a cloud," she murmured, and then, unable to resist, she lifted it and set it against her cheek. She closed her eyes and smiled.

"Yes," he said. "I had the same reaction. It's heavenly stuff."

He opened one of his desk drawers and drew out a pale green shawl. "This is for you." He came around the desk and settled it on her shoulders. She touched his hand. "Thank you. But I am all at sea here. I thought you disliked anything to do with sheep and wool."

"Ah, that was before I discovered the Pride of Stratton Valley. That is what Miss Coltrane calls these woolens. At least I think she is the one responsible for the name. It sounds like her."

"And these admirable woolens come from Will Ridd's sheep?"

"Yes, and they are marketed in London and Leeds, Brighton and Bath. Oh, and Boston." He chuckled softly. "You were right, Lady Roarke. This is not a shabby farm—it is a veritable center of industry."

He briefly told her what he'd learned, of how Will Ridd gave his fleece to the weavers' guild, who then split the profits from the woolens with Myrmion.

"So you are not going to sell off the sheep?"

He tugged one ear. "There's the rub. I want to breed horses at Myrmion, but everyone in the district would prefer to keep things as they are. It requires a man with the wisdom of Solomon to sort it out."

"You have other estates," she ventured.

"None that fit your requirements. Wise requirements, I now believe. The horses should suffer little in the move from Ireland to Devon." He paused. "I am having my man in London draw up the papers, so that your bloodstock can be shipped here as soon as may be."

"But Your Grace—"

"And if you could see your way to remaining here during the transition, I should like it very much." He held her gaze. "Very much, indeed."

There it was, she saw clearly, the bait being dangled in front of her. Sell him her horses, stay here and be courted . . . or refuse the sale and go back to Ireland to face the duns.

"Then what of your bailiff?" she asked cautiously. "What of the wool?"

"I think I have a solution," he said. "In Dartmoor the

land is not so fertile as it is here . . . pasturage can be leased for a song. I'll hire a land agent to find me a farm in Dartmoor and run the sheep there."

"Away from Stratton Valley?"

He shrugged. "The weaving is done here; what matter where the wool comes from?" Before she could protest, he added, "The trouble with my bailiff is that he was thinking on a small scale. These woolens have great potential, ma'am. In the right hands. Of course, the size of my flock can't be increased overnight to meet added demands, but there is the option of blending in other wools. I will expand shipments to Europe and the northern American states. It will require the construction of a weavers' hall, which will bring work to the district. Your prickly Mr. Ridd should approve of that."

Ursula felt the first uneasy shivers of alarm. The duke had a new toy now, and she sensed that she and her horses were about to become yesterday's distraction.

She drew on a mantle of airy poise. "Once the stud is established, I imagine involvement in such a thing might be stimulating. Of course, right now you have other concerns."

"I want to do both. Combine pleasure *and* commerce. Even my grandmother can't quibble with that."

She gave him a half-hearted smile. "It sounds ambitious, two new ventures at once."

"Do you doubt I can accomplish them both? I don't . . . not with you here beside me."

He patted her hand and she nearly snatched it away. "And what of Mr. Ridd?"

"I have no plans to dismiss him. Does that make you happy, my dear Lady Roarke?" His voice sounded almost fond.

"A fair resolution would please me very much."

"Exactly what I have in mind. I'll speak to Ridd in the morning . . . and perhaps afterward you and I can ride out together. I trust you know your way around the old place by now."

Ursula lingered in the front hall the next morning while Will Ridd was closeted with the duke and managed to forestall him as he was leaving. She drew him into the parlor and shut the door.

"Well? What did he say?"

His expression was stark, his eyes darkened to indigo. "He is an arrogant, pompous meddler . . . blatting on about his grand scheme to turn Stratton into a thriving manufacturing town. He intends to move my flock to some nettle-ridden wasteland . . . and increase production by using inferior wool."

Her mouth tightened. "I know. He told me some of that last night. I didn't think you would approve."

"You didn't try to dissuade him?"

"It was all I could do to remind him that he had a prior commitment to my horses. I suddenly feel as though Ardsley has become my adversary as well as yours."

He crossed the room and motioned her to join him on the sofa. "Then let us put our heads together, Lady Roarke. We need to turn him from this ridiculous course."

"I told him about the western property," she said as she settled an arm's length from him. "And suggested he buy it for my horses. Or your sheep could run there instead. Either way, they wouldn't have to leave the district . . . and eat nettles." She grimaced dramatically and was pleased when his face eased into a grin. "But Ardsley was not very cooperative."

He stretched one arm along the back of the sofa and leaned toward her. Even in his rugged work clothes—buckskin breeches, brown boots and old-fashioned frock coat—his natural grace was apparent. "Why do you care, ma'am? Has the old place beguiled you, that you don't want its character destroyed?"

"I don't want my lamb living in a wasteland," she said. "Or any of the lambs." She snatched up the pillow beside her and clutched it to her chest. "I feel so guilty, Mr. Ridd. I came here thinking it would all fall into place—that the duke would buy my horses, and we could build up the stud together. Then in time, he would see how invaluable I was . . . to the stud, to his life." She sighed. "I never expected to bring calamity down on all your heads."

"So you find yourself with divided loyalties?" he asked intently.

"Very divided. If I consider my own needs, which is my habit, I must admit, I should be pleased by the current turn of events. You see, last night the duke indicated some interest in having me stay on—indefinitely."

"Which was your plan all along."

She nodded and then rolled her eyes. "Lord, that does sound calculating. Anyway, if I consider the needs of Myrmion, I should just take myself back to Ireland. The sheep can stay here then. No nettles."

"And without your horses, the duke might just forget about starting up a stud—or becoming an emperor of commerce."

"Precisely. And of course, in addition to the needs of Myrmion, I must also consider your needs, Mr. Ridd."

He shifted closer, sliding his arm farther along the sofa back, and asked softly, "What *of* my needs. Lady Roarke?"

Her throat constricted at his provocative tone. "Why . . . we must arrange things so that whatever happens you are not displaced."

"Too late," he said.

"What do you mean?" When he wouldn't answer, she swiped him with her pillow. "Tell me, Will."

He tugged it out of her hands and set it behind him. "His Grace intends to send me to Scotland. He has a farm property there that is badly managed. I am to resurrect it."

"That is infamous!"

His mouth tightened. "You have no idea, ma'am. Myrmion is the only real home I've ever had."

"Oh, Will . . ."

"I won't do it. I told him I'd have to think it over, just to buy myself some time. But I won't go. I'd rather starve in a ditch than be a dogsbody to that ham-handed meddler." He drew himself up. "Sorry, I forgot I was speaking of the man you hope to wed."

"Need to wed," she corrected him forlornly. "I'm beginning to see that Ardsley is more complicated than I'd first thought. He seemed so . . . so settled when I first met him, not the type to go haring off after . . . glory."

"All men seek after glory, little bear." He leaned forward to meet her eyes. "The trick is not trampling anyone along the way."

His arm was now directly behind her, while his upper body was curled around her. Even though he touched her nowhere, it felt like an embrace. She couldn't stop herself from reaching up and stroking the hair above his brow. It was thick silk under her fingers. He closed his eyes and leaned into her palm for an instant, but then drew back abruptly and stood up.

She blinked up at him.

"Someone's come into the hall," he explained. He went to the door and cracked it open. "It's Miss Coltrane." He stuck his head out. "Ssst, Judith—in here. We are having a war council."

Judith Coltrane, Ursula noted as she slipped through the door, was not in the first blush of youth, but she was slender and long-limbed. Her face was tanned, a bit freckled, but it had good bones, the sort that would allow her to grow more handsome with age. Her dark hair, under a pretty chip-straw bonnet, had been styled into loose curls, and although her walking dress was cut on severe lines, it had been softened by a delicate lace tucker.

Will's face lit up with pleasure as he ushered the lady across the carpet, and Ursula felt their intimacy of the last few minutes evaporate. He made the introductions; Ursula was cordial, but Miss Coltrane seemed a bit frosty. There was an awkward silence after that, and then Will said, "Lady Roarke is on our side, Jude. Now more than ever."

He proceeded to tell her about the duke's latest scheme, and Ursula watched the woman's angular face grow more and more agitated. "Move the flock inland?" she cried at one point, and then, "Blend the wool?" and finally, "Scotlant? *Scotland!*" She'd begun pacing the carpet, but stopped at this last revelation and addressed Will. "He's jealous of you, you know. It's very clear to me. You've been lauded by everyone, so now he wants to put you out of the way and claim credit for all your work."

Ursula found herself unable to argue with this, even though it did not reflect well upon her intended husband. She also noted the way the squire's daughter had leapt to Will Ridd's defense—like a tigress protecting her cub. It occurred to her she ought to say something in the duke's favor.

"Ardsley is not an unkind man," she said. "And he thinks this is an equitable solution."

Miss Coltrane sniffed. "Ignorance is far worse than unkindness."

"Then we must educate him," Ursula said gently.

"We need wool," Will announced. Both women stared at him. "No, I am not out of my head. I wasn't speaking of Stratton Valley wool . . . what we need is commercial fleece. Our weavers can make up some items combining both types—"

"—and let His Grace see the difference in quality for himself," Miss Coltrane finished. She moved to his side and stroked his arm. "That is a capital idea."

"That leaves the wasteland problem," Ursula said, tamping down her resentment at the other woman's easy familiarity with the bailiff. "It might be several seasons before poor grazing affects the fleece."

"It doesn't take an Oxford don to understand that inferior grazing results in inferior livestock," said Will with a scowl.

"Of course *we* know that," Ursula said. "But we are country folk. Ardsley spends most of his time in London. As I said, he needs to be educated."

Miss Coltrane sank onto the sofa and set her hands over her face. "What a disaster. I was sure that by showing him the woolens, he would come around. Give up this idiotic notion of turning Myrmion into a breeding farm." Her head shot up. "Sorry, Lady Roarke, no offense meant."

"None taken," she assured her. "As I've told Mr. Ridd, I didn't foresee any of this happening."

Miss Coltrane shook her head. "No, but you are not willing to find another buyer for your horses, are you?"

"Judith!" Will cried, taking a step forward. "That's hardly fair."

"What's not fair is that our whole world is being turned upside down. At her instigation."

Ursula mustered a mirthless smile. "Mr. Ridd warned me of your habit of plain speaking, ma'am. I have said that I am sorry over this situation . . . that it's gotten so complicated. I told Ardsley I would prefer the farm to remain as it is. Beyond that, there is little I can do."

"Well, there's still plenty I can do," Miss Coltrane declared as she stood up. "Where is the duke?"

"In his study, I believe."

The squire's daughter made a beeline for the door.

"But he is about to take me riding," Ursula called out.

Miss Coltrane turned. "Why? So that the two of you can cook up more ways to harm Will and the people of Stratton?" She flung the door open and marched out.

Ursula blew out a long breath. "I don't envy the duke at this moment."

Will was shaking his head as he approached her. "Never seen Judith like that before. God's truth. She is usually amiable to everyone."

"She still sees me as your adversary, Will." She hung her head. "And maybe she's not far off the mark."

He crouched down before her. "Then I should be the one railing at you. But I'm not, am I?"

She gave him a rueful grin. And then gasped slightly when his hand drifted up over her cheek.

"Come riding with me," he said in a low, liquid voice. "Judith will be in with the duke for an age. And the moor's the best place to settle your thoughts." He stepped back and held out his hand. "Come—"

She was about to reach out and take it when a fearful thing came clear in her head—the enormity of this man's power over her, that she allowed him to touch her so freely, to tempt her so openly. She hadn't offered it to him, but he possessed it all the same.

"You've already shown me the moor."

"Just the well-traveled bits. The moor has other places, little bear, secret places."

"You really ought not call me that," she said.

"Lady Roarke, then. Though it seems you've been calling me Will all morning. Not that I mind . . . much."

He backed up the few steps to the door and opened it. Then leaning the side of his face against the edge, he looked at her through his gilded forelock and murmured, "Last chance."

His face and voice were so childlike, so winsome, it made her heart flutter. Yet there was nothing remotely childlike about the expression in his eyes when she came across the floor to him. The banked, blue flames flared for an instant, and she cursed herself for a fool when she saw how she affected him. It was surely madness to ride out with him after seeing that flash of desire, but that didn't stop her from trailing after him.

They waited beside one of the paddocks that adjoined the stable while their horses were saddled. Imperator had been turned out in this one; he was showing off for the coach horses in the next enclosure, bucking and wheeling, with his black tail an airy plume behind him.

Will Ridd leaned on the fence, watching him with open admiration. "He's a grand beast. And if you promise not to tell anyone, I have a confession to make. I've always pictured horses here at Myrmion."

"I thought you were a sheep man."

"Aye, but horses own my heart. When I was a lad for hire, they'd mostly set me to looking after the work horses. I've got a calming touch, or so Rigger claims."

"What does it mean, being a lad for hire?"

He stretched back from the railing and looked up at the sky. "Oh . . . this . . . and . . . that—"

"—and you don't want to talk about it."

He grinned down at her. "You're a quick study, madam."

She showed her teeth. "And you, sir, are very provoking. I was merely curious about your background . . . how a lad for hire got to know about selective breeding and land management . . . and Lucretia Borgia."

He laughed at that, eyes crinkling, twin dimples carving into his cheeks. "I thought I'd slipped that one past you."

"Not a chance," she muttered.

"What can I say? I've had an unorthodox education. I speak no foreign languages, I have little grasp of politics or higher mathematics. My handwriting is abysmal and my thoughts sometimes become twisted in my head. But I know the land and the seasons, I understand how animals think . . . things you won't learn in a book. Although I like to read . . ." His voice drifted to a reverent whisper. "I do like to read."

"Is that why they beat you?" The question had just sprung from her lips. "Because you were reading instead of working?"

He didn't flare up as she'd feared. Instead he offered her a sad smile. "No, little bear, they beat me because they could. Because they had the power, and I did not."

He pushed off from the fence, went striding away from

her, and she half expected him to keep going, right up the hillside to his cottage. But he only went as far as the stable, where he inquired sweetly of the grooms if they had perhaps lost the use of their limbs since it was taking so long to saddle two horses.

Ursula wondered if he knew how much he had just revealed to her . . . of his past pain and humiliation, of his helplessness in the face of cruelty and, ultimately, of his stoic endurance.

Because they could. She shivered.

It was no surprise to her that the more Ardsley flexed his power, the more Will Ridd resisted. She suspected he would never again let anyone gain that much control over his life. *I'd rather starve in a ditch than be dogsbody to that man.* Or any man, she wagered.

She heard him call to her. He was waiting by the mounting block, holding the bridles of his cob and the gray gelding. She hurried over to him, grappling with the long train of her habit.

"You ought to get a sensible outfit for riding," he said. "That one needs four little page boys to run after you and hold it up."

"I bought it, as you have probably guessed, to impress the duke."

"Pity it's wasted on me then."

But it wasn't. Not at all. She sensed him looking at her several times as they rode along the farm track, his gaze drifting sideways to admire the rise of the fitted bodice where the neckline ended in a spill of lace.

His secret scrutiny thrilled her. And that it shouldn't, thrilled her even more. The duke hadn't exactly been bowling her over with his attention, so it was gratifying to see the masculine approval in Will Ridd's eyes. It reassured her that she had some allurements left. And Will's company was a pleasant diversion. He was the opposite of the duke in every way—candid, cantankerous, playful, challenging— and that intrigued her. Nevertheless, once she and His Grace patched things up, she was sure Ardsley would again be foremost in her thoughts.

And just in case she were to become even a little besotted with the bailiff's crooked grin or the hunger that sometimes sizzled in his eyes, she would remind herself that he was the possessor of many secrets. Just the sort of man she had sworn off.

Ardsley's life, on the other hand, was an open book—a circumstance that was rapidly becoming his chief attraction. As a public figure, his whole history was available to her. There were no secrets there, no scandals or hidden vices, nothing that would spring out and horrify her once she was wed to him.

She consoled herself with this thought as she followed the bailiff down into a shadowed glen.

Chapter Seven

"*J*udith?" The duke looked up from his desk as she came into his study. There was something different about her this morning. The imminent scowl was there, and the ubiquitous carpetbag was still tucked under her arm. Something about her hair, maybe. Shorter, curlier. And her dress was rather newer than the one she'd worn yesterday, and it had a pretty lace collar.

"You're looking well," he said amiably.

"Don't waste your pleasantries on me, Damien."

"I was only—"

"I've just spoken to Will Ridd . . . I know all about your plans for our woolens."

"Ah." He smiled expectantly, awaiting her congratulations, but then realized she was simmering with anger.

"Oh, not again, Judith!" he groaned. "Tell me you're not going to ruin another perfectly good morning with a diatribe on all my shortcomings. Tell you what, I'll ring for cook to send you up some breakfast. I noticed yesterday, you don't talk nearly as much when you're digging into a meal."

He grinned at her. She glared back.

He shook his head, as if to clear out some hobgoblins. "I would ask you to sit, but I see from your face that this is going to be a standing-up sort of conversation."

"You are very glib today. I suppose it comes from your misplaced sense of satisfaction . . . at having in one fell swoop appropriated Stratton Valley wool."

He tried to hold onto his patience. "Judith, they *are* my sheep, as I keep repeating to everyone I meet. And what happened to your offer of friendship? You are hardly behaving like a friend."

"I cannot befriend a man who bullies people."

"*I* bully people? Ho, that's a rare one coming from you."

"Just tell me this, is it true you intend to move the sheep to Dartmoor?"

"I am considering it. However, I do think the idea of blending the fleeces is not so sound, which I believe was going to be your next area of attack."

"Thank God for small miracles." She added darkly, "There is also the matter of the weavers' hall."

"Oh, come on, Jude. You've got to approve of that—a centrally located site, accessible to everyone."

"You mean one of those 'dark Satanic mills' that William Blake wrote about? Most of our weavers need to work at home, especially the ones with children. Some do not own any means of transport. How would they get to your centrally located hall?"

"But this cottage trade is so . . . so haphazard; it limits what I have in mind."

"You don't need the revenue, so why are you suddenly so set on expanding the trade? It serves us just fine. I never thought I would hear myself saying this, but why don't you just focus on your blasted race horses and leave the Pride of Stratton Valley in the hands of the people who created it?"

"You mean Will Ridd, of course. Do you know, Judith, I keep hearing this phrase over and over in my head, like a hopeful prayer . . . 'Let me be well rid of Will Ridd.' "

"That is not even mildly amusing. But I see now that I was right—you *are* jealous of him."

His jaw fell. "Jealous? Of that bumpkin? The man is an insolent agitator. Scotland isn't far enough away for him."

Her dark eyes narrowed ominously. "Will has created something remarkable here. What have you ever done? Passed some piffling legislation in Lords, set the fashion for a new style of neckcloth? However, I will tell you one thing that you manage to do very well, Damien—jumping like a scared rabbit whenever your grandmother snaps her fingers."

He rose from his chair in an angry rush. "Madam, I warn you—"

"William Ridd is his own man," she continued, undaunted by his fearsome expression. "He answers to no one. When was the last time you were able to say that?

When was the last time you stood up to the dowager and told her to go to perdition? Certainly not twelve years ago . . . when she broke your spirit, when she made you . . . made you . . ."

Judith gulped and dashed away the tears that were suddenly coursing down her cheeks.

"You told me yesterday none of that mattered to you," he cried. "That I was hardly worth a mention in your diary. Why do you throw this back at me now?"

"Because I never forgot," she managed to gasp out. "Unlike you, I have not forgotten any of it. Anthony . . . your father . . . me . . . you've wiped us all from the slate of your life."

His face paled as he crashed his fists onto the desk. "I will not listen to this!"

"And now you've got the gall to come back here with your damned plans to wipe away the old Myrmion, to turn it into a showplace . . . when it is perfect the way it is, just as it was perfect all those years ago. But you wouldn't know that, would you? Because you still refuse to remember."

"I *do* remember," he said in a low, shaking voice. "That is my curse. But remembering changes nothing. What I lost cannot ever be returned to me."

She drew in a deep breath and whispered, "No, Damien, it cannot. You've left it too late."

Her words slashed him like a saber stroke. "I think you'd better go," he said without inflection. "There is nothing more for us to say to each other."

She shot him a swift, piercing look, then walked from the room.

He sank down into his chair and realized that his hands were still clenched. He spread them, palm down, on his blotter, trying to ease the rapid beating of his heart. The harsh unfairness of her words still throbbed like a fresh wound. How could she say such things to him? Make such blind accusations?

For one thing, he had stood up to the dowager plenty of times. Though it seemed that the one critical time he hadn't mattered most to her.

"Have you suffered at my hands, Judith?" he wondered aloud.

It had never occurred to him back then how much he

had hurt her. His own pain had been so great, the death of his father, the fading away of his mother's faculties, the ever-present loss of Anthony, that he hadn't the wit or the wisdom to realize the injury he'd done to Judith Coltrane. The proof was before him now, in the tearstains that marked the papers on his desk, in the anguished tone of her voice that still echoed inside his head.

Remorse struck him like a blow.

He had lead Judith on twelve years ago. Though no words had been spoken between them, his feelings for her, his intentions toward her, were in every yearning look. Judith, astute even then, had read the adoration in his eyes, and she had responded.

And he had left her with a promise on his lips that he had never fulfilled.

That omission had wounded her tender young heart. Was it any wonder, then, that she had grown flinty and abrasive over the years? How else was a woman to react after a man raised her expectations up high, and then sent them plummeting to the ground?

Some part of him wanted to run after her, tell her that all the wondrous things he had felt for her could blossom again in time. But then the words she'd just spoken repeated in his head like a knell of doom. *You've left it too late.*

He pushed up from his desk and paced the space before the hearth. It felt as though in a matter of days he'd found her and lost her again. The one woman who could rouse him from his self-imposed reserve. Today she had awakened him to anger and regret. But there was also the promise that hard upon those emotions would come joy and completion.

Too late . . . too late. The crushing weight of her pronouncement nearly made him weep.

But it was not too late for him with Ursula Roarke, he realized with some relief.

It was one thing to unwittingly play fast and loose with a lady when you were callow and inexperienced, but he was neither of those things now. He knew the rules of courtship, knew that inviting an unattached female to your home was tantamount to a declaration in the eyes of society. Lady Roarke would surely have expectations.

As he did himself. He had asked her here precisely to explore the possibilities between them. As yet, however, he had given her little of his time. That would change. His days would be devoted to her. He wouldn't tread carelessly on her feelings as he had done with Judith Coltrane. He vowed he would not make the same mistake twice.

Will led Lady Roarke to one of his favorite dells, where a high waterfall cascaded into an oblong pool surrounded by a grassy bank. He lifted her down, and did not let his hands linger on her waist, even though he very much wanted to.

They left the horses to graze and wandered under the sparse canopy of birch and ash, among the wildflowers and the new-grown grass. The April sun was warm in the clearing; Lady Roarke cast away her bonnet and riding gloves and pushed up the sleeves of her habit. He followed suit and drew off his coat and loosened his neckcloth. He watched as she knelt beside the pool and trawled one hand through the water. The freshet tumbling down the face of the rocks was springfed, and he knew the pool would be deliciously cool.

She turned her head and smiled up at him, her eyes haunting and pale, her skin as translucent as a sea-washed shell. She was Nimue at a pagan well, just as he'd imagined upon first seeing her, a sorceress caught in a moment of repose.

He fell to his knees beside her, inarticulate, worshipful. She shifted up to face him and raised her hand, dripping with chill water, and placed it against his cheek.

"It feels heavenly," she murmured.

"Aye, it does," he said, his voice gone thick and gravelly.

He encircled her wrist and drew her damp palm along his mouth, savoring the coolness of the water and the sweetness of her compliance. She arched into him a little; he heard the whisper of lace against his shirtfront.

He didn't care why she was here, if she was playing him for a fool, trying to make the duke jealous. He only cared that he had tasted her skin and that if there was any rightness in the world he would surely taste her mouth.

He was lowering his head, holding her with his eyes, waiting for some sign of regret or dismay in their pale depths, when the dog broke from the trees. He came upon them in a rush of barking and tail-wagging and general delight at having successfully tracked them from the farm.

Will threw himself backward onto the grass and groaned. "Heaven help us, it's the Pernicious Trial to Mankind."

"He's called Titan now," she reminded him as she roughed up the dog's ears. "Isn't he?" she said, addressing the miscreant, who was trying to lick her face. "Titan . . . son of Snap, grandson of Bobbin."

"Who should have been drowned at birth," Will muttered.

Ursula poked his calf with the toe of her boot. "Hush, he'll hear you."

The dog danced away from her and went to investigate the pool. She stretched out beside Will, propped up on her elbows, and they both watched as the pup ranged along the bank, hunting for frogs and dragonflies in the grass.

Will had a feeling this might be a good time to apologize. Because once he'd said he was sorry for nearly kissing her, he couldn't very well roll over and tug her beneath him and try again. He figured an apology would ensure his good behavior.

But before he'd sorted out the words, she shifted toward him. "That was badly done of me . . . teasing you with the water . . . touching your face. I don't blame you at all for responding. I was being . . . well, coquettish is the word, I suppose. Miss Falkirk says I was a wicked coquette in my salad days. I fear she was right." She sat up and fisted her hands in the skirt of her habit. "And now I am babbling." She looked down at him entreatingly. "Say something, Will."

In answer, he reached over and pried open her curled fingers, smoothing out the tension there. "No harm done," he assured her.

"You always say that," she complained. "And I hope it's true this time. I wouldn't harm you for the world."

"And why is that, Lady Roarke? You have known me less than three days all told."

She tipped her head back, and her brow knit. "I don't know. Perhaps it's because there is a selflessness in you that is very rare in my world. Or because I admire you for having overcome some terrible adversity—"

"In that case, it would be pity you feel."

"Not pity, esteem. For all that you've accomplished."

Will rolled is eyes heavenward. "You do spin a lovely yarn, ma'am. But it's all in your head. I am no different than thousands of men who had to make their way in the world without money or rank. And what is it I've accomplished? A new strain of sheep and a village put back on its feet. Hardly the stuff of legend."

She surprised him by observing tartly, "Miss Coltrane surely sees you in that light."

"Judith? You *are* daft. She thinks I am well enough, I suppose, but lectures me endlessly on my shortcomings."

"And what do you think of her?"

He had to mull this over. "I like her and admire her very much . . . but I suspect she is sad a deal of the time. It might explain why she is forever doing things, trying to outrun her sorrow."

"Has she recently lost someone?"

"The sadness was there when I came here ten years ago. I probably shouldn't tell you this, but rumor insists it was Ardsley she mourned. She helped nurse the old duke before he died, and she and Damien Danover became close. But she has never mentioned it to me . . . and I flatter myself that we are good friends."

"It could explain why she was so hostile to me."

"You think she's been wearing the willow for Ardsley all this time? That doesn't sound like my Judith. Perhaps her melancholy began with the duke, but I think it now stems from frustration—that she cannot cure the ills of the world."

She chuckled. "I hope you are right. It would be difficult to compete with a childhood sweetheart, even one he hasn't seen in years."

"Twelve years," Will stated. "Ardsley hasn't been back here since his father's death. He also avoided the place for a decade before that—after his brother died at Myrmion."

Ursula's eyes widened. "He never told me that, only that he and his brother summered here. Oh, Will, no wonder he wants to make the place over. I am amazed that he ever came back—there must be so many painful memories."

Will stroked the inside of her wrist. "Ardsley must want you very much . . . to face all his ghosts for your sake."

She drew back from his touch. "I'm no longer sure what Ardsley wants," she muttered crossly as she scrambled to her feet.

Will sighed as she went tramping off after the dog. Leave it to him to say the wrong thing. Though the lady might just be entitled to her sour mood. In his estimation, the duke was behaving like a horse's arse—one minute waxing poetic about his precious stud farm and the next spouting rubbish about cornering the woolens market. And ignoring his lady on top of everything else.

He didn't want to think about any of that now, he decided. Myrmion would endure long after both he and Ardsley had gone to their graves. He was here in his favorite spot with a fey creature who enchanted him during the moments she wasn't prodding him over his past.

He watched as she sat at the edge of the pool and pulled off her boots and stockings. She hiked up her voluminous skirts and stepped gingerly into the icy water. He felt the shock that shuddered through her, and then, equally, the relief as the pain gave way to pleasure. She grinned at him from the center of the pool, then moved off closer to the waterfall.

She seemed a complete child now, carefree and playful. It was such a contrast to his first encounter with her—the imperious lady descending from a duke's coach. He recalled her strength and determination when she'd helped the ewe to give birth, and the tender compassion in her voice when she'd asked him about being beaten.

There were so many facets to this woman, and he didn't know which one compelled him the most. That first day he'd mused to himself that he would never tire of looking at her in all her moods. It was still utterly true.

He rolled onto his stomach, facing the pool, and lulled by the sound of falling water and by the wistful memory of his almost-kiss with Ursula Roarke, he drifted into sleep.

It was an odd dream that came to him, not one of the dark phantom dreams; this one began light and airy.

He was a child, racing across the moor on a pony. A young Judith was there, strangely enough, and another boy, who shouted after him. Will couldn't make out the name he called. They rode in great swooping circles over the moor and then down into a wooded dell. He heard the

other two children laughing behind him, but when he swiveled in his saddle, the path had been obscured by twisting
vines. He turned back and saw that they now also covered
the path before him. He tried to push his way through, but
the vines whipped forward like living things, wrapping him
all about, forcing his arms to his sides. He opened his
mouth to cry out for help, but he could no longer speak,
no longer breathe . . . he was suffocating . . . twisting,
thrashing, fighting them off . . . the vines . . . the white
vines . . . the white linen vines—

He awoke with a loud, shuddering cry and sat bolt upright. Ursula came splashing up from the pool and threw
herself down beside him. "Will! Will! It was a dream. Oh,
my sweet Will, only a dream."

He sat there for a moment, his head resting on his palm,
while she crouched next to him, her legs bare, her hem
sopping.

"It was different," he said thickly. At her bewildered
expression, he added, "I dream sometimes of the b-bad
things I can remember. This dream was about a bad thing
I d-do not remember . . . and yet it seemed as though
I should."

"Nightmares are like that," she said, soothing him with
her voice and with one hand rubbing circles on his chest.
"They are so real in sleep, some of them, we think we have
lived them awake."

He pushed up from the ground, suddenly self-conscious
that she had seen him like that—quaking and muddled.
"We should get back."

"Not yet. Please. There's something I want to show you.
In the water." She coaxed him back down to the grass and
leaned over to tug off his boots. He protested, laughing at
her temerity.

"You forget I was wed to a horseman," she said, grinning
over her shoulder. "This was part of my wifely duties."

Once he was barefoot, she took his hand and led him
into the pool. He'd been right—the water was arctic. But
she was used to it by now, and blithely drew him across
the pebbled bottom.

"I can't feel my toes," he announced.

"Such a baby," she said with a teasing look as she shifted
her waterlogged train higher on her arm.

"Here," he said, "let me manage that for you, else you be sucked down and drowned."

"Unlikely in one foot of water."

But she allowed him to drape the fabric over his own arm; it bound them together as they crossed the pool, Ursula a little bit in front of him. Her hair was coming down in the back—shimmering bronze tendrils fell to her shoulders. He wanted to lean into those strands and feel them dance over his face.

"Look there," she said, pointing to a submerged tree trunk.

He craned his head forward. "Very interesting. You don't see many logs like that nowadays."

She poked him in the ribs. "Look closer."

He saw it then, half under the log, a green turtle the size of a small skillet, dappled by the refracted sunlight. It was hard to make out through the rippling water, but Will could have sworn it had two heads.

"Does it—?"

"Yes, two of them. I picked him up just to be sure, but it made him rather grumpy."

He bent down to peer at the odd creature, who scuttled farther back under his haven. "I read somewhere that turtles bring good luck . . . that in China the people keep them in their gardens."

She motioned to the wooded glade that surrounded them. "This could be considered one of Myrmion's gardens, don't you think? Maybe he'll bring you luck, Will. Two heads for twice the luck." She shifted around to face him and set her hand on his shoulder. "Feeling better now?"

"Immeasurably. It's amazing what standing in frigid water does for a man's spirits."

She sputtered a little when he reached down and lifted her off her feet, gathering up as much of her skirt as he could manage. "Shush," he said. "You'll be hours drying off if you walk back across the pond trailing half your petticoats."

She drew her arms tight around his neck, then gave him a sideways glance. "I'm not coquetting you now," she said.

"I know."

"I'm holding on to keep from falling."

"I know."

"Because I fear that if we did something unwise, maybe just once . . . we'd end up not liking ourselves very much afterward."

"I know, Ursula."

He deposited her on the edge of the bank, but stayed in the water, standing a foot or so below her. He welcomed the chill now, needed it to cool his blood. *Something unwise,* she'd said. It brought to mind a world of possibilities . . . unwise kisses and unwise caresses. Unwise passion.

She was looking down at him with a mingling of expectation and caution in her eyes. He felt himself tremble as she started to reach out her hand, and then withdrew it. The chasm between them felt a mile wide, but he knew he could bridge it with a word. What did he care for what was wise or unwise? He had denied himself his pleasure his whole life long, and he found he could not go one more instant without sampling it. Besides, he was so damn tired of being the saint of Stratton Valley.

"Just once," he whispered, promising himself he would not ask for more than that.

And then he tugged her down to him.

She came to him in a flurry of damp skirts and warm skin, her fingers seeking purchase on his wet shirt, while he fisted one hand in her hair, bending her back over the water in the crux of his arm. He looked deep into her eyes for a heartbeat, to assure himself that she was with him in this, completely with him, and then he lowered his head. Her mouth tasted sweeter than spring water when he kissed her, a heady culmination of all his fantasies of what it would be like.

"Will," she murmured, angling her mouth more firmly against his so that a new arc of heat surged between them.

He shifted over onto the grassy bank, dragging her even tighter against him, feeling strangely weak of limb and yet impossibly strong. He couldn't seem to stop kissing her, every slightest movement, every whispering breath, brought a new sensation and a quickening of the desire to taste her endlessly.

Deep, drawing kisses gave way to tiny fluttering ones, which then, when she groaned at the teasing touch of his lips along her throat, became again heated and tempestuous.

when he found her mouth. Their kisses flowed like the cycle of seasons, cool, then warm . . . warm, then hot. God, so hot, so blazingly, achingly hot.

Finally he forced himself to draw back, laying her down on the grass and canting himself up on one elbow above her. Another minute and he would have not been answerable for his actions. As it was, he could not resist a few additional tastes, which Ursula responded to with a soft sigh that twisted his insides.

"Thank you for that," he said huskily, tracing his finger over the curve of her ear.

Ursula raised her head and nuzzled his chest as she twined one arm around his waist. She couldn't bear to lose the contact with his lean body or his enveloping warmth. "Mmm," she whispered. "No, I should thank you. It's been a very long time."

"Has it . . . ? Then your late husband was a fool." His hand stroked along her cheek, warm, work-hardened, and so welcome.

"Let's not talk about Roary . . . or anyone. Let's pretend that we are alone on the planet and that this was the very first kiss in all the world."

"So you liked it then?" he asked cautiously, bending his head close to hers. "It pleased you?"

"Mmm . . . very much."

"Good . . . good."

She was puzzled by his hesitant tone, especially since he had been so overpowering and masterful not one minute earlier. How he could not know that she had been dazzled? She shifted a little so she could see his face, and was surprised by his expression of noticeable relief. Something startling occurred to her.

"Will?" she ventured gently. "*Was* it your first kiss?"

"Aye." His smile was winsome, and, thank heaven, totally without embarrassment.

She sat up, pushing her tangled mass of hair back with her forearm. "God's truth?"

"I wouldn't lie about something like that."

She was stunned. Will Ridd kissed like the most experienced rake in London—and she should know, having been lured into a night garden more than once. How could he have mustered so much assurance, not to mention aptitude, his first time out? Her thoughts then progressed along a logical track . . . if this was the first time he had ever kissed a woman, it was unlikely he'd done anything more advanced along those lines.

It quite staggered the mind.

"I don't know what to say," she uttered. "I certainly have no complaint. Rather the opposite." When she realized how impersonal that sounded, she quickly added, "It was lovely, Will. Absolutely lovely."

The diffidence left his face then; he almost looked a bit smug. And well he should, she thought.

"It was even better than I imagined," he said, stretching out beside her, his hands behind his head. "And I've been imagining it a lot. I've thought about kissing you since the day I saved you from my runaway sheep." He craned his head up. "I was sure you knew."

She was charmed by his candidness. Men rarely spoke of such things, and when they did they were usually gruff and offhand. She decided to be equally forthcoming. "Maybe I did, Will. Maybe that's why whenever we were together it felt like the instant before a lightning strike—when the air positively crackles. You had only to walk into the room and my whole body started to hum."

"I believe some of the crackle comes from you, my lady. I hum like a field of honeybees when you get anywhere near me."

"You do . . . ?" She knew she was grinning like a schoolgirl.

"Though maybe it won't be so bad for us now, since we've gotten this kissing business out of the way."

She nearly goggled at him. Was that how he thought it went? A few heated kisses, and the primal urge disappeared? She'd been close enough to him earlier to know that his body hadn't thought so. But maybe he was being purposely obtuse—out of gallantry. He'd said "just once," and it was clear he intended to stick to that.

If she was wise, she would follow his example.

"I suppose we have," she said. "Gotten over it, I mean."

He lay there without speaking for a time, staring up at the sky. He was so beautiful, truly beautiful in the pure manner of very young children or great works of art. She felt her insides constrict with some inarticulate emotion, and forced herself to look away from him.

He rose eventually and drew her to her feet, holding her hands against his chest. "Ursula, about what you said . . . that we would not like ourselves afterward. I think you were wrong. This felt very right to me."

"Only this once. But, yes, I feel just fine." She reached up and touched his cheek. "And if you promise to stay my friend, Will Ridd, I'll feel even better."

"Done," he said, and then whistled for the dog, who had wandered off to inspect the bulrushes.

They followed the long loop of the southern pastures on the way home, so that Ursula's gown could dry. She displayed only good spirits to Will, laughing when Titan ran off after a herd of deer, challenging him to a race across an empty field, pointing with delight to an eagle gliding overhead.

If he'd been a man of the world, he would have seen the brittleness behind her amiable humor. She was playing a role, skillfully, it was true, but it was playacting nonetheless.

Her feelings were all in a tangle, far beyond her ability to sort them out. Foremost among them was her lingering shock that this engaging, compelling, utterly *desirable* man had never been with a woman. In her social stratum young bucks usually lost their virginity before they entered university. Even among less-exalted folk, sparking was a favorite pastime. What was wrong with the ladies of Stratton Valley? What was wrong with Miss Coltrane? Were they blind, addled, bewitched?

Maybe it was some reticence in Will—a quaint sense of honor that kept him from dallying with a woman. Though that didn't make sense—he'd just dallied the daylights out of her.

Was it something to do with the dark secrets of his past? Had he studied to become a priest in his youth? She could almost imagine, with typical Anglican suspicion, that some penitential Catholic rite had left those marks on his back.

Or maybe—and this answer seemed soundest to her—he had applied all his considerable energies to his work and had allowed no time for the pleasures of Eros. It was a creditable explanation, one that in no way diminished his manliness. In Ireland, some farmers' sons did not wed until they'd inherited their father's property and were often in their third or fourth decade before they took a wife. And she suspected they went to their marriage beds uncouched.

Will Ridd was not an oddity, she decided, merely a man bound to his vocation. The farm was his whole life. Or it had been until their interlude beside the pool. She had a fretful feeling that his appetites, once unleashed, would not quietly subside.

A tremor of guilt rippled through her. She saw she had stirred up his placid, simple life in yet another way. First her horses supplanting his sheep, now passion creeping into his ordered existence like a wolf into the fold.

She renewed her determination to stand up to Ardsley on his behalf. She would never be Will Ridd's lover, but she could certainly be the ally he deserved.

Rigger Gaines was sitting on a hillside above one of the sheep pastures when Will and Lady Roarke rode past below him. They were laughing together, Will with his face turned eagerly toward her, the lady with her head thrown back, her hair all coming down.

He frowned at the sight of them, at the palpable energy that flowed between them. It was what he had feared when he'd first seen the hunger in Will's eyes—that he would foolishly act on it.

Rigger knew full well his friend was untried in matters of the heart. He knew, further, that the lady had a bigger prize in mind than a mere bailiff. She might consort with Will, but she would never have him as her husband. And Will would not understand, because Rigger had made him believe he was the equal of any man. The lad would dash himself against the immutable rules of Society, hoping for some miracle that would allow those rules to bend, and then break.

Will had already suffered a lifetime's worth of pain. It was true he'd come away from it strong and upright, but what he faced now was perhaps even worse. The cane and the whip might mark a man's body, but the insidious worm of love unreturned surely ate at his soul.

Rigger vowed he would do anything to spare Will that

anguish. He was glad now that he'd sent off the letter to Ardsley House, in spite of Will insisting it was no longer necessary. It had become very necessary to get that woman away from Myrmion. Away from Will.

When they came to the stable gate, Ursula felt an imminent sense of loss. She and Will had crossed over into forbidden territory, to a dreamlike place they dared never visit again. But as long as she was beside him, a tangible link to that place remained. When he rode away, that link would be severed.

"Promise me it won't be awkward the next time we are together," she said.

"It's not awkward now, is it?"

"No, not very."

He reached over between their horses and clasped her hand. "How can there be awkwardness? We've managed to find a middle ground despite our differences in rank, and that, I think, is a very rare thing. So we are bonded by more than kisses by a pool. Whatever happens, if I never see you again or if I see you every day for a dozen years, that bond will always be there." He leaned toward her, his eyes bluer than a polar sea. "You are cherished in my heart, Ursula."

This declaration was not exactly what she needed to hear. It made her want to cry. Or embrace him tenderly. Or leap off her horse and drag him to the ground and kiss him until he stopped being so blasted noble and high-minded.

She fell back on her breeding and did not act on any of these impulses. Instead she offered him a gracious smile. "Then you will know I am not avoiding you if we do not happen to meet in the next few days. It's time I focused on my plans for the duke, see if I can't pry him loose from his study and out into the world. Also, I am hoping His Grace will allow me to have a party at the end of next week; that will require some planning."

"You needn't think I will be underfoot," he assured her. "I have my usual duties to attend to . . . and dealing with the sheep issue, of course."

"Fight the good fight," she said lightly.

"You too, little bear."

He nudged his horse away from the gate and rode off in

the direction of his cottage, his head up, his shoulders square. She tried to convince herself that he was not the one playacting now, that his letting go of her had not cost him dear.

You are cherished in my heart.

Ursula turned the gray toward the stable. *Her* heart felt like a lump of sodden peat.

Chapter Eight

*W*ill knew he should get back to work. His dinner lay untouched on the kitchen table, his tea had cooled, and Titan, who'd magically reappeared once the food was laid out, had made off with his ginger crisps.

He heard someone's light footfall coming up the flagged walk. He went into the front hall, his heart pounding, afraid it might be Ursula, praying it would be Ursula.

When he didn't respond to the first knock, the door opened and Judith stuck her head inside. "Will? Oh, there you are, hiding in the shadows."

He stepped forward, about to make some excuse to send her away. Then he noted her strained expression, the lost look in her eyes and the fine lines etched around her mouth. Something had shaken the stalwart Judith Coltrane.

"What's happened?" he asked as she followed him into the parlor. "You look all done in."

She shrugged. "Speaking with Ardsley does that to a person. I've been walking the moors, trying to settle my thoughts. I gather you were out riding again with Lady Roarke. I don't understand how you can spend time with her—she makes me lose all my tolerance."

"You were very rude to her this morning," he said, less harshly than he wanted to. "I am beginning to think she was right when she accused you of wearing the willow for His Grace."

She drew back. "Wearing the willow? For that pompous windbag? Believe me, I have enough reasons to mislike Lady Roarke without adding jealousy to the list."

"This isn't like you, Jude. She is truly upset over what's been happening. Selling her horses to the duke is not a caprice on her part, but a necessity. She was left very much in debt at her husband's death."

"Which will be nicely turned about if she weds Ardsley."

"You're of the gentry, Judith, you know that that sort of union happens all the time."

"So she gets his money . . . what does he get?"

Will dared not respond, but his heart supplied the answer—a woman of beauty and fire, of great charm and easy poise.

"Let's not brangle," he said. "Tell me what happened with Ardsley."

She looked away. "We had a dreadful row. I doubt if he'll even speak to me after this."

He sighed. "You were my best hope, Jude. For getting him to see reason."

"Well, there is *some* good news. He's decided not to blend the wool. Otherwise, he still intends to move your flock to Dartmoor and go ahead with building the weavers' hall. Which will remain empty of workers as long as I have breath in my body."

Will settled on the sofa, gazing up at her thoughtfully. "You really enjoy this conflict, don't you? It gives you a chance to steam and snort and generally be in the thick of battle."

"I don't back down from a fight, if that's what you mean."

"Here," he said, patting the cushion beside him. "Sit a minute." Once she'd complied, he said, "Now, listen to me . . . we've known each other a very long time. I've seen you muster people, and even goad them, but it's been all to the good. We got something started here that enriched both our lives, as well as helping the district. But it's not enriching us any longer, Judith. We've done the best we can, and maybe it's time to let things alone."

He was not surprised by the look of astonishment on her face.

"You mean we should let the duke have his way?"

"There are other paths in life, Jude, ones we haven't explored. We were so busy shoring up Stratton that neither of us took the time to think of our own futures . . . and I fear they are both looking fairly . . . solitary."

Her eyes widened. "William Ridd, if this is a proposal . . ."

He laughed, then shook his head. "Don't fret, it's not.

You know I couldn't regard you any more highly, but my feelings don't tend that way." His voice drifted off. "A pity they don't."

She sighed. "You're lonely, aren't you?"

"Yes."

"So am I, if truth be told. And I suppose that's what you're getting at—we've been too busy to pair off with anyone."

"Now here we are, getting pulled into this new fray. And I have to tell you, I'm afraid it's making you more and more . . . combative. Get yourself a husband, Judith. Go to Bath or to London . . . where your only cause should be finding a fetching bonnet, not saving a town or battling a duke."

He felt her hand on his arm. "You're going away, aren't you? That's where all this is leading."

He nodded. "I think it's time. For one thing, I have a fear that the duke is making all this trouble to punish me. I know that sounds a bit daft, but we didn't start off on a very good footing. Maybe he *is* jealous of my little kingdom, and maybe if I go away, he will lose interest in taking over the weavers. Or be less beastly and bloody-minded about it."

"What will you do?" she asked softly.

"Run my own sheep, I suppose. I have a bit of money put by; the duke is not a nipfarthing when it comes to wages. I know what strains I mixed to create this flock—"

"It might take years before you are producing enough wool for the weavers."

"The weavers will have to fend for themselves." He stood up and moved to the hearth, where he braced his arms on the mantel and studied the etching of Myrmion. "I got fooled, Judith, into thinking this was all mine. But it never was, it never will be. I need to find something to fill that need, something to truly call my own."

She rose and crossed over to him. "I never think about you like that, Will. That you have nothing of your own. I have a manor house and some money to come to me when Papa dies . . . and yet I always envied you because you seemed so much more content than I was."

"Lazy, I believe is the word you used."

She grinned. "No, not lazy. At ease with your life, at

ease with people. I still envy you that gift. It's what made the members of the guild come together. I thought sometimes I had to take a stick to them . . . you only had to smile."

He turned to her and drawled, "Are you *sure* you're not in love with me, Miss Coltrane?"

"No, but very lucky to have you as my friend."

He smiled wanly. "All the ladies want me for their friend. It's a sure sign I need to get out."

Ursula was hurrying to her room to change out of her grass-stained habit when she met Barbara in the hall. Her friend took one look at her and dragged her into her own bedroom.

"Saints preserve us, he's finally done something!"

Ursula blinked. "I haven't a clue what you mean."

"I'd say, by the state of your hair, and by that starry look in your eyes, that someone's finally kissed you properly. And since I can't imagine that great lump of self-consequence that calls himself a duke doing such a grand job of it, it must have been the bonny bailiff."

Ursula sank down onto Barbara's bed and sighed. "He *is* very bonny."

Barbara sat beside her and set an arm around her shoulders. "Oh, pet, what have you gotten yourself into?"

Ursula put her chin up. "Nothing too dreadful. It was just this once, Babs. We both knew that going in. And we didn't do anything but kiss."

"So he'll be fretting for more . . . as men do."

"He won't," she said intently. "Trust me, he won't."

She prayed this was true, for Will's sake. Not ever having had more, he couldn't precisely miss it. Could he?

"What?" Barbara said, shaking her gently. "You've got that cat among the pigeons look. It always means trouble."

"I am just a little tired. And I wish . . . I wish that we had never come here. Everything is falling apart. Ardsley is rapidly losing interest in my horses . . . and he's spent the last two mornings with a woman who was apparently in love with him twelve years ago."

"Miss Coltrane?" Barbara said. "I was in the garden earlier, and I overheard her with the duke. The windows of his study were open and they were arguing rather loudly. There seems to be no love lost there now."

"I'm not so sure. She was cool to me when we met earlier, as if she considered me a threat."

Barbara chuckled. "Sad to say, you do have that effect on some women, Sully. I saw Miss Coltrane as she was leaving . . . she is not an antidote, but neither is she a beauty. I will tell you, though, she said some fairly harsh things to His Grace."

"Is he still here? I need to speak with him."

"No, according to Mr. Gaines, he went off to Barnstable directly after Miss Coltrane left. Gone there to inquire about leasing some land."

"Nettle-ridden wasteland," Ursula muttered darkly. "For Will's sheep." She turned to Barbara and took up one of her hands. "Let's go back to Ireland, Babs. I'll sell the bloodstock off piecemeal . . . I so wanted to keep the stud together, but that might not be possible. Roary's cousin is itching to take over the property, and time is running out."

"But you told me that last night Ardsley has agreed to buy them. And that he asked you to stay on here. It's working out in your favor, could you only see it. But I fear all you can see right now is that braw, blue-eyed man."

Ursula sniffed back her tears. "If I stay on, it will harm him. He'll lose everything he's built up here."

"Then win the duke over, pet. Miss Coltrane's bulldog methods haven't worked . . . but you have a lighter touch."

Ursula recalled what she'd said to Will, that there were other persuasions a lady could use. Only she no longer wanted to ply them on the duke.

"It's not so difficult to sway a man who's in love, Sully. Make Ardsley love you, and you can do good for both yourself and Mr. Ridd."

"What if I find I cannot love him back? What then?"

"You loved Roary . . . and it mattered little when all was said and done. If His Grace proposes marriage, then let it be a union of comfort, of contentment. For both of you. Besides, if you leave now, while Mr. Ridd is still at odds with the duke, he will lose his best advocate."

"Then I will stay on," she said, "and finish what I began—trying to gain the duke's favor."

"There's my girl." Barbara hugged her. "And I am sorry I called him a great lump. He sent me up the loveliest skein of wool this morning. Softer than a bairn's bottom it is."

That night, Ursula managed to hold the duke's attention for the entire evening. Barbara had again retired after supper, leaving the two of them alone in the drawing room.

Ursula responded to his attentive mood and regaled him with stories of her childhood in East Anglia, of her come-out in London, and of her initial, amusing encounters with the various Irish folk who lived around Roarke Stud. She shared with him Roary's favorite after-dinner tale, featuring one Flighty Dean Flynne, the local tinker and sometime horse thief.

"Late one night," she began, "Flighty Dean wandered out from the pub, his head so full of good Irish whiskey that he decided to have a rest in a nearby field. As soon as he lay down in the darkness, he was surrounded by a troop of the little people. They kept their distance, but eventually they spoke to him and promised to impart to him all their fey, fairy wisdom if he would bring back a tribute. He rose up at once and wove his way back to the pub to share his story. ' 'Tis a magical thing, and ye mus' come and see. They're awaitin' us there . . . with all their secrets to tell. But we mus' bring a tribute.' So three men lifted down the enormous, prize-winning stuffed salmon from the wall above the hearth, and they all hurried to the field with a lantern. And there the whole pub saw Flighty Dean's little people—a dozen standing skittle pins that some boys had left behind. But Flighty Dean was not dismayed. 'Ah, d'ye see what's become o' them?' he cried in elation. 'Sure, and didn't I tell ye they was magical?' "

The story had always reduced Roary to helpless tears. The duke's eyes now crinkled merrily. "I take it they then clouted Flighty Dean with the prize salmon?"

"No, that salmon was worth more to the honor of the pub than one bosky tinker."

His eyes darkened a little. "And is there a moral there, my lady?"

She tipped her head. "No moral, except perhaps not to linger too long in an Irish pub."

"Are you sure it's not something like . . . the sheep are

worth more to the honor of the valley than one misguided duke?"

"I would not presume to make such a judgment."

"Not to my face, at any rate." He reached out to her
quickly. "No, don't color up. Though it looks well enough
on you, Ursula." He paused, perhaps so that she could note
his use of her given name. "Whatever thoughts you might
have on this ever-popular subject, let us save them for tomorrow. Will you play for me?"

They adjourned to the back parlor, where there was a small
pianoforte, fortunately not too badly out of tune. Ursula
played a few lilting Irish airs, in keeping with the evening's
theme, and then switched to an easy Scarlatti piece.

He was sitting to one side of her, not fully in her view,
and when she finished, she turned and caught him unawares. His face bore a look of such sadness, such despair,
as he stared unseeing into the hearth fire.

Had she done something to remind him of his brother . . .
or of his father? Perhaps not, she reassured herself. His
expression wore the sharp edge of fresh loss.

She pivoted back to face the keys, relieved that he hadn't
been aware of her scrutiny.

"Do you sing . . . Damien?"

"Not for years," came the soft reply. "My grandmother
has expressed a dislike for it. 'Isn't duke-like to be cater-
wauling for a crowd,' is how she puts it."

"There's only me here," she reminded him. "And I am
told I sing indifferently, so it would be polite of you to
drown me out."

She watched the emotions cross his face and read them
like sentences on a page—reluctance, hesitation, then intent. But still he did not rise from his chair.

"I will begin singing," she said, "and if the mood strikes
you, just join in."

She chose "John Riley," the plaintive ballad of a maiden
whose lost lover was long thought dead.

*A fair young maid all in her garden; a handsome
stranger, came riding by,*
*Saying, "Fair young maid, will you marry me." "Listen,
then," was her reply.*

*"Oh no, kind sir, I cannot marry thee, for I've a love
    who sails the deep salt sea.
He's been gone, these seven years. Still, no man shall
    marry me."*

The duke came up beside Ursula and added his bright
tenor to the song.

*"What if he's died or in some battle slain? Or if he's
    drowned in the deep salt sea?
Or if he's found some other love, he and his new love
    both married be."
"If he's found some other love, he and his new love
    both married be,
I wish them health and happiness, where they now dwell
    far across the sea."
He took her up all in his arms, and kisses gave her,
    one, two and three.
Saying, "Weep no more, my own true love. I am your
    long lost John Riley."*

Her hands dropped away from the keys; she felt the tension humming in the air between them, not passion, but
keen remembrance.

"Do you think," he asked in a constricted voice, "that
lost loves do return?"

She answered quietly, "Often in song, less often in life."

"Except in our dreams."

She raised her face to him, her smile gentle, tolerant.
"Ah, but what are songs but dreams set to music?"

He smiled back, and the faraway look faded from his
eyes. "Sing again, my dear. I will spare you my rusty pipes,
however . . . and though your voice may be judged indiffer-
ent, it is pleasing to my ear."

She sang several lively tunes, and then finished with her
favorite piece, *Jerusalem*. To her it embodied, oddly enough
for a hymn, all the pagan mysticism of England. She had a
sudden longing that Will were there—he, more than anyone, could understand the lure of England's pleasant pastures and mountains green.

Afterward, she and the duke lapsed into easy conversation. They seemed to be finding a relaxed accord for the

first time since he'd left Ireland. When he asked her to ride with him the next day, she did not hesitate. This was what she had come here for . . . not to distract herself with an innocent, intoxicating commoner, but to win over a duke.

When they parted, Ardsley raised her hand and kissed her wrist.

"Good night, my lady." There was warmth in his eyes, but she saw there was still a measure of sadness too.

"I look forward to tomorrow, Your Grace."

She went upstairs then, hopeful and expectant. And maybe a little sad herself. Barbara was sitting up in bed, knitting a collar with the wool the duke had given her. Ursula perched on the edge of the mattress and related the evening's events, including the duke's parting salute. Barbara scoffed and said that wrist kissing was a waste of a good pucker.

Ursula chuckled. She knew a man who might agree with that sentiment.

The next morning the duke rode out with her to the cliffs above the Bristol Channel, where a footman met them with a picnic lunch. They spoke of inconsequential matters as they lounged on a blanket, and she watched with relief as the duke again shrugged off his mantle of reserve.

He laughed over her attempts to lure a group of moor ponies away from the cover of the trees with a bit of bread. She was intrigued by their rugged beauty—the pale dun coats marked with grizzled black upon their legs, the mealy, oat-colored muzzles. The foals in particular looked like overgrown nursery toys.

Finally she gave up her attempts to feed them and returned to the blanket.

"They are brave but shy," the duke observed. "That's what Rigger always said. Brave to face life in the open, but shy of people. Though years ago Miss Coltrane had a herd who would eat from her hand."

Ursula wondered if the duke, likewise, had been as tame to her touch. But she wasn't going to bring up that subject. Instead she mentioned her idea of giving a party for the locals. Ardsley said he thought it a capital plan.

They rode back along the western boundary, Ursula audibly admiring the property. "It's a magical place, with all those eerie rock formations. And the grass must be knee-high. Any grazing animal would flourish there. I can't understand how your family could have parted with it."

"I was a child at the time . . . my father did not consult with me," he drawled. "Still, it might not hurt to have it back again. Restore Myrmion's former boundaries."

Once they were back at the estate, Ardsley excused himself to meet with one of the stud manager applicants. She told herself not to be miffed that he hadn't asked for her assistance. This would be *his* stud, whether he stayed on or not; better if he learned to run things for himself.

She wandered out to the garden and saw Barbara walking up from the home farm beside a thin, long-shanked man who was carrying a basket. He was hatless and the breeze ruffled a sheaf of his dark, graying hair as he walked. Barbara was talking with her usual animation, and the man was laughing, his smile a sudden white slash in his saturnine face.

Ursula went to the garden gate to meet them.

"I was bringing up a basket of eggs for Cook," Barbara explained, a bit breathless after her uphill trek. "Mr. Gaines offered to help me."

The man nodded to Ursula. "Rigger Gaines, ma'am. I look after the house."

"You're Mr. Ridd's friend," she said pleasantly.

She was surprised when he frowned slightly. "One of many, as it happens."

Barbara took the basket from him and with a smile of thanks went off toward the kitchen door. The man's dark gaze followed her, and Ursula was aware that it was not without some appreciation. Had Barbara acquired an admirer? He was wiry and fit, even for a man no longer in his youth, and there was some intelligence in the gaze he leveled on her once Barbara had disappeared from view. "You won't win at this game, my lady," he said bluntly. "There are too many factors against you."

She at once schooled her face into the blandest of expressions. Was he referring to her interlude with Will? Her chances of wedding the duke? Neither of those topics were something she would ever discuss with a stranger . . . with a servant. Ah, but these Devonshire men were not like other servants, as she had quickly learned. They were never obsequious or accommodating; most of them were rarely even polite.

She fussed over a lilac branch, hoping he didn't see her blush of confusion. What was she to say to the man? Finally she looked up. "There are times when winning is the only option."

There, that was nicely vague.

"Winning always means another's loss. Think on that, my lady."

"I don't need to, sir. Loss was my life's study for eight years," she said boldly, recalling that this man knew all about Roary's past.

He grinned. "But that loss was not at your hand. Now you take your own turn at the table . . . but there is another who stands to lose, however the cards lay down."

Now she knew. He was trying to protect Will Ridd.

She thought of how to reassure him. He deserved that much for his concern. "I do not sit at the table with inexperienced players, Mr. Gaines. I learned that much from my late husband."

He bowed his head once. "I never heard that he was a dishonorable man."

"No, he was fair to the bone." She leaned her arms on the top of the gate. "So you can put your mind at ease . . . only two hands have been dealt in this game. And novices are unwelcome."

"And if you should lose all?"

She tossed her head. "I still have an ace up my sleeve . . . or back in Ireland, rather."

"I wish you the luck you deserve," he said cryptically and turned to go.

"Oh, and Mr. Gaines—" she called out.

He stopped a little way down the footpath, his head raised. He reminded her of the moor ponies, eyes dark and wary beneath a spill of black hair.

"She likes gillyflowers . . . just in case you were wondering."

She had taken him unawares, and she knew he didn't like it. His face tightened—in resentment at having been found out, she imagined. A fine sentiment from a man who had practically come right out and asked her not to seduce Will Ridd.

"Gillyflowers," she said again. "And some dandelion wine never goes amiss."

He nodded, and then gave her a close-mouthed grin. "Gillyflowers and wine it is."

That night the duke found her alone in the drawing room just before supper. He told her that he'd had a message from his grandmother, that he had to leave for Bath in the morning.

"What do you mean, you have to leave?" Ursula knew she sounded more than a little shrewish, but this was becoming ridiculous. Once again the dowager had called the duke to her side just when things between them were starting to progress.

"I will be gone less than a week," he said.

She crossed her arms, but tried to temper her tone. "What does your grandmother require of you this time?"

"Who can say? She pleads an ailment. Let me see—" He drew a letter from his waistcoat pocket. "Heart palpitations, it says here. Most likely just too much brandy in her trifle."

"Most likely," she echoed darkly.

"At any rate, you have your party to plan . . . and, if you wouldn't mind it, two more stable managers to interview. Today's candidate will not suit—he's only ever looked after carriage horses. If you get bored, ask Ridd to take you into Stratton. It's a charming place—you could do a bit of shopping and have tea. And you can always call on Miss Coltrane . . . she'll have you to dine at Stratton Meadow." He stopped and Ursula could have sworn he colored up. He said under his breath, "No, perhaps that's not wise."

Ursula was relieved—she refused to be fobbed off on the squire's bad-tempered daughter. "Miss Coltrane and I met briefly yesterday. We did not get on, I'm afraid."

He looked alarmed. "But you will invite her to the party. It will seem odd if you do not."

"Of course. And what of your plans for the sheep?"

"They are well in hand. I found a land agent who knows of several suitable places I can lease in Dartmoor. I've given him carte blanche."

She was about to voice an objection, but realized it would not be prudent to send Ardsley off with ill-will between them. She'd confront him when he returned.

Chapter Nine

*T*he next morning Ursula stood under the porte cochere to bid the duke farewell. He took her hand at parting, but did not kiss her wrist. She was strangely relieved. Once the coach was out of sight, she hurried inside to change into her riding habit—she had a fair idea of who was behind the old woman's intrusion and had every intention of confronting him.

She found Will with two of his dogs ambling along a narrow track behind a clutch of shaggy red cattle.

"You wrote to the dowager, didn't you?" She made no attempt to disguise her anger.

"Not me," he said. "It was Rigger wrote the letter, at my request. He corresponds with Her Ladyship now and again."

"And what about our bargain? I pleaded your case with the duke . . . you were supposed to halt your interference. I trusted you, Will."

"The letter was never sent. I told Rigger it was no longer necessary."

"Well, something's gotten the old lady's feathers ruffled. Ardsley will be gone for nearly a week, and just when he was starting to become attentive."

"I'm sorry about that, about the timing of it."

"I have a bad feeling. The dowager intends to warn him away from me . . . I just know it."

"Ardsley is no schoolboy to be taking orders from his granny."

"He jumps quick enough at her command, though."

Will gave her a lopsided grin and remarked slyly, "The lady is often ailing."

"Ailing, my Aunt Tillie."

He motioned her down. "Come, walk with me a ways. Work off some of your heat."

"Too tame," she bit out. "I need to throw something."

"It's that red hair," he said. "Bound to get you into trouble eventually."

"It's not red. It's brown with auburn streaks."

"Pretty, whatever you call it. Now come down." He paused. "I'll show you how to work with the dogs."

"It's safer up here. This way I don't risk getting trampled . . . or being forced to play midwife." *Or lured back into your arms.*

He tsked. "I thought you stouter than that, Lady Roarke. And these highland cattle are docile." He tugged at the shaggy russet forelock of one of the beasts. It butted gently into his hand. "See?"

When she didn't respond, he moved up beside her horse. His voice lost its teasing edge. "And how do you go on, Lady Roarke?"

She didn't pretend to misunderstand him. "It's a trial sometimes, Mr. Ridd. That bond you spoke of often feels like a burden."

He nodded once. "It does. But you are keeping busy?"

"Distracting myself . . . yes. We are to have a party next week. I wrote out the invitations last night. You are on the guest list."

"That wasn't necessary. And I doubt it's proper."

"It's quite proper. Single gentlemen are never unwelcome at any gathering."

He was still regarding her with concern; her airy tone had not fooled him.

"Ursula—" He reached up to her, but instead shifted his hand to her horse's mane.

"Don't, Will," she whispered raggedly.

She looked down at his fisted hand, long-fingered, tanned, with fine golden hairs lacing the taut skin. It was a wonder of nature in its contours and its strength. She set her own hand over it. Her gaze bore down on him, saying the words she dared not speak. Her look of regret met the blazing light in his eyes and doubled back on her so fast, she was nearly unseated.

Snatching her hand back, she abruptly reined her horse

away from him, kicking and flailing the gelding into a rapid trot—like the worst of cawkers.

She was not usually the sort to flee from danger, but what she had seen in Will Ridd's eyes had been a dark, frightening trap. She'd spent the last two days convincing herself that what he felt for her was mere physical desire—newly roused, and therefore potent—a state he would recover from without lasting harm. But what she'd seen in that burning gaze had been something deeper than desire.

It was surely a trap—one she wanted very much to cast herself into. And therein lay the greatest danger.

Will did not see Ursula again that day, even though he lingered near the house, repairing one of the paddock gates. His work did little to distract him; the familiar comfort in his toil was gone. The dogs whined and nosed at his hand, sensing some inarticulate pain in their master.

It was nearing twilight when Will gave up his vigil and went back to the cottage. He was sitting on his front porch when Rigger went by on the path below. Will had seen him earlier, walking in the lane with Miss Falkirk, but he hadn't wanted to confront him before the lady. He now called out. Rigger came up and settled on the top step. His brow rose when he saw the open bottle of whiskey and the crockery cup beside Will. "What's amiss, lad? I've never known you to take anything stronger than ale."

Will made no answer. Instead he went inside and came out carrying a second cup. He refreshed his drink, poured a healthy tot into the other cup and handed it to Rigger.

"Drink to me, my friend," he muttered. "Drink to the most gullible man in the West Country."

"That bad, eh?"

"You duped me . . . you sent that letter to the dowager, even though I asked you not to. That's why the duke was called away."

"Aye, I did send it. There were things needed to be said."

"I promised Lady Roarke we wouldn't interfere with her if she argued our cause to the duke. She kept her promise. And now you've made a liar of me."

Rigger hitched one shoulder. "I did what I thought best

for you, for the farm, which meant removing her from this place."

"You took a lot upon yourself. Since when have I needed you to nursemaid me?"

"Not for many long years, I'm pleased to say. But this is new ground for you. I thought you might need an ally."

"But not a meddlesome busybody," Will retorted. "She is angry with me. Things were going well with the duke, and now he is off kow-towing to the dowager instead of wooing her."

"And you favor this . . . that she wed with Ardsley?"

"It's what she wants, what she needs to pay off her husband's debts."

Rigger was quiet for a time. "I spoke with her briefly the other day. I'd not met her before that, only seen her about. She is . . . she doesn't miss much. A very clever lady." His voice lowered. "She promised me that she would not . . . encourage you."

Will leapt up. "What bloody right do you have to be discussing me with Lady Roarke?"

"Easy, now. I have a father's right, since there is no other to take that role. I don't want you harmed, Will. A woman like that could rip the heart out of you, and then walk blithely away."

Will sank down again, clasping his cup with both hands to keep them still. "There is nothing between us . . . not now. I admit I was taken with her at first. But I am not so lost to reality that I don't understand how the world works." He laughed softly. "I think she may have forgotten those restrictions more than I did. Which is odd, since she has a lot more to lose."

"You sound fairly sensible—that's a relief."

Will leaned back on his elbows and gazed up at the night sky. There was a thin scrim of clouds, but enough stars were peeking through to guide a man to safe harbor. He swore he was going to find that harbor.

"I'm leaving Myrmion," he said without turning his head. "Before the duke returns."

Rigger didn't respond, just sat and sipped his drink.

"I won't stay here and watch everything I made fall to bits. I think it would kill me."

"You're leaving because of the woman?"

"Maybe . . . maybe she showed me that there are other worlds out there. But mainly I am leaving because I need to work for myself. I have wasted ten years pouring my soul into something that I now find can be whisked away from me on someone else's whim."

"You didn't waste a minute of that time. Whatever you take away with you in knowledge and skill you learned here at Myrmion."

Will turned to him then. "I thought you would be angry at my leaving."

Rigger smiled in the growing darkness. "You haven't left yet, William Ridd."

"What's that supposed to mean?"

"What if I told you that I can give you a place to run the Myrmion sheep?"

"They'd still not be my sheep," Will pointed out.

"You could gradually add your own to the flock. Plenty of cottagers mix their animals in with those of the landlord. You'd be able to stay in Stratton, the weavers would still get their fleece, and the duke could have his stud farm."

"It sounds like a fairy story . . . and things rarely work out that well."

"It could work out, if you stay. If you leave, the sheep will end up on Dartmoor."

"So what is this solution?"

"That land to the west . . . happens I know who owns it. A man who owes me a favor. He will sell me the land and I'll see that your name is on the deed."

Will's fingers tightened on his cup. "And where would you get the money for that?"

"Same place I got the money to pay for your tutors, to rent your room in Barnstable. I've told you before, I came into a tidy inheritance some years ago."

"You should use the money on yourself. If you don't need to work—"

"Every man needs to work. And I like being here at Myrmion, looking after things . . . being with you." He paused. "So will you stay?"

"You will just turn over three hundred acres of prime grassland to me?"

"And who else would I give it to? Listen to me—His Grace was going to lease land in Dartmoor, he can just as easily lease it from you. The money will buy you the beginning of another flock."

"Land," Will uttered reverently. Hard to believe he had somehow found his safe harbor . . . and without setting foot off Myrmion. "God, Rigger, it's more than I can take in."

"It will require some doing . . . we can put up temporary fencing. There's an abandoned cottage where you could set up . . . get yourself away from Lady Roarke if she's to stay on."

Will shifted around. "I told you, she is no longer a problem. And I'm still bailiff here till the end of the month. But this gives me something to think on . . . to plan in the meantime." He gripped Rigger by one shoulder. "Thank you . . . whatever stray wind sent you to me all those years ago, it was the best day of my life."

Rigger tugged at his hair. "Mine too."

Ardsley's grandmother received him again in her bedroom, but he was relieved to see she was sitting up this time. Her wing chair almost seemed to swallow her, and he could have sworn she had shrunk since he'd last seen her. However, even wasted and frail, the dowager was a formidable opponent. His misliked the distempered pull of her mouth as she gave him a tight-lipped greeting.

She was dressed in black, with no embellishment on her gown save a brooch under her wattled chin, a ghastly thing made of strands of hair from his father and brother—light brown and honey blond entwined under glass. It occurred to him that his grandmother darkened every room she entered. She seemed to absorb any available light. He unconsciously contrasted her with the other women in his life—Judith Coltrane, who entered a room like a heartening breeze; Ursula Roarke, who carried dazzling brightness into every space.

The dowager's voice cut into his revery. "It has come to my attention that Lady Roarke is now staying with you at Myrmion."

He nodded. "If you will recall, I am negotiating with her over the sale of her bloodstock."

"Negotiating," she repeated, then cackled dryly. "That's not what we called it in my day."

He tried to hide his annoyance. His grandmother was

clearly not ailing. Once again she had plucked him out of his life and lured him here for one of her tongue-lashings.

"All right," he said wearily. "It is pointless to keep anything back from you, madam—Fouché in Paris had less capable spies. The fact is, I am also considering asking the lady to be my wife."

Her cheeks narrowed severely until she resembled a death's head. "Good of you to inform me of this momentous decision, Ardsley."

"I said *considering*. Nothing's been spoken of on either side. But the more time I spend with her, the more certain I become that she would suit me very well."

"She would *not* suit you. If you are seeking a wife, you can look a great deal higher than the widow of some bog-trotting Irish lordling. Were you to follow such an imprudent course, the *ton* would make a mockery of you."

"I am not interested in what the *ton* thinks."

"That is clear. You would drag us all down, but you do not care one whit."

"This has nothing to do with you. Good God, madam, I am nearly in my thirtieth year. I do not need your permission or your approval when I choose to wed."

She smiled tautly. "She has beguiled you, I see. A red-haired lady of some spirit is what I am told. She is considered fast in Dublin, and that is saying something. You know females there are allowed a deal more freedom. I've heard any number of unsavory things about her—that she frequented gaming hells with her wastrelly husband, that she held dinner parties where she was the only female present . . . and I had it direct in a letter from Sally Jersey that Lady Roarke rode in a match race against a gentleman—and won."

"I'd think less of her if she'd lost," he muttered.

"And I'd think better of her if she'd never mounted the demned horse." The dowager began fanning herself furiously, and the duke feared the onset of an awe-inspiring bout of the vapors. He snatched up her hand.

"For all her faults, real or imagined, she is a canny woman of business. She's kept the stud intact, in spite of Roarke's wastrelly ways. An impressive feat, if you ask me."

"What if she is barren? Eight years wed and no children. You need to think of the succession."

"I am willing to take my chances. Plenty of widows have come from barren marriages and produced offspring with another husband. But if that is the case, then my cousin Harold will be quite happy to take the title."

"Harold be damned." She tugged her hand back with a surprising amount of wiry strength. "You will not marry beneath you . . . while there is breath in my body, you will not."

"I don't see any royal princesses hanging about waiting to be asked," he pointed out. "Surely the dukedom could stand for me to wed a gracious, intelligent woman."

"I will not tolerate it!" She fixed him with one glinting eye, like a heron homing in on a hapless perch, and said in a low, parchment whisper, "Not after I have devoted my life to preserving the dukedom."

He waved away her words. "I know, I know . . . you have sacrificed yourself to be the guardian of my fortune, the watcher over my home, the . . . what else, Grandmama? What else have you done to keep the blasted dukedom intact?"

Her head drew back like an adder poised to strike. "Do not mock me, sir!" she hissed viciously, her fingers biting into his forearms. "You have no idea what I have done for this family. Your line can be traced back to before the Conqueror . . . untarnished, unsullied. You will not be the one to weaken the chain. It's bad enough your father chose unwisely."

"What on earth are you talking about?"

"Your mother was not the woman I would have chosen for him. Oh, she was an earl's daughter, right enough. But she was not strong-minded, as you well know. She bore him a weak son . . . and by the look of you now, perhaps two weak sons."

"Tony a weak son? You are demented, old woman. My brother was brave and clever. He became ill . . . bad breeding had naught to do with it."

"There are things you cannot remember . . . you were too young."

"I remember everything," he growled.

She pushed away from him and fell back against the chair cushion. "You remember nothing. Nothing that matters." Her eyes flashed up at him. "Now you listen to me, boy. I have not risked sending my soul to perdition protecting the Ardsley name just so you could marry a cozening nobody with a mountain of debt. Make her your mistress—"

"Grandmama!"

"—with my blessing. But I beg you, do not bestow our name upon that unworthy creature."

He drew himself up. "I shall do as I see fit. You have called me weak . . . I will prove to you that I am strong. You have bullied me and belittled me for the last time. I am no longer a child of seventeen, too young to understand that your meddling never, ever had *my* best interests at heart. Now I have grown older and see that I must look after my own best interests."

"I am your grandmother, you ungrateful whelp. I will not be opposed!"

He paused, then smiled slowly. "*I* am Ardsley, old woman, not you . . . however much you might wish it. And *I* will not be opposed." He left her without another word, left her speechless, sputtering, filled with rage, but for once without her usual contempt.

The duke then rode down to the dower house, which was located a half mile from the main house. His mother was in the garden plying her secateurs, wearing a large straw bonnet and a white pinafore. She looked like a milkmaid. He hadn't visited her in nearly two years, relying on his grandmother's reports to assure himself of her well-being.

Her companion, Mrs. Camber, a tall, almost brawny woman, was sitting on a bench near the gate. She rose as he came into the garden.

"Your Grace, we were not expecting you," Mrs. Camber said brusquely. "Though she is doing very well today."

He scowled slightly. "I believe *she* can speak for herself." He approached his mother, praying she would recognize him. "Mama?"

She dropped her secateurs and clasped his hands, her eyes alight. "Damien!" she cried softly. "I have missed you so much."

He embraced her, blinking away sudden tears. "I'm sorry I stayed away so long." He pulled back from her and let his eyes linger on her sweet, softly lined face. "You are looking very fine."

She touched the wide brim of her bonnet. "It's hardly the height of fashion, but it does well for keeping out the sun."

He pulled her down beside him on a bench some distance from the sour-faced Mrs. Camber and spoke animatedly about his life in London, of his plans for the stud farm, and of the woolen trade he'd recently taken an interest in.

"Which reminds me . . ." He drew a package from the pocket of his greatcoat and watched her face brighten as she opened it and drew out the rose-colored carriage rug. "This is a sample of the fine wool my sheep produce."

She dug her hands into the soft mass and crooned, "It's lovely. Makes one long for winter." She looked up. "Where are these sheep of yours kept?"

"At one of my estates." No one ever mentioned Myrmion within the duchess's hearing.

But she seemed to know. "Myrmion," she whispered. "The sheep are at Myrmion."

"Yes, Mama."

Her eyes clouded as she laid her face against the soft weave. "Is he there now?" she asked faintly. "Is my boy there now? He was lost . . . but I dreamed he was found again."

Ardsley's heart constricted. This was far worse than her mistaking him for his brother. "No, Mama," he said, capturing her fretful hands and holding them still. "Tony is not there . . . he was very ill . . . and he died."

"No!" she cried and, "No!" again, twisting away from him. "He didn't! He isn't!"

Mrs. Camber was beside her in an instant, pulling her back, hands hard and strong on his mother's frail shoulders.

"You'd best go now, Your Grace. I'll see that she has her tonic. It always settles her right down."

"What tonic?" he cried. "What sort of foul drug is my grandmother feeding her?"

The woman was halfway to the house, hustling his mother forward. "Only laudanum," she called back. "As I said, it keeps her quiet."

He rode off in a blind rage, sending his horse across an open field at a wild gallop. No wonder his mother had remained addled for so many years, if she was receiving regular doses of laudanum. He wanted to ride back to Ardsley House and throttle his grandmother.

But most of his anger was directed at himself. If he'd spent more time here, he would have known how things stood. But that would change. The House of Lords would survive without him. The pleasures of London would not stop in their merry whirl if he was no longer in the city. Not one of his properties required his presence save this one, where his mother dwelled. And his grandmother.

He would have to send her away, he knew. She had spun her web of control and domination through every board and beam of Ardsley House. Only her removal would gain him back his own domain. He'd settle things at Myrmion and then return here. His plans for the stud were already being executed—he'd written to his man of business in London to draw up the checque for Lady Roarke's horses, and the sheep should have already begun their journey to their new home.

He recalled now how Ursula had admired the land to the west of his estate. It rankled him that his father had sold it away from the family. He wanted it back, he wanted Myrmion whole again. He would buy it and present it to Ursula.

Then he'd come back to live at Ardsley House, and he would not be coming alone. He would have a woman by his side, a new duchess. His grandmother's threats be damned.

Damien had given the dowager a wide berth for the rest of the day. Tomorrow he would start back for Devon and it was best that there were no more words between them till then. Once he was at Myrmion, he would write and tell her that she was no longer welcome at his ducal seat.

He hadn't counted on her dogged nature. He was in his study when she tracked him down.

"What are you doing with your father's papers?"

He looked up from sorting through a strongbox. "I need to find a record . . ." he said absently, "for the land that was sold off from Myrmion. I plan to buy it back."

Her eyes narrowed to wizened slits. "You're wasting your time. That land is not for sale."

"And how do you know so much about it?"

"You forget that Myrmion was part of my dowry. I had the disposal of that land—it was never part of the entail."

"*You* sold it?" He couldn't credit that, not his grandmother, who valued property above everything and held on to every crumb of the fat Ardsley loaf. "I don't believe you."

He continued with his search, until her spidery hand gripped his wrist. *"I said leave it."*

His head shot up. Her eyes bored into his. At first he thought it was anger he read there, but as her mouth trembled, he saw it for what it really was. Fear. His grandmother was afraid. He felt his insides quake at the very idea.

"What have you done?" he asked darkly.

"It's none of your concern, boy. Just a debt that needed to be settled."

"But the land is unused . . . it lies fallow. Whoever you sold it to hasn't profited from it."

"Which is why it will never be for sale. The person who owns it does not look to make a profit; I suspect his aim at the time was to take something of value away from our family."

"Who is this man? I can surely reason with the fellow."

"You will not ever learn his name. Even if you find the record of sale, the paper bears only the name of a lawyer who stood proxy for the true owner."

He slammed the lid of the strongbox. "This is intolerable! Are you saying someone was blackmailing my father?"

She shut her eyes for a moment. "Close enough," she said. "But it is ancient history now. You haven't missed that parcel in all this time, why let it bother you now?"

But it did. All during his journey back to Devon he fretted over what she'd revealed to him, that someone had coerced his family into selling the land. As worried as he was over his mother, his thoughts kept returning to this mysterious man who had bested his father and his grandmother. Regaining that land, part of his patrimony, quickly became paramount with him. He wanted it for Ursula, for her horses, and for the additional horses they would breed together.

He purposely didn't dwell on or puzzle over the reasons behind the blackmailing of his father. He'd lost enough in his life; losing his faith in a man he'd always considered strong and upright might be more than he could bear.

Judith had accused him of refusing to remember, but he knew there were some things it was healthier to forget.

*   *   *

The afternoon Ardsley left Myrmion, Ursula had interviewed two men for the stud manager position. One of them seemed a likely candidate—he was Irish, for one thing—and she had told him to return the following week to meet with the duke.

The next morning she was sitting with Barbara in the garden, planning the menu for her party, when she heard a commotion in the lane. She ran to the low wall and was shocked to see three large wagons drawn up beside the nearest sheep pasture. The pasture gate was open, and six men and a number of large, rough-coated dogs were attempting to move the flock into the lane.

She swept out of the garden, calling back to Barbara to find Will Ridd on the double.

"What in the name of all the saints are you doing?" she cried as she stormed up to the burly man who was overseeing the evacuation.

He looked down at her from a lofty height and plucked a toothpick from the corner of his mouth. "Movin' sheep," he said.

"By whose order?"

He dug into his soiled vest and pulled out a wrinkled paper. "By order of Mr. Ralph Llewellyn, land agent of Barnstable. We're to take them to a farm in Dartmoor."

"Oh, no, you're not. This was not approved by the Duke of Ardsley. He owns these sheep."

The man poked a grimy finger into the paper. "That's his name here. He delegated Mr. Llewellyn to remove the sheep. This is only our first trip . . . we'll be coming back all week until the whole flock is moved."

Ursula's head began to reel. She now recalled the duke telling her he'd given the land agent carte blanche. How was she to combat such a thing? She looked desperately up toward the hillside, and then toward the stable. Where the devil was Will?

The man had moved away from her and was now signaling his dogs to bring the sheep up to the foremost wagon. The five other men herded them up a ramp, until the bed of the wagon was a crowded, bleating white mass. Ursula winced when they raised the ramp and slammed home the bolt. She kept scanning the area around her, the hillside, the house, the home farm.

The men began loading the second wagon, while Ursula watched in impotent fury, wondering if there was a gun in the house, wondering where all the Myrmion dogs had got to, wondering where in God's name Will had—

"Morning, gentlemen . . . Lady Roarke."

She spun around. Will was sitting on his cob in the lane, blocking the loaded wagon. He'd come up the track from the south, from the one direction she'd not expected.

"Will!" she panted, running toward him. "They're taking your sheep. I tried to argue with them, but they have an order from the duke."

He reached down and touched the tip of her nose. "Whist, little bear. The sheep are not going anywhere. Not today."

He had such an odd expression in his eyes, one she'd never seen before. If she didn't know better, she'd have called it regal. He did look like a monarch, sitting relaxed and serene in the saddle in his elegant coat and polished boots. It was hard to believe there was a crisis going on under his nose.

He motioned the tall man over to him. The fellow swaggered up to his horse: "Don't be making any trouble," the man said. "I have my orders."

Will nodded. "I'm sure you do. However, I am the bailiff here, and the duke has unfortunately neglected to inform me of his plans. You see there is a slight problem."

The man shrugged insolently. "That's no concern of mine."

"It might be. I've just come from the chemist in Stratton . . . I had some tests done on those sheep and got the results back today." Will leaned forward in the saddle and his face grew somber. "We've got gumpy tail here at Myrmion."

Ursula nearly burst out laughing. She covered her lapse with a look of wide-eyed shock.

"What the deuce is gumpy tail?" the man growled. "I been carting livestock these sixteen years and never heard of it."

"It's a local ailment . . . highly contagious. We've managed to restrict it to this district. But if you carry those sheep across Exmoor and Dartmoor, you could be responsible for spreading it all through Devon." He eyed the loaded wagon in front of him. "And if you wisely decide to remove the sheep, it might be a good idea to wash your wagon out with lye soap. As a precaution."

The tall man stood in indecision. One of his helpers sidled up next to him. "I think I've heard of gumpy tail, Daniel. It's like scours . . . a nasty business. We should go back and tell Mr. Llewellyn. Let him decide."

"You really don't want this on your head," Will pointed out. "If you spread the disease and word gets out, you'll end up carting sh—manure instead of sheep."

The men grumbled as they unloaded the sheep. The sheep grumbled even more at being displaced.

"Just leave them in the lane," Will called out. "My dog will sort them out."

He stood in the stirrups and gave a long, low-pitched whistle. A minute later, Titan appeared on the nearest hillside, running down toward them on the diagonal.

"You'd best put your dogs in the wagon," Will advised the carter.

Daniel sneered. "You're going to need more than one measly beast to move that flock."

"Just watch," he said. He climbed down from the cob and handed Ursula the reins.

Titan had reached the lane and came prancing toward Will. He didn't even acknowledge the other dogs as he passed. Will crossed over to the open pasture gate and sketched a motion toward the field. "Bring 'em in, Titan."

Ursula held her breath.

The dog first collected the sheep, which were wandering among the wagons, into a tight bunch. Then at Will's signal, he prodded them closer to the open gate, and finally, with a great deal of attentive darting back and forth, sent them streaming into the field.

Once it was over, Will turned back to the carter. "One dog," he said. "Not so measly."

He walked back to Ursula, took up the reins of the cob, and with a wink, whispered, "Pretty fair work for a Pernicious Trial to Mankind."

If there hadn't been six strange men standing there, she would have kissed him.

As it was, she couldn't take her eyes off him as he rode toward the stable. Something had happened; something had changed in his manner. It was more than cockiness . . . he'd been plenty cocky to her during their early encounters. He'd been exuding a serene confidence just now, she realized, like a man who had seen his world set to rights.

How remarkable. She wondered what could have happened.

She got her answer that same afternoon. Will came into the library, where she was sketching out designs for the new paddocks. He was now dressed in his work clothes and carried a shepherd's crook; he leaned on it as he told her about Rigger's offer, his eyes bright with excitement.

She set down her pen and gaped up at him. "He is going to *give* you that land?"

He nodded. "He came into some money years ago and has never spent it. If the owner is willing to sell, which Rigger assures me is the case, then the deed will be made over to me."

She leapt up from the table crowing, "That is the best news! No wonder you were so calm with those men. You knew the sheep could stay right here."

"I went off this morning to inspect the land, and stopped in Stratton to order some fencing. Good thing I got back when I did."

"So you'll start moving them today?"

"I was going to wait until the duke returned. But now it appears I'd better do it quickly—before more carters show up." He hesitated. "Still, I don't want His Grace to think I did this behind his back."

"You're the bailiff," she pointed out. "Can't they be moved on your say-so?"

"They are *his* sheep."

She rolled her eyes. "How could I have forgotten."

"But since you are the . . . shall we say, highest ranking person at Myrmion, I would like to have your approval before I do anything."

"Will, you know you have it."

"Officially," he said intently.

"What do you want me to do, tap you with the flat of a sword . . . like Queen Elizabeth?"

"Your hand would suffice."

She grasped his right hand firmly with both of hers and said, "Go forth, William Ridd, and move those sheep."

He raised their entwined hands and kissed both her wrists, slowly, savoringly.

"Don't, Will," she said with a catch in her voice. "You know you must not."

"It's an old country custom," he said, looking up at her through his sun-blond forelock. "To seal the deal."

He took up his crook then, and left her.

She thought of Moses with his mighty staff, leading the Israelites from bondage. There had been a great many Israelites, but she suspected there were even more sheep. Perhaps Moses needed a bit of help if the deed was to be accomplished quickly.

With a determined grin, she headed for her bedroom to change into her plainest riding habit.

Chapter Ten

*I*t took all of three days. Everyone whom Will had ever aided in Stratton Valley showed up at Myrmion during that time. The men from the weavers' guild and the workers from the home farm helped Will and Rigger set up temporary fencing, while several local shepherds came by with their dogs to join the Myrmion shepherds in moving the sheep to the west.

At the end of the first day, Will and Ursula found themselves riding together over the property. He pointed out the tumbledown cottage with a view of the Bristol Channel, and she shared his amazement that this glorious expanse of moor would soon belong to him. He was shivering almost palpably with joy at times, and she rejoiced for him. The first group of sheep that had been moved here seemed to be wandering around in an equal state of delirium, hurrying to feed from one clump of spiky, evil-looking weeds to another.

"You're sure there's nothing harmful here?" she asked.

"That's the beauty of sheep," he told her as they turned toward Myrmion, backlit by the sunset. "They prefer some weeds to grass and can stomach almost anything. Sheep will cleanse a field for other livestock, make it safe for them."

She marveled at this . . . marveled at him, so bursting with pleasure. She told him he reminded her of a child who'd had all his Christmas wishes fulfilled.

"It's more than I can encompass," he admitted. "Especially since it means I get to keep the flock with me."

"Even with the dread gumpy tail," she said.

He laughed, then reined in his horse and turned to her. "Have you ever achieved something that . . . well, that was so good, it surprised you beyond everything? That is how

I feel about breeding these sheep . . . I never expected them to turn out so fine."

"I do know the feeling," she said. He watched intently as she continued. "You see, I have another stallion back in Ireland. He was born with a deformed foot, but his owners thought he might someday be able to race. He has Godolphin Barb bloodlines, so the drive was there. It's happened before—lame horses have been brought along and won races. Finally, when he was three, and it was clear he would never be more than a park hack, they sold him. My husband bought him for me, as a sort of joke . . . got him for a song, bloodlines and all. And I just adored him from the start.

"Then an odd thing happened. One of our neighbors had a few broodmares, but he couldn't afford much of a stud fee. I asked him to let the Magpie cover his mares. A few other horsemen heard about it and bred their mares to him as well. Four years later, the Magpie's get were winning races all over Ireland. That was last year. This year I have a dozen requests to breed him."

"And Ardsley doesn't know?" Will asked with a frown. "He'll want the horse, Ursula. He'll think you held back on him."

She smiled smugly. "He has to marry me . . . then he will get the Magpie. Because right now, that horse is the only thing of value I can call my own. Every last penny from the bloodstock will go to Roary's creditors. But not Magpie . . . he will never be for sale."

He nodded slowly. "So the Magpie is your touchstone, the way my sheep are for me. The thing that keeps you grounded and feeling blessed at the same time."

"That is exactly what he is."

She nearly added, *and that is what you are, sweet Will . . . my touchstone, my grounding and my blessing.*

The next morning Judith Coltrane showed up on a flashy chestnut hunter, impressing Ursula with her seat if not with her temperament. She briskly organized the meals for the volunteers with the ladies of the weavers' guild, setting up long tables in the lane, laden with bread and cheese and cold meats. Ursula wondered why it took her weeks to plan a party, when Judith could serve thirty people at the drop of a hat. It did little to put her in charity with the squire's daughter.

Ursula convinced Barbara to take part in the exodus. The two of them assisted by opening and closing pasture gates, carrying wicker jugs of water out to the shepherds and clearing deadfalls from the paths the sheep would need to follow. They ended up enjoying themselves beyond measure. Ursula did not miss it when Rigger sat next to Barbara during their al fresco luncheon; she also did not miss it when Will seated himself next to Judith. He had been avoiding Ursula all day, but she knew that he had other concerns right now.

On the third day, the skies grew overcast. Late that afternoon, Ursula was riding behind the final group of sheep, watching as they splashed through the stream that bounded Will's soon-to-be property. She prayed that Rigger knew what he was about, that the sale would go through. If it didn't, Will was guilty of trespass, and they'd have to turn around and bring all the sheep back.

Will was up ahead on foot, working three of his dogs, including Snap, keeping the flock away from the sea cliff. Unfortunately, the shallowest ford of the boundary stream was only a hundred yards from the edge of the moor.

The sky had continued to darken throughout the day, and there was now a distinct feeling of rain in the air. Suddenly, the wind picked up. A jagged burst of lightning lit the horizon, followed by a fearful thunderclap. The sheep in front of Ursula began milling in panic; then the formation loosened, and they were no longer a tightly knit pack. Half the flock started trotting, and then galloping, in the direction of the cliff.

Will was calling out to his dogs as she urged her horse forward, racing to head off the runaways. One collie, it might have been Snap, was already at the edge of the cliff, running furiously back and forth, barking in warning. Most of the sheep veered away, but a number of them, carried forward by their momentum, came perilously close to the edge before the dog's diving, biting attacks sent them back.

Ursula threw herself from her horse ten feet from the edge and used her riding crop to beat back the crazed, bounding sheep. Will was there opposite her, using his crook to the same purpose. Each time another rolling crack of thunder sounded, the sheep would again dart in panic toward the drop-off. Ursula thought it was a miracle none of them had yet tumbled over. Snap battled on between Ursula and Will, in a frenzy of barking and nipping, at the very edge of the precipice.

Finally, the three of them—man, woman and beast—managed to deflect the sheep; they veered off as a unit away from the cliff.

Several shepherds had come running up by then, with more dogs, who encircled the exposed flank of the flock. The men offered to bring this last group down to the temporary enclosures. Will nodded and thanked them.

He approached Ursula just as the first fat drops of rain began to fall. "Have you seen Snap? I can't find her."

The anxiety in his voice made something go shivery inside her. The last time she'd seen the dog, Snap had been only inches from the drop-off.

"Let me look for her, Will," she said, placing herself between him and the cliff. "You go see to your sheep."

He brushed past her. "She's my dog."

He knows, she thought bleakly, *he knows she's fallen.*

He knelt at the edge, where the carpet of green grass rolled over into a vertical drop of sixty feet to the rocky shore below. She heard him curse under his breath.

And then he disappeared from sight.

"Blessed saints!" she cried as she ran forward and peered over the edge. He was now ten or twelve feet below the lip, clinging to a withered sapling. Snap lay on her side a few feet below him, her body cradled by a narrow outcropping of roots, her head hanging free. It looked as if the slightest movement would dislodge her.

Ursula crouched down. "Can you reach her?"

Will looked up through the drizzle. "I'm afraid to move her. I need a rope to secure her first."

She jumped up and ran back to her horse, tugging the bridle right off the surprised animal. Then she was back, looming above Will. "Here . . ." She lowered the bridle; he grabbed for it, then quickly tied one of the reins into a slipknot. She watched anxiously as he stretched down and snagged the loop around the dog's neck. Gingerly he raised the inert form from the roots, until Snap was close enough for him to grab her ruff. Then he hefted her over one shoulder.

Ursula held her breath as he slowly made his way back up, grasping single handfuls of wet grass to pull himself higher, his boots trying to get purchase on the rain-slicked turf.

When he was a few feet below her, she reached down and lifted Snap from his shoulder. The dog whimpered, but did not move. Will levered himself over the edge, then lay there panting as the realization of the danger he'd been in finally overcame him.

Ursula had managed to untie one of her petticoats and kick it off; she removed the knotted rein and wrapped the dog in the relatively dry muslin.

Will was on his knees now; he crawled over to her and took the dog in his arms. "She was my first," he said in a wavering voice. "My very first dog . . . not everyone gets the best first time out."

Ursula touched his shoulder. "She's alive, Will. Just shaken and exhausted, I would guess. Use my horse and take her back to your cottage."

She rose and caught the gray by his forelock, then replaced the bridle. She led him back to Will. "Sorry about the sidesaddle; you'll have to ride without stirrups."

She held Snap while he vaulted onto the saddle. After she'd handed the dog up to him, he caught her by one wrist. "Stop," he said brusquely. "Stop being there for me every time I turn around. Stop saving things and rescuing things that I care about. Just keep away, Ursula . . . or you will make me mad with wanting you." He leaned down, his face streaked with rain and mud, washed clean of all its joy. "Do you understand me?"

She nodded mutely.

He never took his eyes from her as he rode off, never looked forward, but kept her in his vision until he'd passed over the stream.

It was a long, wet walk back to Myrmion. She wondered where Will's horse had got to—he'd been mounted earlier that afternoon. Probably some well-meaning shepherd had found the cob and brought him back to the stable. She was alone on the moor now . . . she felt alone in all the world.

Will's words had cut her, slashed at her. Yet they were

so full of harsh truth. He could not have her, however much he went mad with wanting. She dared not have him, even though his presence haunted her, waking and sleeping, and her hunger never subsided.

There had been fledgling desire in the kisses they'd shared, and she wanted to be the one who experienced the rest of it with him—the quickening and the completion. But it wasn't only the pleasure of his caresses she craved, she also ached at times just to be in his company.

It was not love she felt, she told herself. She'd known love with Connor Roarke . . . love was giddy and thrilling. Of course, there had been no impediment with Roary—a baronet and a country gentleman's daughter were fairly matched. These disturbing feelings that Will Ridd evoked were due in part to their different stations; he was only a scant notch above a servant in the eyes of Society. Forbidden territory, she had once called it. And that made it dark and tempting . . . and ultimately bittersweet.

She had tried to be his friend, and she saw now that it hadn't eased him. It hadn't made her particularly happy either. The lightning still crackled whenever they were together. She suspected that was never going to change.

Will knelt on the hearth rug beside Snap, who was now wrapped in a woolen blanket. Rigger and Judith were with him; they had seen him ride in with the dog draped across his saddle and had come up the hill at once. Judith had beaten brandy into some eggs, and Will was trying to spoon the mixture down the dog's throat, but she seemed too weak to even swallow.

He didn't know yet what ailed her, exhaustion or something broken inside her from the fall. Her breathing was labored, nearly audible in his small parlor.

"She's had a good, long life, Will," Rigger said. "If the last thing she remembers is saving the flock, well, a sheep dog couldn't ask for more than that."

"It was my pride that did this," Will muttered. "Made me battle the duke, fight to save the sheep. Well, I saved them all right, and this is my reward."

"This is not some judgment from on high, Will," Rigger protested. "Not some punishment because you did the wrong thing."

"It feels that way. When I was clinging to a sapling, fifty feet above the rocks, all I could think was, don't let me lose her. Because I have lost so much already. My . . . my whole childhood is an empty page . . . not one memory of family or home . . ."

"We know, Will," Judith said gently.

"But dogs love you in spite of that, don't they?" he asked raggedly, gazing up at her. "They don't give a damn about family or money or rank. I . . . I looked at my brave, clever Snap lying there on a tangle of roots . . . and I thought, if I can't save her, I don't care if I die myself."

"Ah, Will . . ." Judith cried. "Don't . . ."

She cast a look of entreaty at Rigger. With a nod of acknowledgment, he crouched down beside Will. He gripped his arm and shook it gently. "Judith and I both know what ails you, William. We understand the loss you are facing. But you have to accept it . . . there's an order to the world we can't alter. And whatever occurs, you will still have the land, a chance at a decent future."

"I can never express what your gift means to me," Will said earnestly. "But the land cannot make me feel whole. I thought it could. For three glorious days I was on top of the world. Now I see there are other things a man needs to fill his soul. More than land . . ."

Both Rigger and Judith were looking at him with open compassion. He realized then that they did understand, that the dog's plight had compounded a loss he was already feeling. "You know what I'm partly mourning, don't you? All my arguments to the contrary, you know how I feel about Ursula Roarke."

"It's there in your eyes . . ." Rigger said. "Anyone who knows you well can read it."

Will put his hands over his face. "I want her. God help me, I feel sometimes that I will perish if I can't have her."

Judith rubbed his shoulder. "The feeling fades, Will. The first hurt seems so deep, but it isn't. Not always."

His eyes flashed up. "Has that been your experience, Judith? Were you able to walk away from Damien Danover with a healed heart?"

After a long pause, she said quietly, "No . . . I was not. So you aren't the only one who has suffered a loss, William Ridd."

"Sorry, Jude. I am a fool to even bring it up." He added

darkly, "Only a fool hankers after something he will never have the stature or the consequence to possess."

Rigger's hold tightened. "Those things I cannot give you, lad. Though I once thought I could. Do you recall when you first came to Myrmion, I asked you if the farm looked familiar? You grinned and said that after being a lad for hire, they all looked familiar."

Will nodded. "I thought it an odd question at the time. Did you really think I should remember this place?"

"Not you, someone else. I . . . I had a foolish hope that you might be a boy I'd lost track of long ago. But you've turned out so well, William, and I am so blasted proud of you. And that other . . . if he is lost to me, then no matter, for you will be always found in my heart."

Will clasped his arm. "Then I am not so alone as I thought." His eyes sought Judith. "Not while I have such friends by me."

It was full dark by the time Ursula reached the path below Will's cottage. She told herself that stopping in to ask after Snap was not a wise idea. Her horse was probably up there, however, which was enough of an excuse to turn her weary steps up the hillside.

The gray was tethered to a bush behind the cottage. She fiddled with the reins, arguing with herself, this way and that, over whether she should intrude on Will. Finally she approached the back door. She truly did want to know how Snap was faring. A quick look in, and she would be on her way.

Rigger Gaines answered her knock. His eyes narrowed when he recognized her. "You are not wanted here, ma'am."

She nearly fell back at the harshness in his voice. "I just thought I—"

"Leave him be," he said. "The old dog is dying. Will's lost enough today. He doesn't need you coming here to remind him of what else he stands to lose."

Judith Coltrane appeared at Rigger's shoulder. "We will tell him you stopped by."

"I can have Cook make up some beef jelly for—"

But they had already shut the door. They might as well have slammed it in her face.

Ursula stumbled back to her horse in a daze and leaned her face against its wet flank. She'd seen the *ton* close ranks against a parvenu and been saddened by it; she reflected now that commoners could be just as callously hurtful.

Will looked up as they came back into the parlor. "Who was it at the door?"

Rigger said, "One of the grooms," the same instant Judith answered, "One of your shepherds."

Will sighed. "You know, you two don't have to lie to protect me. It was Lady Roarke, wasn't it?" Their awkward silence was answer enough. He smiled wanly. "Poor little bear. I left her out there with no horse. I wonder if she walked all the way home."

He felt something warm on his hand and glanced down. Snap was licking the sticky remains of the egg mixture from his fingers. Her eyes were still closed, but her breathing sounded easier to him. He quickly spooned a few dollops into her mouth and was relieved beyond words when she swallowed them.

"Good dog," he crooned, stroking her ears. "Good old Snap."

Chapter Eleven

*T*he next morning Ursula awoke in a mood of such black despair, she doubted she could face anyone. If only she'd come down with a head cold from tramping home in the damp, she could spend the day in her room. However, eighteen years in East Anglia had hardened her constitution against wet weather. She decided to manufacture a headache and sent a message to Barbara that she was indisposed. It was a gray, gloomy day, a perfect reflection of her inner state. She dozed off and on and generally tried not to think of how Will Ridd's face had looked when he'd warned her off. She needed to wipe the image from her memory—of a man equal parts hungry and tormented.

What had happened to him, there on the cliff face, that had brought him back to her with such anguish in his heart? He'd faced possible death, she knew, on that steep, slippery patch of turf. What did a person feel when they stared into the void?

"Regret," she murmured. "Regret over the things we did not do in life."

And then she understood. He had felt the same thing she'd have felt in a dark moment . . . a profound regret that they could never be together, however right that outcome might seem.

This felt very right to me, he'd said by the pool.

Just this once, she had answered. But she'd never believed that . . . it would always feel right between them.

She wriggled back into her pillow, wondering if she dared consider the possibility of forever with Will Ridd. The very notion sent a thrill coursing through her.

Will had cast her away because he believed he could never have her. What if she told him he could? Did she have the courage to fly in the face of Society's rules—and a lifetime's beliefs—and ally herself with a man of the lower classes? She knew no one personally who had ever done such a thing. Members of the gentry married up or they married down, but always within their own strata.

But Will had land now; that gave him some stature. She had the Magpie. It was a beginning. And if there was one thing she had learned about Will Ridd, it was that he could make great things grow from tiny beginnings.

She was sorting out the possibilities of this uncertain future when Barbara came sweeping into the room, wearing an expression of barely suppressed glee. "Get yourself up, pet. The duke is come home, and he has specifically asked to speak with you."

Ursula groaned. "Not now . . ."

But Barbara prodded Ursula from her bed and whisked her into a muslin gown sprigged with periwinkles.

Ursula sat before her mirror like an inanimate doll while Barbara fussed over her hair. There was no color in her cheeks, no sparkle in her eyes. All her dreams of Will Ridd suddenly seemed like foxfire—burning bright, but so unreal. This was her reality she saw—a daughter of the gentry, waited on by servants, coddled by her companion, and now, it at last appeared, wooed by a duke.

She went listlessly down the stairs and into the drawing room. Ardsley was there, still dressed for the road, his driving coat thrown over a chair. He bowed, then handed her a glass of cordial. "My dearest Ursula."

"Your Grace," she said, mustering a smile. "I trust your grandmother is improving."

He shook his head, then chuckled. "No chance. Worse every time I see her. Her character, that is . . . her health remains ironclad."

Was he actually grinning at her? The dour duke seemed almost lighthearted. She sipped at her drink, wracking her brain for something to say. "I suppose you noticed the sheep are gone."

"Are they?" he said absently. "The rain's coming down so hard, you can't see your hand before your face. Well, then, good for Llewellyn. I like a man who acts with dispatch."

She shook her head. "It wasn't Llew—"

"Never mind that. Now sit here, dear lady," he said, practically dancing her into a wing chair, "and let us speak of what is in our hearts."

Ursula gulped. "Our hearts, Your Grace?"

He smiled down at her. "What's in my heart at any rate." He coughed slightly, and his face grew earnest. "I doubt this will come as any surprise to you . . . not after I invited you here to my home. I understand what such a thing implies in our world."

"Our world?" she repeated blankly.

He leaned forward from the waist. "I am asking you to marry me, Ursula."

"Oh." Her glass clinked down on the side table.

He stood there waiting, an expression of keen anticipation on his face. Finally she stood up and set her hand on his shoulder. "Are you sure, Damien?"

"I should have followed my instincts in Ireland and asked you then. But a man learns to go cautiously . . . a waste of time in this case, since you have never failed to impress me." He cocked his head, and doubt stole into his eyes. "Though if you require more time, I understand. I . . . well, I had reason to think my sentiments were reciprocated."

"And what *are* those sentiments?" She'd spoken more sharply than she intended.

He drew back from her, and some stiffness returned to his posture. "I won't insult you with moon-calf expressions of infatuated adoration. I believe we are both beyond such things. I see in you a woman with whom I can share my future, someone of beauty and intelligence, who will grace my home, enrich my life and be a loving mother to my children."

"You have listed my virtues . . . my values," she observed dryly. "Yet you still do not speak of your feelings."

He looked rattled for an instant; then his chin set. "I would think my desire to marry you speaks volumes on that score." When her probing expression did not alter, he added, "For one thing, I admire you for holding Roarke Stud together. You see, I know all about your husband's gaming debts. Not that they matter to me." He tapped his chin. "What else? Ah . . . I enjoy your amusing way with a story." He added with a sly grin, "I even like your singing. The truth is, you please me in innumerable ways. I think we could have a good life together. You will have every comfort—"

There it was, that dry, dusty word Barbara had used.

"—and never lack for anything."

Except love, the voice inside her head taunted.

She clasped her hands before her, forcing herself to remain calm. "Damien, I won't fob you off with some nonsense about the signal honor you have done me. Although it is an honor, truly. But I need some time to think . . . just a little time. Things here at Myrmion have been at sixes and sevens since you went away. I need to shift my focus away from Will Ridd's problems and back to my own life."

He bowed rigidly. "As you prefer, ma'am. Though I see I have one more complaint to lay at that blasted bailiff's door."

Ursula flung out one hand. "No, please. You misunderstand."

She wanted to shout in vexation. How the devil had she let his name slip out? Up until this moment she was certain the duke had no idea there was anything between her and Will Ridd.

He was watching her closely; she raised one shoulder negligently. "Your bailiff merely required my assistance on several matters . . . after all, you were not here to make decisions."

There, she'd put the onus back on him, on his defection earlier that week.

Ardsley's face relaxed. "I'm pleased, actually, that you were willing to help with the running of the place. More proof of what an admirable duchess you will make."

Ursula was trembling as she walked from the drawing room. Thank God the duke still had no idea of her feelings for Will. It had felt like a near thing, though. Then she realized his self-consequence would never allow him to consider such a possibility. What would he have done if she'd announced boldly, "I cannot marry you, Your Grace. I am in love with your blasted bailiff."

Ardsley had done nothing to deserve such a low trick. If she'd never met Will Ridd, never fallen under his considerable sway, the duke's proposal would have charmed her. All she could muster now was a bleak acceptance that it had finally come to pass.

Still, it wasn't his fault that her feelings for him had faded, her budding affection replaced by confusion, and then near apathy. He was a pleasant enough companion when he relaxed his guard; he'd even shown occasional bursts of humor. She'd enjoyed picnicking with him and playing for him. Nevertheless, it had felt both times as though he was the preamble to the play, and that the real drama would take place at some later time. How could she devote her life—her future—to a man who was nothing more substantial than the fish course?

She might have laughed at the irreverent image, but she was too close to tears. Suddenly, the dark, low-ceilinged house felt suffocating. She hurried across the hall and flung open the front door. It was as dark as twilight outside, the storm clouds hugging the hillsides. Mindless of the rain, she ran down the front walk and out into the lane.

This was what she had plotted and schemed for, she reminded herself. It had taken four months to bring her plans to fruition. And now she held the Duke of Ardsley in the palm of her hand. He'd offered her release from all her debts, the chance to keep her horses and a status in the *ton* most women would sell their souls for. She would be a fool to say no.

"Nerves," she muttered as she paced along, swiping the rain from her face. "I am merely suffering from a bout of nerves. He caught me unawares, dreaming dreams I had no business indulging in."

The stable yard was deserted; all the grooms had wisely sought shelter. She stopped beside Imperator's paddock. He danced toward her, and then feinted back. She smiled weakly. He did not own her heart as the Magpie did, but she would miss him if she refused the duke and ended up back in Ireland.

It began to rain harder; she clung to the fence, shivering now, her mind racing with questions. Was it fair to marry Ardsley while she pined for another man? Was it fair to her? And, oh God, was it fair to Will?

She recalled the torment in his eyes yesterday; the image shattered her all over again. She blinked it away, and still it prodded her. She was weeping now, her cheek pressed against the slick wooden railing as she gasped out her pain. Thunder rumbled overhead; lightning bisected the slate-gray sky. She thought she heard someone call her name.

Strong hands griped her shoulders and spun her around.

"What's wrong? Why are you out here . . . ? God, you're soaked to the skin."

He tugged off his long canvas drover's coat and pulled it around her. She felt the warmth of his body in the heavy fabric. She looked up into his eyes, so blue even in the gloom of the storm.

"The duke's asked m-me," she managed to get out between chattering teeth. "I haven't accepted yet, but he's asked me."

He didn't say anything. His hands rose, fingers splayed, to bracket her head, gripping it tightly as he stared intently into her face. The rain pelted down on them, running in rivulets along their cheeks, but neither of them moved to wipe it away.

"I haven't accepted . . ." she repeated.

Please, Will, her eyes pleaded, *tell me to refuse him. Say the words that he couldn't bring himself to say . . . tell me that you want me, that you love me.*

He lowered his head, his mouth close, so close to hers, but still he said nothing, did nothing. She felt his whole body tremble as he battled the power of the link that bound them together. It hummed and crackled in the air between them, as tangible as the storm that raged overhead.

"Will . . ." she sobbed, her hot tears mingling with the icy rainwater.

She knew it the instant the resolve solidified in his face, the instant she lost him.

His hands dropped away from her. He took a step back and nodded his head once. "You are to be c-congratulated, Lady Roarke."

He swung away then, disappeared into the veils of slashing rain.

She went back into the house, still sopping wet under Will's duster, and found the duke in the library. "I will marry you, Your Grace," she said from the doorway.

He came forward and swept her in a half circle, laughing

and chiding her for being such a goose that she had to get soaking wet before she could decide. "We will announce the betrothal at our party," he said. "You have pleased me very much, my dear. I have been trying to read and cannot keep my mind on it."

"Are you truly happy, Damien?"

He seemed puzzled. "Why shouldn't I be? You will make the most beautiful duchess in Danover history. I will order a portrait of you for Ardsley House . . . perhaps all in white, as you were the day you arrived here. And I have a splendid betrothal gift in mind, but you will have to wait a bit." He raised one finger to his lips. "It involves lawyers, and you know how complicated that can get."

He sent her upstairs to change out of her wet gown, but she fell onto her bed still fully clothed, and proceeded to cry for an hour. Barbara tiptoed in, but Ursula waved her away without raising her face from the pillow.

The duke was out early the next morning. Weeks before, he had commissioned his architect at Ardsley House to come up with a suitable stable design for Myrmion, and he now carried the completed sketches. He was standing in front of the present stable, determining in which direction the new structure should face, when Rigger Gaines came up behind him.

"You won't recognize the old place when I'm through with it," the duke pronounced over his shoulder.

"That is a thought that occurs to me from time to time."

"And now with the sheep gone off to Dartmoor, we can start tearing down the old pasture fences."

Rigger harrumphed. "I was sure Lady Roarke would have told you by now, Your Grace. The sheep are not in Dartmoor. They were moved to that stretch of land west of here—Will Ridd's land."

The duke pivoted around. "What do you mean 'Will Ridd's land'?"

Rigger's dark eyes glinted. "The owner of that parcel is deeding it to him."

Ardsley felt his face grow red. "That's preposterous. Where would Ridd get the money to buy so many acres? And, furthermore, how dare he move my sheep without permission? That's one step away from thievery." The duke's head jerked toward the outcropping of rock, where Will lounged in the sun. "And there he sits, blithely eating his breakfast, like a lord instead of a laborer. It's long past time I had things out with him."

The duke started away, but Rigger caught him by the arm. "It won't change anything. The land's been promised to Will."

Ardsley's expression brightened. "Then the sale's not completed yet? Good. Because I intend to buy that parcel as a gift for Lady Roarke. I will double any offer he can make."

Rigger poked the toe of his boot into the sodden earth. "Happens it's not for sale to you."

"The devil it's not! That bit of moorland's belonged to my family for centuries. I vowed to get it back, and I will not stand by and watch it sold to that lout."

"You don't have a choice. You see, the land was always intended for Will. He's just never needed it until now."

"Then it belongs to *you?*"

"It will go to Will Ridd. That is all I am able to say."

Ardsley wanted to shake him by the throat. "The dowager all but admitted to me that the owner of that land blackmailed my father. That he forced the old duke to sell because he wanted to take something of value away from the Danovers." His cheeks narrowed. "Was it you, Rigger, who schemed away part of my patrimony?"

Rigger smiled grimly. "I've only ever worked to benefit the Danovers . . . as you know, Master Damien."

The duke cursed under his breath and stalked away.

Will saw Ardsley striding up the path toward him. The dog lounging beside him snarled a little, but Will calmed him. "Not quite a wolf, Titan," he whispered, "more like a very testy badger."

"Come down from there!" Ardsley called from the path. "I have a small bone to pick with you."

Will sighed as he made his way down the rocks. When he reached the duke, he touched his forelock, and then put his hands behind him. He had the oddest urge to fetch His Grace a mighty blow on his patrician chin.

"You directly disobeyed my orders to Mr. Llewellyn. The sheep were to go to Dartmoor."

Will scratched the back of his neck. "Seems to me I

could hardly disobey orders that were given to a man in Barnstable."

"Don't try to flummox me, Ridd. I wager the instant I was gone from here, you sneaked those sheep off my land."

"Not sneaked, Your Grace. Hard to sneak anywhere with fifteen hundred sheep. But don't fret, I won't charge you much for the grazing rights."

Ardsley canted back on one leg. "Oh, you're very smug now, aren't you, Mr. Ridd? Odd how a bit of land can give a nonentity notions of grandeur, the idea that he's the equal of his betters."

Will looked him hard in the eye. "I don't aspire to be you, Ardsley. Not that. All I want is a piece of something to call my own. Can you, who have so much, begrudge me that little?"

"I begrudge you anything that rightfully belongs to my family. I understand the transfer of deed has not been finalized. My men in London will make sure that it is held up—indefinitely. That's the beauty of lawyers, you see . . . they take so wonderfully long to do things."

Will took a step toward him. "I found a compromise . . . are you so blind that you can't see that? The sheep will remain here on the pasturage they are used to, the grass that makes such fine fleece for Stratton Valley wool, and you will have Myrmion for Lady Roarke's horses."

"It wasn't a compromise," the duke seethed, "it was a damned underhanded way to gain control of my sheep. You are lucky I haven't called the constables. As for that land to the west, my wife-to-be has expressed a liking for it, and she shall have it. This I promise you."

So she's accepted him, Will thought numbly. He felt a cutting resentment stir in his gut.

"And since you are not yet the owner of that property," the duke continued, "nor ever likely to be, I suggest you not camp out there once you are gone from Myrmion. Which should be some time this afternoon, if I allow you half a day to pack up your things."

Will's brows rose loftily and he drawled, "So, the dukeling is dismissing me—*again.*"

Ardsley's mouth twisted. "Furthermore, I'll see the sheep gone from here. And they will not be bound for Dartmoor this time, but for the slaughter yards in Barnstable."

Will's hands fisted. "No . . . I don't believe you would do that."

Leaning forward provocatively, the duke hissed, "Is your hearing addled as well as your wits?"

Will hit him then, sending Ardsley reeling back into the pasture fence behind him. He retreated a little and stood, legs apart, nursing his fist.

Ardsley dragged himself upright. There was a smear of blood on his lower lip. To his credit, the duke did not threaten him with repercussions for lashing out. Instead, he flung himself at Will, landing a punishing uppercut to his chin. Will staggered back, but did not fall.

"Again," the duke taunted. "Come again, and see how a gentleman conducts his sport."

Will's eyes blazed at the challenge, but the fury inside him was cooling. "No . . . you are still my master till I leave Myrmion. I will not strike you."

He tried to brush past the duke, but Ardsley caught hold of his arm. He jerked him close and whispered, "You think you are so noble? You are nothing, Will Ridd. A misbegotten, misplaced accident of nature."

Will pried the man's fingers from his coat and walked away before the devil inside him forced him to lash out again. Rigger always said to laugh. He couldn't laugh. Not now.

At the turning of the path, he swung around. "You can take away my position here," he said with studied care. "You can take away the land I crave and the sheep I bred. But in the end, Your Grace, I possess something you want . . . want badly . . . that you can never take from me."

Ardsley snarled, "There is nothing on this earth you could possess that I might want."

Will's mouth quirked slightly. "That remains to be seen."

Ursula came out of the breakfast parlor at the sound of voices and found Mrs. Hutchins trailing after the duke, clucking in concern as he crossed the front hall. Ursula was shocked to see that his lower lip was swollen and oozing blood. She knew instantly what had happened; he didn't have to mutter as he passed her, "Ridd and I got into a tangle. It's nothing . . ."

She followed him upstairs, followed boldly into his bedroom—noted the stately bed with its ancient tapestry hangings—and went to his washstand to fetch a dampened towel. "I said it's nothing," he grumbled from his chair.

"Oh, hush, Ardsley," she said as she dabbed at his lip. "If you're going to be fighting like a young boy, you'll have to take some mothering without complaint." She stood upright when she was done and studied her handiwork. "And how is Mr. Ridd's face?"

"Insolent as ever," he said darkly. "Though I did fetch him a tolerable blow to the chin."

"And now what? What's to become of your bailiff?"

"I've dismissed him . . . for the last time, I might add."

She sighed. "Is that why you were fighting?" Somehow she couldn't see Will initiating a bout of fisticuffs over the loss of his position—he already had one boot out the door, so to speak.

The duke looked away from her. He was still shaken by the cruel things he'd said to the man. Wretched, spiteful, ignoble things. No one in his life had ever provoked him to such rage. Well, perhaps his grandmother, on occasion, but he would never say to her face the things he'd said to his bailiff.

"I don't want to talk about it," he said. "We never got on, not from the first. So here's an end to it. And now I can truly say I am well rid of Will Ridd." He gazed up at her, hoping for a grin.

She was scowling, just as Judith had done. God help him, she even made the same response. "That is not even remotely amusing—Your Grace."

She dropped the wet towel in his lap and marched from the room.

Will took only his books and his personal effects away from Myrmion—and his dogs, including Snap, who looked to be recovering nicely. He spent the next three days cleaning out the abandoned cottage on the moor and making some basic repairs. Several times each day he patrolled his boundaries on a hack borrowed from the Coltranes, carrying a horse pistol in his saddle bag. No one was going to take his flock off to be slaughtered.

He got word of the goings-on at Myrmion from Rigger, who came by each night. Lady Roarke's upcoming party had set the house in a tizzy. Will pictured her in the thick of things, preparing to take on her role as duchess. He hoped she was happy. The last time he'd seen her, she had been miserable—crying, clinging to a fence in the rain. And he had done the only honorable thing. He had torn himself away from her.

It would have been easy to take her from Ardsley at that moment. He wasn't sure he would have acted so nobly now. But she had been confused and upset, and he'd refused to play on those weaknesses. If she ever came to him strong and sure, he knew he wouldn't have a prayer of turning away from her.

On the evening of the third day, Rigger rode up to the cottage with a wide grin and handed Will a sealed packet. "This came in the post today. The land is yours, free and clear."

Will gripped the packet to his chest. "But what of Ardsley's threat to hold up the transfer?"

"Bluster," he said. "Just as it was bluster that he was going to fatten the infantry on your flock. I think you can relax your vigilance."

Once he'd gone, Will opened the deed and read it by candlelight. The wording baffled him—Rigger Gaines was listed as the previous owner. Will gnawed his lip. Why wouldn't his friend have told him if he'd owned the land all along? It didn't matter, he decided. Rigger's extreme generosity overrode any questions he might have.

He set the paper on the upturned crate that served as his table and stared at it for a time. Such a small, insignificant object to hold as fine and glorious a thing as freedom. He wanted to march into the duke's study and slap it down on his polished desk. But as he thought a while longer, a startling idea occurred to him. The more he chewed on it, the surer he became that it was the only course he could take.

Chapter Twelve

*U*rsula had thrown herself into her party plans with a vengeance—for one thing, they furnished her with a prime excuse to keep away from the duke. There were meetings with Cook, daily trips into Stratton. She had to instruct the grooms on the handling of the guests' conveyances and the household staff on the serving of supper in the garden. There were a million little details, as she frequently explained to the duke.

The oddest thing was, once she'd accepted his proposal, all Ardsley's reserve had fallen away. He'd become jocular and attentive. She wished him at Jericho. *She* was now the person with her guard up . . . avoiding him whenever possible. It occurred to her that he must think her an avaricious harpy who, having got her claws into him, could now dismiss him at her whim.

On the third day after Will's departure, the duke managed to track her down. He surprised her making lists in the morning room. "It's very clear you've been avoiding me."

"The party—" she said lamely.

"Hang the party. I believe I understand the reason you are keeping to yourself. You are angry over the way I treated the bailiff. I know you admired him—"

Ursula swore her heart went cold.

"—that you valued something in his character that I could not see. And it made me angry . . . because I feared you did not value me in that same way. You think I blundered with the sheep, that I had no right to interfere with Miss Coltrane's weavers."

She shrugged lightly. "You came about, though . . . and it's all turned out well. The sheep are close by, the new paddocks are being built, the stable design approved."

"So do you admire me now, Lady Roarke? Now that I've 'come about'?"

The tension inside her eased. "That you are having this conversation with me is quite admirable. But do *you* think yourself worthy of my esteem?"

"To tell the truth, I'm not sure." He turned his face from her. "I said terrible things to your Mr. Ridd that morning, Ursula. Unforgivable things that still trouble me. The harsh words, the anger boiled out of me. It wasn't just his usual insolence that drove me. I was . . . jealous of him . . . of your high regard for his work here. And of his taking that land away from me when I wanted so much to buy it for you."

Her eyes softened. "You never told me that."

"That was to be my surprise," he said wistfully.

She reached for his hand; she couldn't help it. He was so clearly troubled.

"My grandmother, whom you will someday have the misfortune to meet, is a terrible bully. I thought I had distanced myself from her in every way possible. Then last week Judith Coltrane called *me* a bully. I've been wondering these past few days . . . if I was treating Will Ridd that way . . . you know, as a sort of whipping boy."

"For one thing," she said after some reflection, "these Devonshire men you employ take a bit of getting used to. Rigger Gaines behaves as though he's lord and master here. So maybe Will Ridd's direct approach is what riled you . . . right from the start."

"You liked him, though, didn't you?"

"Oh, yes," she said softly, unable to lie.

"I've come to trust your judgment, as it happens. You saw something in the fellow that I could never grasp."

"Everyone saw but you, Damien."

"Make me understand, please. He's gone now, and we are unlikely to meet him again, except in passing. But I'd still like to know . . . what is this power he possesses?"

She thought for a moment, tempering her words so that the duke would never know of Will's power over *her*. "Mr. Ridd is one of those people who knows how to think outside the accepted channels. He would have done well in intelligence work, I believe. Or as a diplomat. He is not the sort to follow orders and just march along." An apt

nalogy occurred to her. She smiled and leaned toward
im. "Think of it this way . . . Will Ridd is the sheep dog,
ot one of the sheep."

Ardsley sighed. "I suppose I wanted to be the sheep
log."

She laughed. "I've learned there's room for more than
ne on a farm, sir."

That was when she realized she truly liked the duke.
After he'd confided in her, he was very comfortable to talk
vith. She wished she didn't feel like such a Jezebel, though.
he could never as easily confide in him how she felt about
Will. Yet the more she saw of the warm core inside the
ool Duke of Ardsley, the more she wrestled with her prob-
em. She honestly didn't wish to hurt him.

Of course, marrying one man while you were helplessly
n love with another was a sure way to do harm. Ending
heir betrothal would also cause him pain—he was truly
ond of her, even if he could not articulate it.

The question gnawed at her . . . should she seek security,
s she'd promised herself she would do, or should she
ledge herself to Will—and a life full of chance? Chance
ad never favored her husband, and she had grave doubts
he would be any luckier.

The morning of the party dawned clear and bright. As
he went about her final duties, Ursula had a fidgety feeling
hat something bad or momentous—she had no idea
vhich—was going to happen. It kept her on edge, so that
y the time she was getting dressed that evening, she was
bit waspish. "Wear the blue," Barbara coaxed after she
ad rejected all her other dresses. "I know it's a winter
own, but I can't imagine why you brought it if you didn't
ntend to wear it."

Ursula looked at the four rejected gowns on her bed,
umbled there like offerings from a greenhouse—apricot,
rimrose, violet and rose blush. She had to admit, the deep
lue that Barbara held was her favorite. Even if she had
vorn it the night she met Ardsley.

"Very well, the blue it is," she said, "with the Roarke
iamonds."

Barbara laughed. The Roarke diamonds, as they both
new, were now only a high-quality paste copy. By this

time next year, she might be wearing real diamonds again.
Or she might be living in a hovel in Ireland with the Mag
pie stabled in the next room.

It seemed only a remote possibility that she would be
sharing a sheep farmer's cottage—even though there were
still moments when she ached to walk out of the house
over the moors and across the stream that bounded his
land. There would be no coming back, she knew. She
hadn't yet found the courage to do it. She didn't know i
she ever would.

Once she was dressed, she went downstairs to make sure
everything was set up properly. She checked the back par
lor, where the card tables had been arranged, and the draw
ing room, where the carpet had been rolled up to make a
space for dancing. The front parlor, now awash with flow
ers, was where the guests would assemble. She had done
little rearranging there, except for carrying in the painting
of Damien and the miniature of the duchess, which were
now displayed below the last duke's portrait. She though
it made a nice family gallery.

Ardsley found her in there, and nodded his approva
when he saw the paintings.

"What did Anthony look like?" she asked. "You men
tion him from time to time . . . and I would like to have
an image in my head."

She thought he would balk, but he merely said, "He wa
rather more like my mother than I am, with her wide
spaced eyes. They were a bright blue and his hair wa
honey colored, fairer than mine. He was more sturdy than
I was . . . I think he would have grown up tall."

"So he was not disfigured in any way by his illness?"

"No, not at all. I suppose you are wondering why there
are no pictures of him here. There are none at Ardsley
either. I think my grandmother had them removed."

She reached up and touched his cheek. "Thank you.
am glad you can speak of him to me."

He leaned against the mantel. "It's the oddest thing, Ur
sula. Since I've been back at Myrmion, I swear there are
times when I feel him here with me. Not as a child, bu
grown up. Can ghosts age, do you think?"

"No, but maybe our minds age the people we haven'
seen in years. When I think of my school friends, I se

them as women grown, though I have rarely met any of them since we were girls."

He pushed forward and took her hand. "I think I hear someone at the door. Shall we go and greet our first arrivals?"

Will borrowed Judith's gig and spent most of the day in Barnstable, making preparations for the upcoming night. He arrived at the door of Myrmion at nine and handed his invitation to the hired butler, who then directed him to the parlor, where the guests were assembling.

Will was nearly to the door when Rigger came into the hall. He caught hold of Will and dragged him under the staircase. "You can't do this, lad," he whispered sharply. "Thank God I was here to stop you."

Will tugged back from him, smoothing the sleeve of his black cutaway coat. "And why can't I? I was invited . . . at the future duchess's request."

The older man's eyes pierced him. "It's to see *her* that you came, isn't it?"

"Just once more," Will said truthfully. "Because we never parted properly. Besides, I wanted to let Ardsley greet his new neighbor." His grin faded. "Ah, Rigger, when have you ever known me to be vindictive or malicious? I'm not here to make trouble. Let me pretend for one night to be a real gentleman. Tomorrow I will be Farmer Will again . . . and happy in that role."

Rigger's frown eased. "You are the equal of any of them," he said. "But some may not see it that way. Keep your wits about you."

Will laughed softly. "I am hardly entering the lion's den, old friend. Just the testy badger's lair."

By nine o'clock the parlor was full of guests. Ursula feared it was going to be a crush. Sir Harris Wainwright, a distant connection of the duke's, had come over from Barnstable with his wife. The vicar was there with his wife and two daughters, one of whom was flirting with Mr. Draycott, a prosperous young merchant. Barbara Falkirk was listening attentively to Lady Winifred Castlemaine, a towering matron in a plumed hat, who had come in the Wainwrights' coach. Mr. Spathe, a solicitor from Lynton,

was having an animated discussion with Squire Coltrane.
Last of all, the room was graced by the presence of two
strapping militia officers from Minehead, whom Ursula had
met while awaiting the duke's coach. Barbara had thought
it very fast to invite them, but the duke insisted it never
hurt to be hospitable to the military.

As Ursula drifted past Sir Desmond Coltrane, he broke
away from Mr. Spathe to compliment her on the party. The
squire was a lanky, lantern-jawed man with a head of thick,
iron-gray hair. Ursula liked him almost immediately, especially when he was able to recite Impy's bloodlines off the
top of his head.

"My daughter does love those sheep," he remarked, "but
I'll take a raking hunter any day of the week. Judith goes
her own way . . . and it is usually in the opposite direction
from me." He leaned closer. "The truth is, I am pleased
as can be over how my girl turned out . . . how she supported Will Ridd in all his schemes. I was hoping they'd
make a match of it, but things never blossomed in that
direction, more's the pity."

"You would have let your daughter marry a common
bailiff?"

He winked at her. "Ah, but Will Ridd is an uncommon
man, my lady. And you know my Judith—if she'd wanted
Will, no one could gainsay her, least of all me."

"I am sorry she was unable to attend tonight," Ursula
murmured, trying not to let the squire's words tweak her.

He shook his head. "She's been blue-deviled over something lately. I thought this party would cheer her up. But
she took to her bed and would not be budged."

Ursula was about to excuse herself and move on when
the squire gave a gusty shout. "Ho, now! See who's just
joined us. And looking fine as fivepence."

She craned her head around. Will Ridd was standing in
the doorway. The floor seemed to undulate beneath her
slippers, like the deck of a tossing ship, and she nearly
tipped her champagne onto the squire's pristine shirtfront.
She watched in dumb wonder as the vicar, and then the
squire himself, approached Will and shook his hand. Several other people in the room began to notice him; a little
buzz filtered up from the general conversation.

Lord, how could they *not* notice him? He looked like a young Apollo come down from Olympus—gilded, bronzed, shimmering. His severely tailored black coat made the startling blondness of his hair more apparent, while his dove-gray inexpressibles and gleaming Hessians showed off the length and muscled contours of his legs. When her gaze at last moved to his face, however, she nearly frowned.

In a better, fairer world, he would have been looking at her with hungry longing in his eyes. But he was not. His interest was fixed on the squire. She imagined Will asking after the health of Sir Desmond Coltrane's daughter. She imagined herself flinging Judith Coltrane into a deep, dank well.

"He's the duke's bailiff," Lady Winifred whispered loudly. "In London, he wouldn't be allowed upstairs. But you know county society, the rules are sometimes lax . . ."

"Do I suddenly detect the odor of sheep?" a masculine voice behind Ursula inquired. Muted laughter followed.

She was about to move forward to greet Will, as was her duty, when Ardsley blocked her path. He was also looking quite fine in a seal-brown coat worn over a blue-and-gold satin waistcoat. His expression, however, was not at all fine. "This is very awkward, Ursula. Why has he come here?"

She swallowed hard. "I invited him. It never occurred to me not to. It was before . . . before you dismissed him."

"He doesn't belong here."

She clutched his arm. "Please, Ardsley, don't make a scene. He has friends here. He will not be out of place."

His frown deepened. "I wasn't going to tell you this . . . but there are ill feelings toward him in the district. The other landowners consider him an upstart. They don't like it when someone of his background sets himself up as a gentleman."

"Look at him!" she stormed softly. "Is there any man here who is his equal?"

Ardsley gaped at her in astonishment, and then turned his gaze to the tall man who still hovered near the entrance. It was as though he were truly seeing him for the first time. He noted the angular, sculpted face, the wide-set blue eyes, the gilded hair. He saw the crooked curl of his mouth as he grinned down at the squire.

Ardsley felt a buzzing begin in his head . . . a curious imbalance of time and place. He quickly shook it off, attributed it to inferior champagne.

When he looked back, Will Ridd was crossing the floor, coming directly toward him.

"Lady Roarke," he said, bowing low. "Your Grace," he added with a practiced smile. "I believe I need to have a word with you."

"Ridd," the duke acknowledged gruffly. "This is hardly the place to conduct business."

Will Ridd's mouth twisted as he rubbed his chin, which still bore the faint traces of a bruise. "I think we got our business out of the way last time we met. There is still one small matter, however."

The duke gritted his teeth. What was the fellow up to now? He would bear with him for Ursula's sake, but his patience was not unlimited. He turned and asked her to excuse them.

"This concerns the lady, as well," Ridd stated.

Ursula knew the duke was going to balk. She saw the irritation building in his eyes. She quickly nodded to Will and led them to the fireplace, away from the other guests.

"I see you brought in some of the family portraits," Will said to her.

The Roarke diamonds flashed at her wrist as her fingers brushed the miniature of the duchess. "I thought the old duke could use some company."

Ardsley cleared his throat. "*Mr.* Ridd . . . if you would just tell us what—"

Will drew a folded paper from his waistcoat. "It's the deed to the western parcel. Three hundred acres of prime grazing land."

"I know how much land is in that parcel," the duke snapped, "to the last square yard."

His cheeks narrowed as Will offered the paper to Ursula. Her eyes darted up. "What are you about, Will Ridd?"

"Freedom," he answered in a low voice. He was looking right at her now, the keen light of vindication shining in his eyes.

"I'm very pleased," she said. "I understand what this means to you." She attempted to hand it back, but his fingers closed over hers, pressing the deed into her palm.

"You don't understand at all, my dear Lady Roarke. This is *your* freedom. Open it."

Her hands were trembling as she unfolded the paper. It was a transfer of property from William Ridd to Ursula, Lady Roarke. Her heart bucked once again and then began a rapid tattoo in her chest. *Freedom, indeed!*

She wanted to cry out and fling herself on him . . . for this gift, this gesture that had cost him more dearly than all the diamonds in the world.

The duke now snatched the deed from her hand and thrust it back at Will. "Your jest is ill-timed, sir. And now Lady Roarke and I must get back to our guests."

"No—!" Ursula cried, trying to turn back as Ardsley drew her away.

"If you are wise, Mr. Ridd," the duke uttered over his shoulder, "you will leave this house. Before I call my footmen to . . . escort you out."

Will watched as he tugged Ursula across the floor, keeping her at his side with a steely grip. She was trying to fight back, but was too well-bred to make an outright scene. He'd hoped that after seeing his gift she would stand up to the duke, scene or no scene. He hadn't deeded her the land as an enticement to come to him—he never expected that. Rather, it had been to give her a choice, so she could take a husband out of wanting, not out of needing.

Perhaps she had made her choice, he thought bleakly.

Most of the guests were staring at him openly now, no doubt wondering what he had done to rile their host. He didn't care; he'd been stared at enough in his lifetime—and by a better class of tormenters than anyone in this room.

The duke turned, halfway across the floor, and glared at him. Will raised his chin and smiled mirthlessly at the man. Then he shifted around and with great care laid the deed upon the mantel.

He looked at the portrait above him, seeing for the last time the handsome, careworn face of the duke. Will knew he would never return to this house. His eyes drifted to the painting of the young Damien, and then to the miniature of the chestnut-haired duchess with her wide-set blue eyes, her slightly lopsided smile—

Something constricted sharply in his chest . . . pain and not pain. He grappled with his neckcloth as his breathing faltered. His vision clouded as dizziness swept over him. Images flashed past in the dark recess of his brain. A woman crying . . . a young boy hammering on a door . . . a man sobbing at the side of a child's bed . . . chestnut hair, tawny hair . . . fair-skinned faces, wide-eyed faces . . .

He shook away the images, forced his eyes open, but they were still all around him—the man, the woman, the boy—there on the wall, there on the mantel. Tremors began to course through him, small ones, but he knew they would soon increase in strength.

No-o-o! he screamed silently. Not here, not now . . . it had been so long . . . they had been gone from him so long . . .

A loud, ragged cry broke from his throat as his fisted hands pressed his temples in a desperate attempt to drive out these old familiar demons. He pivoted around and staggered a few feet from the fireplace, the guests nearest him hurriedly backing away. He raised his eyes to the duke and reached out one hand toward him, the fingers curled in entreaty.

Ardsley's eyes were black with horror, his mouth hanging open. Yet he swiftly closed the ten-foot gap between them, reaching for Will's hand, reaching back across the long, endless space.

Will clasped that hand, tightened his fingers around it like a lifeline. "Help me, little badger," he rasped out. "Help me—"

Ursula cried out as Will collapsed to the floor. She pushed past Ardsley and cast herself down beside him as his arms and legs began to spasm. The two militiamen came forward then and attempted to drag Will to his feet. "Drunk, I expect," one of them muttered. "We'll put him under the pump."

"Please . . ." Ursula insisted, "set him down on the couch." They ignored her. She rose and placed herself in front of them. With the voice of an Irish sergeant major she barked out, *"Set . . . him . . . on . . . the . . . couch!"*

Once Will was stretched out there, she called for a blanket and a handkerchief. Ardsley crouched down beside her, his face ashen, sweaty. He appeared to be ill. "Let me get Rigger. He'll know what to do."

"No . . . I will take care of him. It's just a fit, Damien. My aunt's housekeeper in Kerry suffered them. I know what is needed." She reached past him to take the squire's proffered handkerchief and quickly folded it into a pad. "Here," she said to the duke, "we must get this into his mouth, else he might bite his tongue."

She marveled at how firmly yet tenderly the duke manipulated Will's jaw. She gingerly set the pad between his teeth. Will's eyes were open, but they were unseeing. When his head began thrashing from side to side, she set a cushion beside it.

She looked up to ask Ardsley for a blanket, but he was no longer there. Her eyes sought Barbara in the crowd, but she too had vanished. The party guests were now backed against the door, several of them audibly incensed over what they considered an ill-bred display.

"Please," she said, as she forced herself to her feet. "He needs quiet. If you would all go into the drawing room, His Grace will be with you shortly."

She returned to the couch, bracketing Will's restless head with her arms. From the corner of her eye she saw the vicar moving about the room, extinguishing most of the candles. She felt his hand brush over her head, heard him whisper, "Peace be with you both." The squire spread a woolen blanket in soft autumn hues over Will's body, and then the two men went out, gently shutting the door behind them.

"Peace, Will," she murmured against his hair, her bright Apollo turned to shuddering, unlovely Vulcan.

Rigger had been lurking in the hall, fretting over Will, when he heard the lad cry out. He'd ducked his head through the parlor door just in time to hear the urgent plea upon Will's lips as he staggered toward the duke.

It was the sign he'd been awaiting for fifteen long years.

Once he'd seen that Lady Roarke had taken Will in hand, Rigger singled Barbara Falkirk out of the crowd and all but dragged her from the parlor. It was an ally he required at this moment, someone level-headed and practical.

"Lady Roarke will need me," Miss Falkirk protested.

"There's another lady who needs you more. Will you come away with me?" He grasped her wrist. "No questions now . . . all will be explained soon enough. I need you to fetch your cloak and be quick about it."

Her eyes narrowed and her bosom swelled. "Is this an elopement, Mr. Gaines?"

He spared a moment to grin. "Not this time it isn't, Miss Falkirk, more's the pity. 'Tis a sort of friendly abduction I'm planning, and I need you to aid me. Your Scots pluck and your fine Scots heart will both be in demand."

Barbara hesitated. She knew without a doubt that Mr. Gaines's urgency was directly related to the occurrence in the parlor, when for one instant the entire room had stood transfixed as the duke clasped Will Ridd's hand. Something very strange was afoot.

She weighed her options. She had always been a practical woman; as a governess turned companion, she'd had little occasion to dream. Yet she discovered at this moment that she harbored a secret yen to go adventuring—most especially with a dark-eyed, piratical man.

"Very well," she said briskly. "I will fetch my things."

Ursula knew that Will would sleep deeply once the fit passed. And that he would awaken with little memory of what had occurred. It was nature's small recompense for making a man thrash and twitch against his will, for making him an object of ridicule to any stray onlooker.

Not that she was distressed by his seizure, except for the pain it had caused him. Rather, she was feeling oddly serene. A great many things had come clear in her head. For starters, she'd just gotten an answer to one of her most vexing questions.

Will Ridd had been beaten as a youth because he suffered fits. "I'll beat the devil out of him!" she'd once heard an Irish drover bellow as he pummeled his flailing son with the butt end of a bullwhip. It was ignorant and cruel, but it was a time-honored method to subdue anyone so afflicted.

She sat up a little as his body began to ease out of its strange possession and removed the folded pad from his mouth. The danger was over.

Still, it was a wonder to her that he, who was so strong and powerful, could also be so frail. Not much different from her race horses, she realized. Strapping, vibrant creatures who were notably susceptible to the smallest rock, the shallowest gopher hole, the tiniest shred of moldy hay.

She sat tucked up beside him, watched him curl into the

back of the sofa as the healing sleep overcame him There was time now to reflect on what he had done for her . . . the gift that lay on the mantel. It was still more than she could absorb. A man who owned very little, suddenly rich in land beyond his wildest imaginings . . . then giving it away. To a woman who had done nothing to deserve it, nothing but confuse and tease and torment him.

"And love him," she whispered aloud.

He stirred at the sound of her voice, twisted his head around and looked up at her, his blue eyes sleepy still, his expression puzzled. He said nothing, just gazed around the room as though he expected the party to be going on, the guests still chatting and laughing.

"What's happened?" he asked as he pushed himself upright.

"You had a fit, Will. I sent everyone to another room."

He put his head back and laughed almost noiselessly, a strange, bitter sound. "So this is what my playacting the gentleman's come to—I am made the fool again."

"You don't know yet what it's come to, Will Ridd," she said as she unfolded her legs and rose from the sofa. She moved away from him for a moment, then came back and plucked up the autumn blanket. "Come, let me take you home . . . to the hillside cottage."

She took his hand, tugging him gently toward the door. She managed to get him through the hall—deserted now, no sign of anyone, not even the servants—and out the front door. The stables were lit, but there were no grooms about.

The night air was chilly as they made their way toward his cottage. She draped the woolen blanket over both their shoulders, but he shook it off and grumbled, "I can see myself home, Lady Roarke. I'm sure the duke will be looking for you."

"He's disappeared," she said musingly. "Barbara, too. Everyone's disappeared."

It was what she'd wished for at the pool, that they might become the only two people in the world. The ground mist swirled around their legs as they walked, increasing her sense of being isolated in a strange, foreign landscape. He didn't say anything more, didn't press her to leave, so she just kept on beside him, holding the skirt of her blue gown away from the dew-wet grass.

"Go lie down," she said, once they got to his front door. "I'll brew you some chamomile tea."

"I'm not a blasted invalid, Ursula."

Her temper flared a little. "For all that you are kind-natured, you rarely say thank you." She didn't dwell on the one time he *had* thanked her, after he had kissed her in the dell. "Is that why you don't like it when anyone helps you, because then you have to show gratitude? Does that weaken you, Will, or make you less of a man?"

"You saw me tonight," he shot back. "You tell me how much of a man I was, writhing on the carpet."

"Oh, pish," she said. "Flighty Dean Flynn, our local tippler, has it all over you every night outside the pub. And that's just him trying to get his breeches fastened after a trip to the privy."

She heard his low chuckle, saw him grin in the darkness. "Go on inside," she said with a hand on his shoulder. "This fine coat of yours is getting damp."

She stirred up a fire in the cold kitchen hearth. When she carried the tea into his bedroom with a lit candle, he was fast asleep, sprawled on his stomach across the feather comforter.

Setting the candle on his nightstand, she knelt down beside the bed, cupping the mug in her hands. She watched the steady in-and-out motion of his ribcage beneath his cambric shirt. His coat and waistcoat had been neatly hung on one of the wall hooks.

She had it in her to love a tidy man, one who cared for the things he possessed . . . one who cherished them in his heart.

The sound of hoofbeats roused Ursula some time later. She started awake, confused, clouded. The candle had burned down a bit, she saw, but it was still lit. The room around her was shadowy, though in a comforting way. She heard the hoofbeats again, but they seemed to be receding now. Reassured she snuggled into her pillow, thankful for the warmth at her back, and drifted again into sleep—totally unaware that she was lying on the edge of Will Ridd's bed, prevented from tumbling off only by the lean arm that was wrapped around her waist.

Chapter Thirteen

The Duke of Ardsley rode like a madman in the dark . . . across Myrmion, down along the stream boundary, and then doubling back toward Stratton. His lathered horse, however, could not outrace his tumultuous feelings. He was desperate for someone to talk to, someone sane and strong and practical. He needed Judith. God help him, he needed Judith Coltrane.

He slewed his horse to a halt in the drive of Stratton Meadows, reeled onto the porch and began thumping frantically on the door. Hannah, Judith's old nurse, finally answered his pounding, wearing a dressing gown and a frilly cap.

"I'm sorry," he panted as he careened into the hall. "You must fetch Miss Judith down to me. I know it's beastly late—" He caught her by one arm. "Please, Hannah, it's urgent."

After helping himself to a glass of the squire's brandy, he paced in agitation across the parlor floor until Judith appeared. She also wore a dressing gown, but no cap. Her hair was a halo of dark, disordered curls around her face.

"Damien!" she cried, rushing forward. "What's wrong . . . something at Myrmion?"

He stood there trembling, unable to speak. "It's Will," he said at last. "Will Ridd . . . Oh, God, Judith . . ." He clunked his glass down on the drinks tray. "I . . . I don't even know how to say this."

Her face blanched as she grasped his wrists. "Tell me quick! For the love of god, Damien, tell me if something's happened to Will."

He drew in a long, shuddering breath. "He isn't Will Ridd," he sobbed hoarsely. "He is my brother, Anthony."

Judith reeled back several feet, clutching the edge of a

wing chair to keep from falling. "Why would you say such a thing? How could you even think it?"

He swept across to her and practically bellowed, "Because it's true! My brother is alive, Judith. I don't know how or why, I only know that tonight I saw him and I knew. Without any doubt."

"But you were having a party . . . when did this happen?"

He laughed darkly. "In the middle of the party, of all things. Under the very noses of Stratton Valley's elite, the true Duke of Ardsley reappeared."

She blinked rapidly. "Will claimed to be the duke?"

"No, it wasn't like that. I don't think he has any idea. He suffered a fit, Judith, a falling-down fit. And that's when I remembered—as you have been nagging at me to do. It came back to me that a short time after Tony first got sick, he started having fits . . . terrible, frightening fits."

Judith bit her lip. "Damien, plenty of people suffer fits. It doesn't mean that—"

He grabbed hold of her, tugged her up close and set his mouth against her ear. "What did Tony call me when we were children together?" He purred, "You remember, don't you, Judith?"

She arched her head back. "I was only six . . ."

The duke fisted one hand in her hair and drew her head back. "What did he call me? When he wanted to tease me or vex me?"

"Little b-badger."

He nodded. "Precisely."

"Oh, Damien, did Will really call you that? You're not mistaken?"

"Not now . . . I will never be mistaken about him again. He staggered toward me, Judith, trembling and weak, and as he reached out his hand, he cried, 'Help me, little badger.' "

"Oh, my God," she whispered. She pushed away from him and fell back into the chair. "I need to collect my thoughts. Dear God . . . how can this be?"

He knelt beside her and clasped her hands. "Think about honey-brown hair turned to gold, fair skin tanned by the elements . . . the man lives outdoors, Judith, in the sun. Think about that crooked grin of his . . . it is my mother's puckish smile, to the life."

"Your smile too," she pointed out. "And he does have your mother's eyes. But he looks nothing like any of you in the lines of his face. When he first came here, I used to think he looked rather like a beautiful martyred saint." She paused, then set her hands on his chest. "You can't know this . . . but Will has no recollection of his childhood. Rigger Gaines found him working as a lad for hire near Tiverton and took him as his ward—"

"Rigger Gaines," the duke repeated with a little venom. "I've lately suspected he was involved in some scheme against the Danovers."

"He loves Will," she protested. "If Will were the true duke, don't you think Rigger would have come forward and proclaimed it before now?"

Ardsley raked his hand through his hair. "I'm damned if I know what to think . . . or to do." His eyes sought her. "That's why I came here. I always come to you in a crisis."

She lowered her head. "I didn't think you would even ever speak to me again. I said those wretched things to you . . . hurtful, unfair things. You must have such a disgust of me . . ."

He touched his hand to her dark curls. "That could never happen, Judith."

Something like joy suffused her face for an instant, but then it grew anxious again. "When are you going to tell Will?"

His face tightened. "This is where it gets difficult. As unbelievably delighted as I am at having my brother back, there is a slight problem."

"Oh, you mean because now he will get the dukedom?"

"Hang the dukedom," he said intently. "But I have a feeling he has already gotten Lady Roarke. You see, I left the party tonight in a state of shock and rode off. When it came clear to me that the only answer was that Will was my brother, I went looking for him. I suspected he'd have gone back to his old cottage and sure enough, I rode below it and saw a light in the bedroom. I went up the hill . . . and as I rode past the window—"

"What?" she prodded.

"Lady Roarke was with him."

One hand fluttered out. "Looking after him, surely, watching over him after his seizure?"

Ardsley shook his head slowly. "She was lying on the bed . . . in his arms."

"Oh . . . oh, my."

The duke gripped her shoulders. "I am sorry, Judith. I know how you feel about him. I suppose we were both blind to what was going on."

She sighed. "Damien, some day, some precious day, you will look beyond that fine patrician nose of yours and see what is *really* going on."

He cocked his head, and his insides lurched a little when he saw the bemused affection in her eyes. Affection for him? God, maybe it wasn't too late. "You mean you're not—?"

"No, not a bit. Never. Will was merely the brother I never had."

He chuckled. "If I'm correct, he's also the brother *I* never had. At least not for twenty-odd years. Ah, can you imagine it, the three of us together again?"

"I can," she said. "Well, more like a foursome now. I am sorry about Lady Roarke . . ."

He looked down. "It's not that I am crushed by her betrayal or anything so melodramatic. But I was very taken with her, you know. And lately I thought we were getting to be friends. Almost as good friends as you and I once were. I trusted her—"

She preempted him gently. "Will's been in love with her . . . almost from the beginning. And I suspect the sentiment is very much returned."

Damien recalled the day they'd fought, the taunting words Will had thrown at him. *I have something you want badly . . . that you can never take from me.*

Ursula Roarke's love.

He blew out a breath. "Will came to the party to give her the deed to his land . . . did you know that? Talk about the grand gesture. Though she won't require it now. She'll have a Duke of Ardsley one way or another. I think it was always her plan."

"But she couldn't have known—"

"Of course she couldn't, which is to her credit—that she was willing to give up marriage to a duke for the arms of a farmer."

"Are you feeling calmer now? You should focus on your

happiness, Damien. This is a momentous night." She touched his sleeve. "You must go to Will in the morning—"

"I'm thinking I should go to my grandmother . . . bring her here. I have to make her acknowledge Will properly before anything else can happen."

"Why not bring Will to Ardsley House?"

"No, she's too strongly entrenched there. I want her at Myrmion . . . where she'll have to face the ghosts."

She shivered, a reaction so unlooked for in his stalwart Judith, that he had to steel himself not to take her in his arms. "I'll leave tonight . . . give my pique at Ursula and Will a chance to cool. By the time I return, I can greet my brother with a whole heart."

He moved to the door, then hesitated and pivoted around. "I say, Judith, you wouldn't by any chance fancy a trip to Ardsley House? I could use a dragon slayer."

"I'd like to take on your grandmama," she said with relish. Then her face fell. "But you're not serious—the two of us traveling to Bath alone? What of the impropriety?"

"When did you ever give a damn about that, Miss Coltrane?"

He swept back across the room, hauled her up from her chair and kissed her hard on the mouth.

Her eyes widened. "Damien? What was that for?"

He tapped her mouth with his fisted hand. "That was for a blind, foolish seventeen-year-old boy who didn't know enough to hold on to you." He turned her about and prodded her toward the door. "Now go get dressed. And Judith . . . leave the blasted carpetbag behind."

Chapter Fourteen

*W*ill awoke from a favorite dream—one where Ursula was asleep beside him, tucked under his arm. He sometimes had other, more vivid dreams of her, ones where they went beyond shared kisses . . . oddly specific dreams of touch and reciprocal response, as if his mind knew the delicate intricacies of those things his body had never experienced.

When he opened his eyes, he saw the lit candle on the nightstand. He also realized with shocked surprise that there *was* a woman sleeping, relaxed and warm, beneath his arm. The auburn mass of her hair was a millimeter from his nose. From where he lay, he could just see the curve of her cheek and the rounded whiteness of her throat, bared by the low neckline of her gown. The diamonds she wore glittered there, but they could not match the luminescence of her skin.

He inched his head forward until his face was nestled in her hair, and breathed in the scent of her, like a sultry night wind from some exotic land, redolent with jasmine and gardenia and dark, woodsy myrrh. The fabric of her gown was as soft as suede beneath his fingers.

He shifted forward to rest his head lightly upon her shoulder. He watched her breathe, soon matching the rise and fall of her chest with his own, fascinated by the contrast of the velvety, deep-blue bodice against the smooth alabaster of her breast.

He ached to kiss her there, to taste the cool skin and warm it with his mouth. And then to slip the gown away from her and know the flavor of every lush curve and every shadowed recess.

The feelings that had begun to ripple through his body were not strangers to him. He was unfledged, but still a man for all that. He'd just never imagined the acuteness of those stirrings when there was a woman's scent and a woman's warmth close up against him. Much more than that, it was Ursula here with him, the Ursula of his dreams who lay in his arms.

It was like to drive him to madness, in truth, if he couldn't feed the craving for her that was growing stronger with each insistent heartbeat. If he couldn't lose himself in her . . . sink into her until there were no barriers, no obstacles, only the inevitable surrender to the immutable link that bound them together.

At that heady thought, the arm curled about her waist tightened reflexively.

She came awake all at once, craned her head around and gasped softly when she saw him.

"Oh, goodness . . ." she said hoarsely as she tried to push up from the mattress. "I am sorry. I was watching over you and got so sleepy. I must have shifted onto the bed."

She was trying to disengage his arm, but he tightened it with purpose, drawing her down and pulling her back against him. "Whist, little bear."

Once he felt her relax, he leaned over her and touched his mouth to the soft flesh of her ear. "Let me pretend," he whispered, his voice a low rumble. "For just a bit longer, let me pretend that you are mine."

"Ah, Will," she murmured as she shifted to face him, her quicksilver eyes glittering in the candlelight. "You don't need to pretend."

His heart soared with joy, almost bursting inside him.

Then her eyes grew fretful. "But are you sure? I know you were vexed with me. You gave me something so . . . precious, and I let Ardsley thrust it back at you." Her voice caught, and she looked away. "And I . . . I didn't stand up to him."

"I knew I was taking a chance, sweetheart, that there was no guarantee you would accept my gift."

To his surprise, she reached into her bodice and withdrew the folded paper. "I took it before we left the parlor—" She hesitated. "If it's still mine to take."

He nodded. "And no strings, little bear. Sell it, live on it, lease it to His Bleeding Grace of Ardsley. You need that land more than I do. I've no one to look after. You've got Miss Falkirk . . . and your workers in Ireland."

"Why, Will? Why did you think you had to save me?"

It was his turn to look away. "Because of your face that day in the rain, when you told me he'd asked you to wed. It nearly killed me, how you looked. Still, I couldn't say what you needed to hear, not then. But I decided I could free you from him another way. If you wanted to be free—"

"What if I don't want to be free?" she cried softly. "What if I want there to be strings?"

He nearly stopped breathing. "Be careful what you say. I am not a man to take those words lightly."

"I would not say them lightly. I know I've toyed with you, Will, and made you angry—"

"No." He took her face between his hands. "Not angry . . . never angry with you, Ursula." He grinned crookedly. "Not even when you called me a dolt less than five minutes after we'd met."

Her mouth opened in protest. "I never did."

"God's truth," he said—and then swooped down to take her mouth. She groaned as his lips met hers, a low, shuddering moan that tightened the coil of heat deep in his belly. She strained up against him, twining her arms around his back, gasping, crying out as his fingers bit into her side.

He started to pull away . . . she panted, "No. Don't let go . . . please, Will, don't let me go."

"Then stay with me, Ursula," he breathed against her lips. "Give me this night . . . give me all your nights."

"Yes." It was the merest susurration of her breath.

He tugged her roughly into his arms then, trailing hungry kisses across her face, down her throat and along her white, white breast. She arched again, and he found the deep cleft above her bodice and traced it with his tongue. The shudder that coursed through her swept him into even greater need.

One hand reached down, bundling the rich fabric of her skirt, finding the slim, silk-clad legs beneath a half-dozen lacy petticoats, then the soft warmth of her thighs.

She was moaning his name. *"Will . . . ah, Will,"* and between her cries, biting at his throat. Her hands ranged over his body—dear God, everywhere—touching him, urging him on. Such sweet, unimaginable torture.

He barely recalled undoing his breeches, his only awareness was the heat that drove him, the desire that had overridden every thought but the need to possess her. When he found the heat that matched his own, his blood roared in his veins.

"Ursula," he cried raggedly, fisting one hand in her hair, holding her still so he could look into her eyes. Those Nimue eyes, so haunting, so frighteningly full of a woman's wisdom. "Will you have me?"

She smiled a half-moon, sorceress smile. "If you will have me." She tugged his head down, boldly, and he felt her tongue dance against his.

He took her then, with primal instinct and fierce tenderness . . . and the connection that blazed between them was so strong, so true, he felt rapture pierce through him like a spear.

She guided him, though he was not aware of it in fact. Rather, there were nuances he read, and he strove to respond to her subtle navigation—his mouth eager on her throat as he found his own rhythm, then urgent on her breast as the rise and fall of his body intensified. Finally, as he felt himself being pitched into a screaming, pounding, endless void, she arched up, caught his mouth in a breathless kiss—and brought him to shivering completion.

They lay there unspeaking, entwined in a tangle of clothing—mostly petticoats—until the candle guttered out. A bit of light filtered in from the distant kitchen hearth, but the room was mostly soft shadows.

"Are you still alive?" she whispered against his ear.

"Barely," he said. "You are a rare, cruel woman." He found her mouth in the near darkness and kissed her deeply. "I am truly blessed."

He stroked her breast, feeling pleasure shudder through her. The velvet of her gown beneath his fingers was warm and lush. He raised his head and asked peevishly, "Why are you still dressed?"

Her fingers flexed on his shirt. "I could ask the same of you."

"I might have been a bit hasty," he said. "But, God

in heaven, it was worth it. You are a fine, lusty wench, Ursula Roarke."

"Will!" she cried in mock outrage. She came at him then, fingers digging into his ribs. He tried to deflect her but she persisted with her gouging and tickling until he was curled up at the foot of the bed, breathless with laughter.

"Dolt," she muttered fondly as she collapsed back on her pillow.

He moved up beside her, still laughing softly, to light the spirit lamp on his nightstand. Then he shifted her onto her side as his hands sought the tabs of her gown.

"What are you doing?"

"I am pretending to be a lady's maid. It's the devil's own work. But worth it in the end, I suspect."

Once he had undone the top of her gown, he slipped it off her shoulders and ran his mouth along the satiny skin there. She was purring now, languid and relaxed.

"You see I noticed something earlier . . ." he continued in a low voice as he raised her and tugged the gown from around her hips.

"Mmm?"

"You were not undone at the end, not as I was." He swiftly untied the laces of her corselet and drew it away from her. "And it occurs to me that when a man is learning to pleasure his woman in bed . . ." He untied her petticoats and gathered up the folds. "Then he had better make sure she is . . . satisfied." He raised her again and tugged them away.

She was trying to sit up. "No, Will . . . I was . . . I mean, it was splendid and you—"

"Hush." He caught the hem of her silk chemise beneath his palm and drew it slowly up along her body, over thigh and belly and rounded breast. She arched beneath his hand, and he whisked the silk over her head.

"There are those who say I am slow-witted," he continued softly as his hand slid along her thigh, to discover the hidden source of her heat. "But I find that if I apply myself . . . and try again . . . and yet again . . ." He caressed her there, and his breathing hitched when she gasped. ". . . I usually get it right."

It was morning, the encroaching light of dawn reminding them that there was a world to face beyond the cottage walls. Ursula drew on her chemise, then sat on the side of the bed, trying to tame her hair with the few pins she had managed to locate in the bedclothes. Will was sprawled behind her. She felt his eyes on her and turned to glare at him through the curve of her upraised arm.

"What are you looking at?" she baited him. "You are supposed to be getting dressed."

He lolled back on one elbow. "I am admiring your . . . physicality."

She grabbed for the nearest pillow and thumped him with it. In retaliation, he threw himself at her and dragged her shrieking and laughing back down on the bed. He wrestled with her until he was canted above her, holding her arms down on either side. "It's a wonder, but I've still not had my fill of you."

She frowned. "I think I need to find myself an older man . . . one who is not so impetuous."

"No," he said slyly as he pressed his hand upon her belly. "It's me you want."

Her teasing expression faded. "Always, Will," she whispered. "Always and forever."

He traced his other hand over her brow and along her cheek. "Do you want me to tell him?"

Her eyes clouded. "Perhaps it would be better coming from me."

"I'm thinking it would be cowardly to let you face him alone. What do you say we go down there together?"

She smiled. "I would say thank you. My heart is already in my throat."

"No," he said as he leaned down and kissed her tenderly. "Your heart is held in my two hands."

Mrs. Hutchins met them in the hallway. Her eyes bore no hint of accusation, though her expression was troubled. "The duke is gone," she said. "It's the oddest thing—he sent over a note from Stratton Meadow, it's in his study. And Mr. Rigger left right after you took sick, Mr. Will. He drove off with Miss Falkirk in the duke's coach. But he wouldn't tell anyone where they were going."

Will turned to Ursula. "Gretna Green, do you think?"

She stared at him. "I have no idea."

Mrs. Hutchins was still fussing. "And all that great mass

of food left over. The guests never went in to supper, you see . . . they all went home after Mr. Will's unfortunate episode. A terrible waste, I say."

Will was already heading toward the duke's study. "Send out word in the district, Mrs. Hutchins . . . to everyone who helped us move the sheep. Tell them that there is to be a party at Myrmion tonight. They'll make short work of the duke's banquet."

Ursula followed him into the study, saw the note lying on the blotter. He picked it up and handed it to her, but she shook her head. "It's addressed to you."

Bewildered, he took it back and read it. His expression grew even more puzzled. "What do you make of this, ma'am?" He read aloud, "My dear Will, Circumstances have called me away from Myrmion for several days. I sincerely hope that you have recovered fully from your attack, and if so, I ask that you remain there to look after Lady Roarke. When I return, I will need to speak with you on a matter very much to your benefit. Please tell Lady Roarke that I understand how things are and that I am not angry. Your most humble and obedient servant, Damien Danover."

Will let the note slip from his fingers. "I think he's gone mad."

"Maybe it was something in the champagne . . . he told me it was making him see things."

"And how the devil did he know about us?"

She winced. "Last night, before you woke up, I thought I heard a horse moving outside the cottage. He could have ridden up and seen us through the window . . . together on your bed."

Will cursed softly. "That's a wretched way for a man to discover he's been tossed over."

"Do you think that's why he left?" She sank into a chair. "Oh, bother . . . I was so hoping not to hurt him. I know he is pompous and pigheaded at times, but I was actually growing to like him."

Will paced the small room. "It must be something else. Ardsley's never been afraid to face me over any issue. I will give him points for that." He snatched up the note again. "But I still don't understand his tone . . . it is almost obsequious. 'My dear Will' . . . 'your most humble and obedient.' And he signed it with his name and not his title."

Ursula frowned. "Just one more mystery to add to the pile."

The groom who had ridden to Stratton Meadow to invite Judith to the party came back with another strange story. Miss Coltrane had gone off in the middle of the night with her father's coach. It was rumored that she had been in the company of the Duke of Ardsley.

"Another elopement?" Ursula asked Will, who was helping her carry the food out to the long tables they'd again set up in the lane.

"Well, she was in love with him all those years ago," he said. "And took her time getting over it, if I'm any judge. Maybe his being back here stirred up something between them."

"But apparently all they ever did was brangle."

He laughed and caught her about the waist. "Rather like it was for us in the beginning, Lady Roarke. You with your cutting remarks—"

"And you with that insolent grin." She set her hands on his shoulders. "Are you sure you don't mind if they have run off together? I always thought you fancied Judith."

He shook his head. "You are the only woman I've ever fancied, little bear." He tugged her closer. "Now kiss me quick before Mrs. Hutchins comes out and catches us. I'm thinking we need to be discreet."

Ursula nearly laughed. She doubted there was even one skivvy at Myrmion who did not know she had spent the night in Will's cottage. She leaned up and pecked his cheek.

"Discreet," she said as her eyes danced. "*No, Will!* What if someone sees!"

It was too late; he had caught her up in his arms and was kissing her like a man possessed.

The impromptu party was an unquestionable success. Nearly two dozen people, farm workers, weavers and shepherds, came pouring in at dusk. Soon a fiddler started playing, and couples began to dance, swirling around the dusty lane as though it were a London ballroom.

The food held out for most of the night—the fine hams, rare cuts of beef, baked salmon, dazzling confections of meringue and spun sugar that Ursula had spent so much care choosing to impress Ardsley's guests. She realized that these simple people were more impressed by the generosity of Myrmion than by the quality of the meal.

Will moved among the merrymakers, totally in his element. She hung back a little, preferring to watch him rather than be in the thick of things. But at one point he caught hold of her and plunked her down beside him on a bench. "Tell them the story you told me last night," he coaxed. "Of Flighty Dean Flynn and the little people."

She rallied for his friends and did her best with the tale. Two of the weavers actually fell off the bench, they laughed so hard, and Will's eyes gleamed in the torchlight.

Ursula began to enjoy herself after that. Just as the first party had distracted her from dwelling on her betrothal to Ardsley, this one gave her an excuse not to fret over his cryptic note. She only wanted to feel happy and tried all night to push away her edginess.

But something was surely brewing; she felt it in the air around her, like the eerie quiet before a violent storm. Too many people had disappeared from Myrmion, apparently within minutes of Will's episode in the parlor. There had to be some connection. But try as she might, she could make no sense of it.

Once the last weary guest had wandered off home, Will drew her into the shadowy garden and settled her on a stone seat. She was wearing a muslin frock with two wide ribbons down the front, and he toyed with them as he spoke.

"Remember when we were by the pool, and I had that wretched dream?"

"You said it was a bad thing from your past you couldn't remember."

"There is something you need to know about me if . . . if we are to be together. The fact is, I can't remember anything about my life before the age of ten or eleven. I've tried these past twenty years to recall who I was, where I came from. You see, at the time I was living in a place . . . an evil place." He paused. "I was an inmate . . . in a lunatic asylum."

She gasped slightly, and then cursed herself for letting it slip out.

He seemed undaunted. "If you misbehaved, they immersed you in icy baths . . . or poured steaming hot water over you . . . or beat you with a cane. I tried to be good, but sometimes the fits came and I lost control. I think that's what happened, why I can't remember. They must have beaten me too harshly or kept me under water for too long. I w-woke up tied to my bed . . . and I had no idea who I was. They called me William, but the name meant nothing to me. At any rate, no one would tell me who I was . . . if they even knew or cared."

Ursula was weeping, and she felt his fingers brush over her cheeks. "I didn't tell you this to make you sad, sweetheart. It's long over."

"Is that where Rigger found you?" she asked with a little sob.

"No. A few years later, the superintendent decided to send me out to labor for the local farmers. I'd always been strong and fit, and I made money for the asylum, working in the fields or loading wagons."

"But you were just a boy," she said.

He shrugged. "That's where Rigger found me, toiling in a barnyard. I learned recently that he was looking for someone else . . . but I was the one he took away." He laughed ruefully. "I was a sorry thing, gaunt, covered with weals. I'd also developed a terrible stammer. Rigger rented me a room in Barnstable and hired tutors . . . oddly enough, I knew how to read and write. My landlady had been a governess . . . she schooled my speech until my stammer almost disappeared."

He knelt down in front of her. "He remade me, Ursula. Gave me a fine Devonshire name to call my own and believed in me totally. But until last night I was fully convinced that the kernel of madness dwelled inside me."

"Last night? You mean the fit?"

"No. Just before that, I had . . . a sort of vision. I saw myself lying in a bedroom, a man and woman beside me weeping. A young boy was pounding on the door to be let in." He grasped her hands. "I knew then that I had been ill as a child . . . that the sickness had not been born in me."

"Oh, Will, now I understand what you told me last

night . . . about that day in the rain, when you couldn't say what I needed to hear."

He nodded. "I told myself I had to resist you, Ursula. I dared not be with you or love you . . . I couldn't risk bringing another afflicted child into the world. But last night changed that. I knew somehow, knew absolutely, that I didn't carry madness in my blood."

She curled her arms around his neck. "Did you ever really believe that? You must have seen how different you were from the others in that terrible place."

"You have no idea how normal some of them seemed. Still, their madness inevitably surfaced in delusions, violent rages. My only symptom was the seizures. But someone had put me there . . ." His voice broke as he leaned his head on her shoulder. "My mother . . . my father. Someone believed I was mad."

He was trembling now, and she tightened her hold on him. "It doesn't matter any longer. You've remade yourself, as you said. Strong and wise—and beloved, Will. Beloved by so many. Those people who were here tonight, they are your family now. And Rigger."

He raised his head. "And you, Ursula? Do you still want to ally yourself with—what was it Ardsley called me . . . a misbegotten mistake of nature?"

She growled a little. "I hope that was when you hit him."

He gave a low chuckle. "Thereabouts. But you still haven't answered my question."

She rose and pulled him to his feet. "Let's go up to your cottage, Will Ridd, and I will give you your answer. In the dark."

Their next three days together were nearly idyllic. She and Will spent the daylight hours riding over his property, overseeing the building of the new sheep enclosures, working with the dogs, eating their meals sitting on a log or sprawled in a shady grove. They spent their evenings before the parlor hearth in his cottage talking, laughing, sharing confidences. Ursula told him about Roary, his kindness and his killing vice. He told her about the beginning of his wondrous flock, how he'd managed to buy a dozen merino sheep, the strictly guarded pride of Spain, who had swum ashore after a shipwreck on the south Devon coast.

At night they lay side by side whispering in the dark, touching only at their fingertips, until the whispers turned to sighs, the sighs to moans, and when at last they joined together, touch became a moving stream of sensation until there were no longer any boundaries of flesh.

Ursula had never known such completion, even in the heady, early days with her husband. Those few years with Roary had schooled her to swift passion, but not to the delicate butterfly touch of tenderness. She was already learning from Will how exquisitely passion could be prolonged, that by going gently and slowly, he could eventually drive her into a sort of mindless, incoherent oblivion.

It was lovely. He was beyond lovely. In their short time together, he'd become the center of her world, its fixed, grounded core. There was no mood he could not tease her out of, no problem he could not sort out. He might have had a dozen secrets, a thousand secrets, but she trusted that he would gladly share them all with her as long as she remained at his side.

She thrilled to his simplest touch and delighted in his pet name for her—little bear, spoken always as an endearment. She recalled now, as she lie in the dark beside Will, that he had called the duke something similar just before he'd been taken by the fit. What was it? She'd nearly forgotten that night, pushed aside the dark memory during the glorious days that followed.

"Little badger," she murmured in the darkness.

She sat up with a startled cry, pressing one hand to her mouth. She again heard Ardsley's voice in the coach, when he'd spoken of his brother's teasing. *And now, little badger, you can pretend to be a laundry maid.*

She slipped silently from the bed and went to huddle on the parlor chair. Her mind leapt furiously from one bit of evidence to another . . . Ardsley's pale, sweaty face after Will had called out to him . . . his abrupt disappearance . . . his oddly conciliatory note to Will . . . Will himself, the man with no childhood memories, who read the classics and who spoke in the accents of a gentleman.

It was inconceivable. Still, the pieces meshed together. The heir had died of a horrid ailment, Estelle had told her. What if he had not died, but had been placed in an asylum so that the healthy son could inherit the title?

She wanted to run back to Will, shake him awake, ask him if this could possibly be true. But then reason overrode impulse, and her composure returned. Will had lived at Myrmion for ten years. He'd known Rigger even longer. Surely during that time he would have remembered the house where he'd summered as a child or at some point recognized the man who had been his personal groom.

Or was it possible, she pondered, that Will's memory had simply not been sparked by these things? In the garden, he'd told her that Rigger was searching for another boy, but had taken Will instead. She knew now whom Rigger had been seeking—Anthony Danover. Was it possible that he was mistaken, that Will *was* the boy he'd sought?

She had such a strong intuition that it was the truth.

Then she realized something—she could never share her suspicions with Will. He might think she'd chosen him only because she thought he was the true duke. He had to believe absolutely that she wanted him for who he was now, not for who he might become.

The next day Ursula seemed a bit fretful to Will. It had been a warm, hazy afternoon, and when she insisted on a visit to the waterfall so she could wade in the pool, he instantly complied. He again lay on the bank and watched her as she crept through the water, skirts raised above her knees, looking for her two-headed turtle.

"He seems to have disappeared," she complained as she bent closer, her face only a foot from the surface. He had a rather nice view of her rounded backside, but he chose not to draw her attention to this.

"That's because you manhandled him last time," he said.

"I notice you never object to being manhandled," she said wickedly.

He shrugged lazily. "That's because I have more sense than a turtle . . . even one with two heads."

He was amazed that they had settled into such an easy camaraderie. They were never far apart from one another, and he had only to catch her eye across a room to be reassured that she had no regrets. She was both friend and lover, and for the first time in memory, he felt truly cherished by a woman. He remembered using that word with her, but he'd never dared imagine she would one day make him feel the same way.

In the evening, she would lie before the fire with her head in his lap and tell him about her horses and her life in Ireland. He would hold her close, breathing in the heady scent of her, and wonder anew at his good fortune. She dazzled him with her presence—as though a rare, exotic bird had settled on his hand and refused to fly away.

Most important of all, being with her made him feel utterly normal. He no longer feared the phantoms of his past, she was no longer the grand lady of the manor—they were just a cottager couple going about their daily work. And coming home together to fall wearily, most happily, into bed. Not that they slept much, he reflected. A proper farmer's wife would never keep her man up until all hours with sporting and such. But no other farmer was lucky enough to have Ursula Roarke in his arms every night.

Every night . . .

He liked the sound of that. Tomorrow he would ride over to the vicarage and ask to have the banns posted. In three weeks time, they could be wed.

He folded his arms and laid his head on them, musing over the life they would make together, he running his own flock, Ursula with her stud horse and maybe a few broodmares to start with. They would have to give the farm a name . . . a proud name for their livestock to carry. He thought a bit, chewing on a blade of grass. There was something he'd said to her about his sheep and her stallion—he'd called them a touchstone. Touchstone Farm. He liked the sound of it, and he had a feeling she would—

"Mr. Will! Mr. Will! You're wanted at the house."

He sat upright and shifted around. One of the grooms from Myrmion had ridden into the clearing. "You must come now, Mr. Will. The duke is home and he's asking for you."

"We'll be along directly," Will called out as he rose to his feet.

Ursula stepped up onto the bank, her expression unreadable as she wrung out her skirts. She came up to him and slid her hand into his. "I have a bad feeling about this, Will."

He stroked her hair back from her brow. "I told you, we'll face him together."

But her mouth remained grim all the way back to Myrmion.

Chapter Fifteen

*A*rdsley was pacing in the drawing room when they came through the door. She noticed that Will kept her a little behind him as they approached the duke.

"No, no," he said. "You don't need to protect her. I am over my anger. These things occur between people and who am I to question them? And perhaps it's for the best . . . Miss Coltrane and I . . . well, nothing's been said yet."

He came forward then and gripped Will by the upper arms. And grinned at him broadly.

Will started back. "Your Grace?"

Ardsley drew in a breath. "Ah, Will . . . I don't know quite where to begin. Miss Coltrane says you have no recollection of your childhood. I might be able to furnish you with a few of the details."

Will reached for Ursula's hand, and she gripped it tightly. Suddenly, her wild conjectures of last night no longer seemed so preposterous.

The duke fidgeted. "I wish Judith was here with me, but she's in the parlor, standing guard over my grandmother." He leaned forward and whispered gleefully, "*Our* grandmother, Will."

"What is that supposed to mean?" Will muttered. "Are you suggesting I am one of your father's byblows?"

"No . . . you are my father's true son . . . my brother, Anthony Danover."

Will tugged away from Ursula and closed in on the duke. "What new mockery is this, Ardsley?" He swung back to her. "Do you have any idea what he is talking about?"

She nodded soberly. "Just listen to him. I have an idea where this is leading."

He sank down into a chair then, and listened in numb disbelief while Damien Danover spun his tale of a duke's young heir who had suffered some strange affliction—to the great distress of his family. He'd been pronounced dead, but in reality had been taken from his home and sent to recuperate with a farm family.

"I haven't sorted out all the pieces," Damien said. "Haven't got a clue how my family lost track of you. I suspect Grandmama can fill in some of the blanks. But I think that's the gist of the story."

"Not *my* story," Will spat out. "And stop grinning at me, Your Grace. It's unnerving."

Damien shook his head. "The more I am with you, old fellow, the more convinced I become that you are Tony. You can have no idea how thrilled I am . . . how many years I have prayed for this."

Will pressed his palms to his eyes. "This is all a dream . . . it must be a dream."

"And I have saved my trump card for last," Damien continued, unfazed. "At the party, when you cried out to me . . . the name you spoke was Tony's pet name for me— little badger."

Will looked up. "I can explain that. I'd been thinking of you as a testy badger all week. Ask Rigger . . . I called you such just before I went into the parlor that night."

"Rigger's not here," Ursula reminded him. "But what if he's right, Will? What if you are Anthony Danover?"

He laughed mirthlessly. "And donkeys shall dance."

She looked directly at Damien for the first time. His eyes were full of forgiveness, and she nodded once in acknowledgment. "You have to realize," she said, "that if this is true, it isn't necessarily good news for Will. You and I, Damien . . . *we* would expect a person to rejoice at such a thing, but he might not wish to be elevated in that way."

"It's not good news or bad," Will snapped. "It is wholly preposterous. I am no duke's son."

"You don't know for a fact that you are *not* my brother," Ardsley pointed out. "You don't know if you're *anybody's* brother. It's a dashed shame that Rigger's taken himself off . . . I wager he knows a great deal about this. Meanwhile, we must face the dowager. She put up some fight over coming here, I can tell you. Good thing Judith was with me to, er, help things along. At any rate, I told the dowager everything I've just told you, but she has refused to speak on the matter. I'm hoping the sight of you will jolt her out of her silence."

Will got to his feet. "Time enough, when Rigger's come home, for us to sort this out. I have sheep to tend."

The duke's face contorted into a comical expression of great long-suffering. But Will was not smiling; his face was set and full of caution.

"One thing you need to learn, Will Ridd. You can't put your sheep before the dowager. Even if they are probably better company. Come along now. I . . . I just wanted to break it to you first."

Will muttered something under his breath, but followed the duke from the room.

Ursula trailed behind them, fighting the urge to drag Will away from here . . . far, far away. She was more fearful than ever that their idyllic world was teetering on the brink of a precipice and would soon plunge down and be shattered on the rocks below.

Will didn't want to go back into the parlor, with its portraits, its memories of his strange vision . . . of his reaching out to Ardsley. He knew he was already beginning to fasten onto this nonsensical idea. Out of desperation, he was sure, some childish yearning to discover his true family. Then it occurred to him that in finding his family he would also be facing his betrayers. So there was not even any solace to be had in discovery.

He pushed past Ardsley and went into the room first, determined to get this over with.

"Hullo, Will," Judith said, rising from the sofa. She also wore a look of barely restrained delight, a mirror image of the duke's foolish expression.

Ah, but there was no pleasure in the severe countenance of the old woman sitting upright in a wing chair. Her face was that of a crabapple doll, lined and creased. But the dark eyes were alive—vividly bright above the dull black of her gown—and harshly judgmental.

Ardsley saw Ursula to the sofa, then moved to the old woman. "I hope the tea has calmed you, Grandmama. Now, if you will allow me to present Lady Roarke and Mr.—"

"I will not," the old woman snapped. She levered herself

out of the chair and tottered toward Will, one withered finger raised in accusation. "*This* is who you name my grandson?" she uttered. "This . . . bumpkin, with leaves in his hair and grass on his coat? You might have dressed him in something a little finer . . . if you were so set on passing him off as your late brother."

The duke's face colored. "I am not 'passing him off,' madam. I am presenting him to you as your grandson, Anthony Danover."

She spun to him with surprising agility and spat, "Anthony Danover is dead. His casket lies in the crypt at Ardsley House. This man, this bailiff, is a pretender. You told me that he himself admits he has no memory of his childhood."

"He *knew* me, Grandmama, as I've already explained."

Her eyes grew canny. "Anthony had a scar on his shoulder . . . from a fall when he was an infant."

"Would you show her, Will?" the duke asked with a grimace of apology.

"I cannot say if it is still there . . . my back is a bit of a shambles."

"So you won't even let us examine that possible bit of evidence?" the old woman purred.

"No!" Ursula protested, half rising. "Please don't make him—"

But Will had already peeled off his coat. He untucked his shirt and drew it over his head, then turned so that his back was facing the old woman. It was one of the hardest things he'd ever done, baring himself in front of these people, but he wanted this interview over.

Ardsley cursed softly at the sight of the crisscrossed purple weals, but the dowager merely nodded. "You are right. There is no way to see if the older scar remains."

"Tell them about your dream by the pool," Ursula urged him. "The bad thing you thought you should remember."

He shrugged as he drew on his shirt. "I was riding across the moor with two other children . . . one of them may have been Miss Coltrane. We rode into a dell that became filled with vines. They wrapped all about me and turned into bands of white linen."

Ardsley spoke up eagerly. "The last time I saw you, Will, you'd been bound tight with sheets. I know you hated it, I saw it in your eyes. You seemed to be saying 'Free me, Damien.' "

He hung his head. "I have no recollection of anything like that."

With a cackle of triumph, the dowager returned to her chair. "This is a waste of my time. This buffoon offers nothing to support his claim."

"It's not *my* claim," Will fumed, glaring at the duke.

Some raw emotion began to clamor inside him. He thought of the years he'd lost, the memories he'd misplaced, all the pain he had suffered. The resentful anger boiled up in him, keening to be heard. Rigger wasn't there to soothe it away, and within seconds it had mastered him.

"But I *do* have a claim against someone," he said fiercely, fisting his hands before him. "I want a reckoning with the person who decided that a boy who suffered fits was mad."

"Will—" Ursula flung her hand out.

"I want to know what sort of creature would cast a child into a . . . a lunatic asylum."

"What do you mean asylum?" the duke cried. His gaze darted to Judith. "You told me he'd been a lad for hire . . . I assumed he'd been off living with a farm family."

Judith looked stricken. "Is it true, Will? What was this place?"

"Hell is what I called it," he said. "But the name over the gate spelled out Chenowyth."

The dowager's startled gasp seemed thunderously loud in the still room.

Will moved toward her like a man in a trance. When he reached her chair, he leaned down, braced his hands on the arms, and set his face directly before hers. "Was it you who put me in that foul hole, old woman? Is it you I have to thank for the marks on my back . . . for the blank, empty spaces in my head?"

"Nay, lad. It was me who put you in that place."

Will rose and turned around slowly. Rigger Gaines now stood at the threshold.

One lone question pounded in Will's brain—had this man, who had become his savior, first been his jailer? He felt his world shift, felt the solid core inside him begin to crumble.

Rigger came forward. "Yes, it was me put you there . . . and then cursed myself every hour of every day for six years afterward. When I could stand it no longer, I went back, against the orders of my betters, and tried to find you. There'd been a fire at Chenowyth . . . the superintendent had perished, most of the records had been lost. No one there remembered the day I'd carried Anthony Danover through those gates. So I looked over the boys who seemed the right age . . . but not a one of them could have been Anthony."

He drew closer to Will, his eyes hollow. "I was about to leave, heartsick that I had failed, when a groom approached me. 'There's another boy lives here,' he said. 'Not violent or troubled, but a tall, strong boy. When the fire started, he was the one got most of the inmates safely away. They send him off to work for the local farmers, who task him something cruel . . . and him a gentle lad, who's got a real way with horses.' "

Will heard a woman's low sob; he didn't turn his head to see if it was Ursula or Judith. He couldn't seem to look away from Rigger.

"And that's where you found me," he said, "hauling bales of hay. The best day of my life, I told you. But you never told me the truth . . . never admitted who you thought I might really be."

"I wasn't sure who you were, Will. I didn't want you to get your hopes up. You had the look of the duchess in your eyes . . . but I couldn't be sure."

"Then why did you take me away from there, if you thought I was just another madman?"

His mouth tightened. "The groom had spoken so well of you . . . and I thought, let me have the saving of one fine young fellow, even if Anthony is beyond my help. And so I took you off. Five years later, I brought you to Myrmion, hoping that once the clouded parts of your mind were free of Chenowyth, your memory would come back. Especially here, in this place you'd once loved."

"What a disappointment I must have been to you. When I did not know this house . . . when I could not recognize the portraits of the Danovers."

"Until the other night," Ardsley interjected. "You were looking at the paintings—of me, of our parents—and you gave such a horrific cry. I think you knew then, Will. Some part of your brain began to put the pieces together."

"Don't," he said softly. "Don't call them our parents. You still cannot know if those things are true."

"Of course they're not true," the dowager said. "And Rigger Gaines can spin all the tales he likes, but his own past could do with some examining."

"Tell them," Rigger said in a voice of ice. "I don't care if they know."

Her mouth pursed. "I swore to my son I would never reveal your past."

"A woman of principle," Rigger drawled. "Very well, I will tell my own tale. Thirty-two years ago, I was a sailor in the King's navy. We were about to set sail from Portsmouth when I got word that my father was dying. I abandoned my post, struck down the boatswain, and rode off to Ardsley House where my father was head groom for the young duke. The navy sent men to fetch me back—I would have been shot for desertion, most like—but the duke protected me. I owed him my life after that . . . I owed him my obedience."

"Christ Jesus," Ardsley murmured. "Was it my *father* who ordered you to take Tony away?"

"Your brother was not improving. Your grandmother"— he snaked a hand out toward her—"that noble, high-bred lady, convinced the duke to send his son somewhere out of the way, to pretend he had died. Especially since there was a healthy son to inherit the title. They settled a large endowment on Chenowyth, and for my part in the deed, they offered me a sum of money. I also asked for that parcel of land west of here. The dowager had no choice but to oblige me."

She pushed up from her chair, thrust past Rigger until she was positioned to face them all. "Do not condemn me!" she cried. "Don't you dare condemn me. Anthony Danover was beyond help, beset with fits and convulsions, freakish distempers . . . until he could barely recognize those around him. The dukedom could not support such a creature at its head. I made the decision to send the boy to a discreet establishment that catered to wealthy patrons who were . . . so afflicted. I still don't regret it."

"Heinous," Judith whispered loudly.

"Prudent," the dowager retorted. "And painful, yes . . . the boy had been a favorite of mine as much as anyone's."

"And what of my mother?" Ardsley demanded. "Did you not think of how it would affect her? If her firstborn had not been so rudely snatched from her, I doubt my father's death would have driven her inside herself as it did."

Rigger clasped his wrist. "She is not so bad as that, Master Damien." He stepped back to the parlor door and opened it. "Ladies . . . you may as well come inside."

"Mama!" Damien cried as the duchess swept through the doorway with Barbara Falkirk at her side.

The dowager's eyes narrowed. "Where is Mrs. Camber? You cannot be unattended, madam."

Her Grace smiled archly. "We left Camber—and her laudanum—at home. Miss Falkirk and I have been listening in the hall." Her voice lowered as she approached the dowager's chair. "Yes, listening . . . to how you discarded my son as though he were a troublesome puppy." She drew her arm back as if to deliver a mighty blow, then lowered it again.

"No," she said, almost to herself. "You are an old, old woman. Any punishment I could mete out pales beside that of the Great Judge you will soon face. He will surely know of the sins you committed against my family."

"Not sins," the old woman hissed, "salvation. I was saving the family . . . saving it."

But the duchess had dismissed her. She moved on to Will, studying him, her eyes sad and wistful. He unconsciously reached for her hand. "Madam," he said as he bowed over it.

She raised her free hand and traced it slowly over his face, as though her fingertips were recording every contour and angle. Then she leaned up and kissed him on each cheek. "Anthony William Marsden Danover," she murmured. "My own Tony come back to me."

"This is a farce," the dowager cried. "A madwoman and a madman . . ."

The duchess slid her arm intimately through Will's. "He is the image of my father at that age," she proclaimed. "There is a portrait of him at Peete Castle, in case you doubt me. 'My bright angel,' Mama called him when they were courting." She beamed up at Will. "*My* bright angel."

He shook his head and pushed gently away from her. "You cannot know, madam . . . there are too many questions."

She disregarded his protests and moved to clasp her other son's hand. "I thank you, Damien . . . for seeing the truth and acting on it. Few men, I think, would have had the courage or the conscience to do what you have done."

He bowed his head as her hand drifted over his hair. "And what of my father? How can we ever forgive him?"

She pointed to the dowager. "She held great sway with His Grace, I am sorry to say. And I was so distraught over your brother's illness . . . I suppose he thought it a kindness to end my pain, to send Tony to a place where he could be properly looked after."

Ursula spoke up, her face flushed with righteous anger. "Did no one ever think to check up on the boy? To make sure he *was* being looked after? Or even to see if he had made a recovery?"

The dowager glowered at her. "What—and have every nosy parker in Devon wondering why the duke's people kept visiting a madhouse? I believe the superintendent reported to Rigger."

He nodded. "For five years he wrote to me, claiming Anthony had continued to go downhill. A lie, obviously, since he'd been sending the boy out to work. Then a year passed when I heard nothing. That's when I decided to visit Chenowyth myself . . . and learned about the superintendent dying in the fire."

Will felt his breathing falter, felt the walls closing in on him. He pushed his way past Rigger and the duchess until he reached Ardsley.

"Let me go," he entreated him. "This is not my past . . . nothing I have heard here convinces me of it. Every one of you is looking for someone to ease your guilt." His fevered gaze slid to Rigger. "You, because you abetted that old woman's terrible deceit." He shifted back to Ardsley. "And you, sir, because you did not feel you had the right to take your brother's place." His gaze sought the duchess. "And perhaps even you, dear madam, need a balm for your guilt. Because a wife must surely know what darkness lies in her husband's heart, even if he does not speak the words."

"I did know," she said. "The night he died, my husband swore to me that Anthony was alive. But no one would believe me. The dowager duchess convinced everyone that I had lost my wits— "

"She's rather good at that," Ardsley muttered.

"She had me dosed with laudanum . . . until I truly did become disordered."

Ardsley swung on his grandmother. "Miss Coltrane nursed Papa that last night. Were you afraid he'd also told her? Is that why you kept flogging at me to forget Judith, spewing hateful nonsense about how unworthy she was? Well, what is done can sometimes be undone, and I intend to marry Miss Coltrane—"

"Damien!" Judith cried, sitting suddenly upright.

"And you, madam," Ardsley uttered, pointing one trembling finger at the dowager, "will be sent to my estate in Scotland."

"Scotland!" she echoed. Her head reared up. "I most certainly will not."

"Oh, Scotland's nae sa bad," said Barbara Falkirk, as she came forward and patted the dowager's hand. "Th' haggis is a treat, if ye can get used tae it, and th' oatmeal warms yer belly better than a briary old tartan. An' ye'll be needin' it when the winters blow in sa frosty from th' north."

The old woman jerked her hand away. "You have *all* clearly lost your wits. I am going to my room."

She squared her narrow shoulders and moved toward the doorway. Halfway across the carpet, her eyes hooded over. She tottered to a halt, and her gaze slid slowly back to Ursula.

"You were to be Damien's bride," she said silkily. "He told me as much at Ardsley House."

Will saw the stricken look in Ursula's eyes as the woman closed in on her. He sensed great danger there, but could not seem to move forward, not even when the dowager reached out and stroked a finger over Ursula's cheek.

"But you did not wait faithfully for his return, did you? I see the hungry way you look at the bailiff—and he at you. Damien told me you were clever." Her eyes narrowed. "Clever enough, I see, not to waste any time climbing into the real duke's bed—"

"Leave her alone!" Will cried.

She leveled her glinting gaze at him. "Ask her, Mr. Ridd. Ask Lady Roarke if she hadn't already guessed your true identity before today. She was at the party . . . she saw how my grandson reacted when you called him that foolish name."

The room seemed to be holding its breath, awaiting Ursula's response.

Will's eyes pleaded with her. *You don't have to answer.*

Ursula shook her head. "No, it's a fair question." She drew in a long breath. "I did suspect something odd was going on regarding Will . . . too many people disappeared directly after that incident at the party. But I didn't have my answer until yesterday, when I recalled Damien mentioning his brother's pet name on the day we arrived." She looked directly at him. "You must believe me, Will . . . I did not make the connection until last night."

The dowager gave her a close-mouthed smile. "How convenient for you then, that you accidentally found yourself compromised by the true Duke of Ardsley."

Ursula leapt to her feet. "What is between Will Ridd and me is no one's business, least of all yours, you poisonous little banshee. First you insist that Will is not the real duke, then you imply I turned to him out of avarice. Which is it, old woman? If he is *not* your grandson, then I have chosen to ally myself with a sheep farmer. Proudly, I might add."

The dowager touched the brooch at her throat. "Even more proudly if it turns out he is the Danover heir—which my family seem to think is the case."

"Whether he is or not, is immaterial to me," Ursula said. "Will knows that," she added under her breath as she sank back onto the sofa.

"I think you'd better go, Grandmama," Damien said curtly. "You've done enough damage."

She moved again toward the door, then paused beside Will. Her head jutted out and she whispered, "Still, it's food for thought, eh, Mr. Ridd?"

Ursula flew to Will's side the instant the door closed. She snatched up his hand, cradling it between hers. "Are you all right?"

He looked down at her and for the first time ever had no idea of what to say.

"Tell me you're all right," she gasped. "Tell me it will be like it was before."

There was a leaden thudding in his chest that whispered nothing might ever be right again. "I don't know, little bear," he answered truthfully. "I don't know anything."

Ursula's cheeks were ghostly pale now, her eyes bright with unshed tears. She was all but crying out for reassurance, but he would not let himself touch her. She was so beautiful to him, in every way, but sometimes beauty was a lie. And sometimes a withered old crone spoke the truth.

No, he dared not examine Ursula's motives now. Betrayal was too much on his mind . . . he might easily tar her with the same brush. And why not? Nearly everyone else he'd loved had betrayed him—father, grandmother, adored boyhood groom.

He also refused to think about this title they seemed determined to thrust on him. He knew full well what Ursula Roarke would urge him to do, but he had to make his own decision. He would not let himself by influenced by her many persuasions.

"I'm going to my cottage," he said gruffly as he disengaged from her. When she started after him, he shook his head. "Alone, if you please. I need time to think things through."

Rigger reached out for him as he neared the door, but Will twisted away from him. "Alone," he said again. This time it was almost a snarl.

Ursula stood there in numb disbelief, only half aware of Rigger slipping through the door, of Barbara going after him. Everyone else seemed frozen in place. Finally, Judith put her arm around Ursula and drew her back to the sofa.

"Did you see his face?" Ursula said in a faint, faraway voice. "That childlike, untouched look he's always had, that was so much a part of him . . . it's gone now, just wiped away."

"I thought he'd be pleased," Damien said under his

breath as he went to the drinks tray. "It never occurred to me he'd take it like that." He stopped with one hand on the brandy decanter. "I never realized how ugly it would get."

"Nonetheless," Judith said, "I could just throttle Will. He didn't have to lash out at Ursula."

She shook her head. "No, this was too much for him to take in. And I know there are times with a man when it is best to stand away—"

"There are also times when they need a clout in the head."

Ursula tried to muster a smile. "It feels like I'm the one who got clouted."

Damien handed her a glass of brandy. "This might help. And I really must apologize for my grandmother."

The duchess settled beside Ursula and sighed. "It occurs to me lately that perhaps she's the one who ought to be in an asylum."

"When did you learn of this, Mama? You seem quite calm, considering everything."

"Rigger told me most of what had happened on the journey from Ardsley House. I had some time to get over my shock. Though my poor Tony did not take it at all well."

Ursula leaned toward her. "You honestly believe he is your son?"

"A mother knows her own child, Lady Roarke. And there is that uncanny resemblance to my father. You'll see, he will come to believe it himself before long."

Damien knelt down and took Ursula's wrist. "Don't fret, Ursula. Something will jog his memory, now that we are all here together. Some tiny detail will part the haze . . . and it will all come clear."

"I just hope I'm still in the picture when it does." A tiny sob escaped from her throat.

"Don't," Judith said soothingly. "Don't let the old harridan's words frighten you. She was bound to strike out at you . . . you are the only person in Will's life she hasn't targeted. The rest of us are armed against her by now." She grinned. "Lord, I still can't believe you called her a poisonous little banshee."

"That was the only high note of the whole afternoon," Damien muttered, and then added, "Listen to me, Ursula . . . you of all people must know that Will is too grounded to heed her foul whisperings. You must trust him."

Damien was right. She had to stay strong. There were such strong souls all around her in this house—the duchess, Judith, Damien, Rigger Gaines. As Judith had pointed out, every one of them had been damaged by the dowager's manipulations. Rigger, especially, had been coerced into outright betrayal. Yet not a one of them had allowed the old woman to prevail in the end. *She* was certainly not going to do so.

And so what if Will had turned away from her? She would borrow from the strength of these people, Will's family, Will's friends. Barbara would be there, too, staunch and wry as always. She was not alone in this battle.

Chapter Sixteen

*W*ill did not appear for supper, as Ursula had hoped he might, and the dowager had wisely remained upstairs. It had been a subdued meal, everyone still shaken by the ugly thing they had seen uncovered that afternoon.

Ursula couldn't blame Will for not wanting to sit at the head of this family. Still, his father was dead, as the grandmother would soon be. His mother and his brother had not been party to the deception . . . and they both clearly longed to have him back. Damien seemed quite willing to forfeit the dukedom out of love for his brother. And she suspected the duchess wanted Will to take his rightful place not only as restitution, but also so that he could regain his family. It was what Ursula wanted for him above everything.

He must be feeling very torn right now, she thought. Give in—and accept obligations and responsibilities he was scarcely prepared for. Or refuse—and spend the rest of his life wondering what he had missed. If the door had never opened to that rarefied world, he would have been quite content as a farmer. But it had opened, and there was no going back now.

Will might not refuse outright, but she had a feeling he would resist. For a man who had instituted so many improvements at the farm and in the Valley, he mistrusted any changes that were beyond his control. She had only to think of the day he'd spoken of being beaten. *They had the power and I did not.*

No, he would not welcome being caught up in the machinery of elevation. He would not view the dukedom as a prize, he'd see it as a snare.

Nevertheless, understanding these things in her head did not stop her heart from twisting whenever she remembered how he'd dismissed her. His turning away from Rigger was understandable considering how fresh and raw his pain must have been. But why had he turned from her? Was it only because of the dowager's horrid words?

No, she thought wretchedly, it was also because he still viewed her as one of *them*—a member of the upper classes, one of the enemy . . . who wanted yet again to wrench him away from his secure existence and cast him into a frightening, unfamiliar world.

Four days passed and Will never came down from the hill. Every now and then, someone caught a glimpse of him riding off toward his property in the west. Ursula wondered why he had not gone back to his cottage on the moor. He seemed to be somehow taunting them all by remaining so close and yet staying so aloof.

Rigger went about the house like a wraith, his mouth grim, and even Barbara seemed unable to coax him out of his dark mood. Damien, meanwhile, was getting reacquainted with his mother now that she had emerged from her drugged shadowland. Often Judith joined them, her bracing good humor bringing both mother and son some measure of normalcy. Ursula had grown to like Judith enormously; partly because she realized what her friendship had meant to Will and also because Judith now offered that same staunch support to her.

The dowager had been sent to Scotland, as promised. Ursula watched from the parlor window as Damien saw her off in his coach—the woman's face had never relaxed its expression of muted rage. Ursula had to give her points for strength of conviction. Even with her whole family aligned against her, the dowager still believed that she had done no wrong.

By the fourth day of Will's self-imposed exile, Ursula's spirits had begun to flag noticeably. Judith suggested brightly that she busy herself around the house. But she found she had little heart for putting up preserves or organizing the books in the library or making lavender sachets for the linen closets.

This is ridiculous, she told herself as she stood in the kitchen beside Cook, covered from collar to hem with sticky strawberry jam. She was a horse breeder, not a blasted dessert chef. Without even untying her apron or washing her hands, she stormed out the back door, went marching through the garden, along the lane, and then up the hillside path.

She didn't even knock.

"It's time I had this out with you," she announced as she plunged into his parlor. "I've waited as long as any woman should have to wait. It's enough, Will Ridd."

He looked up from his notebook. "Have you fallen into the pudding?" he asked calmly, eyeing her smeared pinafore.

"Did you hear what I said? I am done with waiting. They are all afraid to come up here . . . they don't want to risk hurting you . . . or upsetting you again. Well, the Danovers may tread lightly around you . . . and so they should, I'm thinking. But I have done you no wrong, William Ridd, and so will not be shunted aside."

He closed the notebook and got up from his writing table. He was unshaven and looked a bit gaunt, she noted, and there was a quiet tension in his manner that made her very uneasy.

After gnawing his lip a moment, he opened his mouth as if to say something, then shut it again. "I'm still sorting things out," he said finally. And shrugged.

"That's it?" she asked incredulously. "I cool my heels for four days . . . and you shrug."

"There's been an outbreak of foot rot in some of the ewes. I've been distracted."

Ursula had a sudden, profound sympathy for Damien, back in his days of having to reason with his sheep-crazed bailiff.

She took a steadying breath. "I'm sorry I came storming in here, but we are all worried about you. The dowager's been sent to Scotland, if that's any solace. Besides, you can come down from your mountaintop and dine with us without having to make any proclamations."

He moved to the window and set his hand upon the crosspiece. "It's dark down there, Ursula." He looked at her over his shoulder. "I need to be up here in the light."

She knew he wasn't being cryptic; she understood perfectly what he meant.

"And am I part of that darkness now?" She'd managed to speak the question evenly, but her insides were quaking.

"I don't know." He leaned one shoulder against the window frame. "In the beginning I was afraid, because I knew you were bringing change to Myrmion. I had no idea, though, that there would be changes coming that would shatter my whole world."

She took a moment to congratulate herself—it was indeed change that he feared.

"I came here to sell my horses, Will. I'm not responsible for these other happenings."

When he met her gaze, his eyes were full of sadness. "Aren't you, my dear? There was one 'happening' that you alone created. It was when you made me want something I'd never dared to even dream about. And you offered it to me, and it was so . . . so fine and grand . . ." He paused.

"And . . . ?"

"And now it's over."

Ursula felt her breathing stop. Stop dead.

She put her chin up, striving for some dignity, even smeared with strawberry jam as she was. "Do I get the courtesy of an explanation?"

He looked away from her, out the window again. "You know," he mused, "it's odd how sometimes a poisoned seed will take root and flourish more easily than a healthy one."

"The dowager's innuendo," she bit out.

He gave her a wistful smile. "You're a quick study, Ursula. I'm going to miss that."

"So you believed her? After all that was revealed to you that afternoon, this kernel of untruth is what you carried away with you?"

"I carried it all away with me . . . but strangely, that was the part that hurt most. Just the thought of it. More than knowing what my grandmother and father did to me, more than knowing my mother had been virtually imprisoned. They were and still are strangers to me. No, it was having my trust in you wrenched away . . . and yet aching inside, whenever I remembered how good it felt to hold you as I slept, or how wonderful your mouth tasted—"

"Stop it!" she cried. "Do you think those things meant nothing to me?"

He almost sneered. "Oh, I'm sure you enjoyed them. As I pointed out, once upon a time, you are a lusty woman."

She stepped forward and hit him, slapped him as hard as she could muster. His head recoiled as his face tightened.

"You know there is nothing I can say," she raged, "nothing I can do, to prove that your wretched grandmother was wrong. That is why she is so incredibly evil, because she is clever with it. She swayed your father and overwhelmed your mother. She thwarted Damien with her poisonous insinuations." She flung one hand toward him. "Aha! You yourself just called her words a poisoned seed. If you think that, then you must know she was trying to corrupt you."

"I know what *she* was trying to do," he said hoarsely. "What I need to hear is what you were trying to do."

"I was trying to marry Damien!" she shouted back, nearly sobbing. "But his bailiff kept intruding in my thoughts and my dreams, until he was all I could see and hear and feel."

He grasped her by both elbows, his fingers digging into her flesh. "And you swear you didn't come up here with me the night of the party—didn't crawl into my bed and love me, make me love you until I could have wept from it—knowing that I was the Duke of Ardsley?"

She struggled to pull back. "I won't even dignify that question with an answer. You dishonor us both . . . that you could voice such suspicions and that I could be so cold-blooded and calculating."

He closed his eyes for a moment; she felt him trembling. Then his hands fell away. "Go now, Ursula. I need to think."

"Oh, no," she said. "You get up to terrible mischief when you do that." She nodded to the sofa. "You need to talk . . . *we* need to talk. Just sit a minute and I'll make us some tea."

She escaped into the kitchen, and then reeled back against the inner wall. Lord, that had been a near thing. It was fairly clear that he'd been testing her, and though she should be angry at him over it, she was just relieved to have cleared all her fences. Well, at least she hoped she had.

There was no possible way she could prove her integrity to Will, but it seemed a proper shouting match had at least allayed the worst of his suspicions. Oh . . . and a clout to the head.

Maybe Judith was right on that score after all.

* * *

Will sank down onto the sofa, all his festering doubts now leeched away. It had been despicable to put her on trial like that, but it was the only solution he could think of—especially considering his lack of experience with human females. Sheep dogs, now, you tested them again and again, until you were sure it was safe to leave them with your flock. Certainly his heart needed the same assurance before he placed it in her keeping.

No, he admitted to himself, that had been accomplished many days ago. Ursula possessed his heart, would always possess it. But to live like that, loving and doubting—as though the pure and the impure had somehow been fused together—it was unthinkable. That was the dowager's great dark gift, he saw, to so combine sound reason with sly insinuation that her victims believed, almost beyond questioning, that her slanders were the voice of truth.

But, unlike some members of his family, he *had* questioned the old woman's words, thank God. And so he'd goaded Ursula, as unfair as that was, to get an answer.

She had been combative, not cozening; her strongest persuasion had been the heat of her outraged feelings. She'd shown no dismay at the notion of losing the honey pot, only at the possibility of losing his love. If those fierce emotions she'd flung at him had been a schooled and polished performance, then she rivaled Mrs. Siddons as actress of the century.

Will went into the kitchen, where she was fussing over the tea tray. He slid his arms around her from behind and tucked his face into her neck. God, he had missed this— the feel of this woman under his hands, against his body.

"Forgive me," he said. "For doubting you, for hurting you."

She shifted to face him. "Of course," she said. "We all doubt at times, Will. But doubting should never make us strike out at the ones we love." She paused. "I think your family learned that . . . they doubted your sanity to the point that they sent you away forever."

"As I nearly forced *you* away. I'm not going to blame it on some wretched Danover family weakness. I was being a dolt, pure and simple." He gripped her by the arms. "Ah, Ursula . . . how did things between us get so tangled?"

She lowered her eyes. "I should have told you the night I first suspected. You'd have seen in my face how utterly stunned I was by the notion."

"I might have been better prepared to face my family if you had." He tipped her head up and stroked his knuckles over her throat. "Then again, I might have called you daft and taken you back to bed."

She caught his hand and raised it to her mouth. "I've missed you like the very devil," she said against his warm skin. "Every night I wake up reaching for you, needing to touch you . . . and . . . the bed feels a mile wide."

"I know . . ." His arms gripped her so tightly, she could barely breathe.

Without another word, he drew her through the parlor and into his bedroom. She was silent as he sat her on the edge of the bed. Her pinafore was sticky with strawberries, and he tsked as he knelt before her to untie it and gingerly pluck it away.

"Blame Judith," she said. "She's had me making preserves to keep from fretting myself into a state."

"You know I like you grubby." He ran his mouth along her wrist, kissing away the sweetness on her skin. "Grubby and delicious."

He kissed his way up to her face, where she had managed somehow to smear the jam on her cheek and brow. He licked at those sticky spots, making little noises of hunger and delight in the back of his throat. She thought she might swoon from the effect.

She untucked his shirt, then slipped it over his head. Her fingers reached around, to trace gently over the raised weals on his back. His eyes closed as his head relaxed to one side. She knew the marks no longer pained him, but they were sensitive to her touch. He nearly purred like a cat as she stroked him there.

"You were so brave," she murmured, "that afternoon in the parlor. I know how hard that was for you . . . to show your back to that old woman."

"I'm glad there was no childhood scar for her to see," he said gruffly. "Now she can spend the rest of her miserable life wondering . . . is he my grandson or is he an upstart?"

"That's fairly wicked of you."

"Or wickedly fair," he responded as he stretched out on the bed, then drew her down beside him. "But enough talk, Lady Roarke. We've other things to say to each other."

He slid over her, his welcome weight sinking her deep into the featherbed. And when he kissed her mouth—a long, slow, penetrating kiss—he tasted of sweet strawberries and sweeter passion.

She sighed and stretched, watching him dress from her comfortable hollow. He'd tugged his shirt carelessly over his head, and she had to reach out and smooth down the comical disarray of his hair. Her hand stopped abruptly at his crown as she was suddenly overcome by a craving for this man's child—one with wheat-gold hair and bright blue eyes, who would tease her into laughter and run to her arms each morning—and most likely drag puppies all through the house.

This desire was so strong, it left her with a sweet, sharp, needling sensation deep in her belly.

Will cocked his head. "What, little bear?"

She slid her hand along his softly bristled jaw. "I was thinking how much I want to have a child with you."

He pulled back a little. "Even if it were no more than a farmer's child?"

"So you've decided, then?" She tried to keep her tone light.

He fiddled with a buckle on his boot top, then got up. He went to his wardrobe and pulled out a fresh neckcloth. "I am nearly there," he said as he knotted it before his shaving mirror. He turned to peer at her. "What? No opinions, Lady Roarke?"

"It is fully your decision."

"But you want me to do this, don't you? You always wanted to snare a duke—"

She was about to flare up, when she realized he was grinning. "I would take you whether you were a tinker or a tradesman . . . a rag-and-bone man or the landlord of an inn."

His face lost some of its humor. "And I would rather be any of those than a blasted duke."

"It's a frightening prospect now, but in time—"

"Go ahead," he said. "I knew it was only a matter of minutes before you started in on me."

She snatched up her chemise and wriggled into it. It was difficult to have a proper argument when one was naked.

"Please listen, Will," she said, rising on her knees to face him. "When two people are allied as we are, they should help solve each other's problems. Roary shut me out . . . he refused to let me help him. I wanted us to go away from Dublin, somewhere where he would not be tempted to gamble. But he insisted he knew best—and then he died a week before Christmas, climbing the ice-slicked bell tower of the local church—on a bet."

"Bloody fool," he murmured.

"I am a strong-minded woman, and I believe that together we could have gotten past the worst of it. But Roary scoffed at my offer. As you are doing now . . ."

"No, not scoffing, not shutting you out. But you cannot know what a burden this is." His voice grew full of entreaty. "My life was my own, Ursula, simple and uncomplicated. That last day by the waterfall, I was plotting out our future on the farm . . . when we were called back to Myrmion. Called back to face this insanity." He sighed. "I see now that my dream would never have made you happy. You were meant for wider worlds."

"Will Ridd!" she cried, scrambling off the bed to stand toe to toe with him. "Don't you dare tell me what I was meant for. Do you think I lived like a princess at Roarke Stud? I was up at dawn every day, overseeing the stable lads, doctoring ailing horses, helping mares to foal. I attended auction sales, brangled with horse dealers. I am no hothouse lily that needs to be wrapped in silk. But I will tell you this—I do like silk and other fine things . . . and I don't think there is any shame in that, either."

His eyes danced in spite of his baiting mood. "Am I being a dolt again?"

She wrapped her arms around him. "You are just confused and overwhelmed."

"None of this would have happened if Damien Danover hadn't gotten that farfetched notion into his head. Even if it was the right notion."

"You can't keep holding them away. Damien wants his brother back, and I . . . I . . ."

"What do you want, little bear?"

"I want you to be happy."

He chuffed once. "If only it were that simple. Whichever way I turn, Ursula, I lose something. If I stay a sheep farmer, then I will spend my days wondering what I forfeited. If I accept the dukedom, I give up this life that has meant everything to me."

"What if we *were* to have a son? If you don't accept, he would be done out of his rightful inheritance."

"I've thought of that . . . I imagine you would like that for your child."

She shook him. "You have again painted me the grasping harpy. If I had a child with you, I would want him only to have his father's love. Title or no, that is all I would require."

"Then I will turn down Damien's offer."

"But—"

He raised one hand. "See? Already you object."

"I was going to point out," she said with great forbearance, "that it's only been four days. Take some time before you decide. Damien wants to show you your other properties. Once you've seen them, the farmland . . . the sheep . . . all the other livestock, you may change your mind."

His voice rose. "I want nothing to do with Damien or the Danovers, can't you understand that? I wish they would just take themselves off and leave us here together, as we were before. They mean nothing to me . . . they are strangers who have disrupted my life." He paused and shook his head wonderingly. "Though Damien has a good advocate in you. How strange that two weeks ago, you were *my* advocate with him. Still, there is nothing you can say that will convince me. Damien and his mother might not have betrayed me, but I cannot find it in me to care about them."

Ursula saw then what she would need to do. The thought of it nearly made her reel.

"I must go back to the house now," she said, pulling away from him.

"I think you should stay," he said. "After the dowager's revealing little speech, no one would be at all surprised if you took up residence here."

"I can't, Will."

"But it feels as though you've only just come back."

Her eyes sparked a little. "I never went anywhere.

You're the one who disappeared." She drew on her gown, fumbling with the tabs. "Anyway, I must consider your mother's sensibilities, even if you do not."

"One more reason to resent them," he muttered. "But you will do what you think best."

Just then she wanted to kick him. "I'll see you tomorrow," she said. "Who knows, maybe you'll even venture down to the house."

"Not until they have taken themselves off. Christ, with six properties, you'd think they could find somewhere else to stay."

She went to the front door, lingered there, but he did not come after her. Something inside her broke apart a little at his utter dismissal. She went out onto the porch and was halfway down the steps when he caught her from behind.

"Come to me tomorrow," he said urgently, tugging her back against him. "I'll take you out in the old duke's ketch. There's an island full of puffins in the Channel, you'd adore it. I rarely find time to sail . . . but I'm not a bad hand. Rigger taught me . . ." His voice drifted into silence.

She craned her head around. His eyes looked so lost.

The tears were already welling up in her throat; she had to get away now. She cupped his cheek for an instant. "Tomorrow, Will."

She made herself walk calmly down the path, forced herself not to look back.

Will waited all the next day, but she did not come to him. The following morning, he busied himself near the stable, hoping to waylay her. Imperator was out in the paddock; Will spared a few minutes to scratch his ears. He didn't hear Damien approaching until he was right beside him.

"Ursula left him behind for me," he said without elaborating.

He didn't need to. Will felt the dull pain that had been weaving itself around his heart lash inward, sharp and deadly.

"Yes, she's gone home to Ireland," Damien continued. "Went off at first light yesterday with Miss Falkirk in Squire Coltrane's coach. She said she was needed back at

Roarke Stud. Got to empty out the place for her husband's cousin."

Will was trying to hold on to his composure. He was damned if he was going to crumble in front of this man. But Damien merely put one arm over his shoulder and turned him toward the house. "She left a note for you, though. Come inside, there's a good fellow. You look as though you could use a drink."

He left Will alone in the study with a glass of brandy. Will took one long, burning swallow, drew in a deep breath, and then unfolded Ursula's note.

Dear Will, she'd written in an elegant sloping hand.

After a deal of soul searching, I have decided that my wisest course is to go back to Ireland. My presence at Myrmion was only serving to confuse you. There are answers you need to discover, decisions you need to make, that I was sorely tempted to influence. To be quite candid, I wanted you to take the title. My financial requirements, alas, have not changed. But now that I am out of your life, your choices will be wholly your own.

I will be busy clearing my effects from Roarke Stud, and then, perhaps, I will cast myself on the mercies of Dublin society. My friend, Lady Whitley, has written to tell me that a wealthy, widowed viscount with four children is there now, looking for a wife.

In case you are thinking of following me (and I do not believe you would be so imprudent) I must tell you that I cannot respect anyone who has not come to terms with his past. I married a man with one dark secret . . . I dare not ally myself with another who remains a cipher. If your memory were ever to return, why then, who knows what might be possible between us?

I wish good things for you, Will Ridd. There truly was a bond between us, and to borrow your own words . . . even if I never see you again, that bond will always be there. But life intrudes on these wistful dreams, and I must look after my own needs now.

Will wanted to cast the note into the fire, but feared that as the days passed he would doubt what he'd read and would need it to refresh his anger. Instead, he flung his brandy glass against the hearth. It made a satisfying crash that brought Damien charging in.

"Don't worry," Will said, as he stuffed the note into his waistcoat, "I am not running riot in here."

Damien touched his sleeve. "What did she say?"

"She left because I won't accept the title. I must give her points for honesty."

"And you won't have her on those terms?"

"Would any man?"

"I was willing to marry her . . . knowing full well she was after my blunt."

Will nodded curtly. "So you were. You are a better man than I am, it appears."

"No, just not so bloody high-minded. You spend enough years in the *ton,* you get used to women eyeing your purse. After all, they do have to insure their futures."

Will had never quite seen things this way, that even fine ladies depended on men for their very bread. But Ursula still had her stud horse in Ireland and the land he'd deeded her; she was not so destitute that she had to barter herself to the highest bidder.

"She also said she cannot respect me because I don't remember my past." He growled softly. "Can you believe she makes that a condition? That I attain something I've struggled in vain for twenty years to discover?"

Damien gave him a tight smile. "Perhaps she wants you whole again, Anthony William."

"She doesn't want me at all."

"I wager she would if you accepted the title. Won't you even consider it? It would gain you so much."

Will gripped him by the shirtfront. "You haven't a clue about the world you are asking me to leave behind. How it pleases me, validates me."

"Then show me," Damien said reasonably. "Let me discover your world, and I in turn will show you some of mine."

Will scowled as he pushed past him. "Not in this lifetime. I want nothing to do with the damned Danovers."

*   *   *

The following morning, as Will was setting out toward his property, Damien rode up beside him and asked if he couldn't tag along. Will knew what he was about, but said, "I can hardly stop you."

Damien dogged his heels the entire day, watching, learning, asking questions now and again. He showed up the next day and the next. By the end of the week, he was down off his horse working the dogs, seeming to take great pleasure in it. Will kept forgetting to scowl.

Another week passed, and Will began taking his meals at the house. The duchess played for them in the evenings and once had Will sit at the piano, to see if he recalled any of his childhood music lessons. "I can barely write a legible hand, madam," he protested, but then surprised himself when he was able to pick out a tune by the end of the night.

The duchess had ordered the portrait of her father sent from Peete Castle. When Will was called into the parlor to view it, he nearly swooned from shock. The duchess's memory had not been faulty—the earl was a golden-haired, broad-shouldered man, with piercing blue eyes and high cheekbones. It was as close to looking in a mirror as Will could have imagined.

He had just come in from riding, late the following afternoon, when Damien called him into the library. "There can be little question now that you are my brother," he said. "The rightful duke."

"It hardly matters. You are the one who was given all the preparation."

"Truth to tell, I never felt comfortable with that much responsibility. Maybe I always knew you'd come along and take over."

Will scratched his ear. "You seemed quite at home in the role when you first arrived here. Insufferably arrogant, as I recall."

Damien's mouth twitched. "I was trying to impress Lady Roarke with my command and my consequence."

"It definitely got my dander up," Will laughed softly. "I still can't believe I hit you."

"I can," Damien said. "I imagine if we had grown up together, we'd have enjoyed our share of fisticuffs. I loved you, but you still made my blood boil at times."

"Maybe that explains why we were always sparring when

you came back here. Still, I don't see how you could give it all up. You always seemed so . . . territorial. About Myrmion, about the sheep." He purposely didn't add Ursula's name to his list.

Damien took his time before responding. "I was very jealous of you. I saw a man who was passionate about something in his life. No matter that it was those blasted sheep, the passion was there. I felt trapped by my duty. You, on the other hand, seemed to relish yours."

"How can you compare my running a sheep farm to your duties as duke? I could afford to be so focused, Damien, because my world was so small."

"No," he said earnestly. "Your world was London, Leeds, Brighton, Bath—and Boston."

Will still looked dubious.

"No, listen to me. I once asked Ursula why everyone thought so highly of you. She said it was because you knew how to think outside the accepted channels. That you were the sheep dog, not one of the sheep."

"She said that about me?"

Damien nodded, then smiled ruefully. "I am one of the sheep, Anthony William."

"No—"

"And that is why you must take the title. Because if you could make a forgotten little farm and a worn-out little town in Devon flourish, if you could send goods out into the world that are finer than any of their kind—well, by God, just think what you could do in the Lords."

Will felt himself blanche. "I am not setting foot in Parliament. I—I can barley speak in front of the weavers' guild."

"Oh, tush, tush. You've waxed eloquent to me defending your sheep. Surely affairs of state would stir you—almost equally."

Will cast about for something to say. He felt the trap closing about him. "I . . . I should warn you . . . I often find myself with Republican sympathies."

Damien burst out laughing, then clapped his hands slowly. "Oh, how splendid! I must write to Grandmama in Scotland and tell her. She will choke on her oatmeal." He set a hand on Will's shoulder. "You forget you won't be alone in this. I am not running off to America . . . you can look to me for any guidance."

"And what of the *ton?* How will they react to an up-start duke?"

"With much blatant toadying . . . to your face. And what do you care if they talk behind your back?"

Will tried a new tack. "What about you, Damien? How will you fare with your social consequence so reduced?"

He shrugged negligently. "If they dare to mock me, I will bring the wrath of Miss Judith Coltrane down on their heads. Well, I do hope she'll be Lady Damien by then. But you see my point."

"Frightening concept," Will agreed. "Have the two of you set a date?"

"No, the lady requires courtship, if you can credit it. Twelve years wasted, and she still wants to be wooed." He shifted on his feet and gave Will a probing look. "And speaking of the ladies—"

"Oh, no. I'm not discussing that situation. Not with anyone."

"Not even Ursula, from what I hear."

Will glowered. "Has she been writing to you? Well, that's a damned irritating thing to discover."

"We are business associates, in case you have forgotten. I've just finalized the sale of her horses. My income will be reduced, of course, so the revenues from the stud farm will come in very handy. For one thing, Judith has suddenly discovered a taste for fashionable bonnets."

"Stay here," Will said suddenly. "Keep the stud at Myr-mion. Even if I decide to take the title, I will deed the estate to you. I can buy some property near here; we will be neighbors then, whatever I decide."

Damien's eyes brightened. "Done," he said. "But you still have the property across the stream."

"It currently belongs to Lady Roarke . . . whom I am not going to discuss."

Damien grumbled at this; then his cheeks narrowed. "Will, I've just thought of something—you *must* take the title. If you don't, you will be perpetrating as great a lie as our grandmother did. Just think about that."

"I realize that." He added softly, "I am afraid, Damien. As I have never been before. Not even in Chenowyth did I feel the future looming over me." He laughed bleakly. "Most likely because I had no future in that place." He reached out and grasped his brother's hand. It was pale against his own sun-browned fist. "Listen to me, this is your chance . . . to do what you were unable to do for me the last time we were together as children." He murmured intently, *"Free me, Damien."*

Damien swallowed hard. "This *would* free you . . . to follow any dream you chose."

"It's not a dream to me, it's a burden. One I do not want. I am a farmer."

"So was the Regent's father. Farmer George, they called him. He did all right as king."

Will nearly groaned. "He went mad, Damien! And so shall I if I have to reinvent myself again. I've lived four lives so far—duke's child, asylum inmate, lad for hire, and now bailiff. I think that's b-bloody well enough for one man."

He grabbed up his hat from the library table and went striding from the room.

Damien sat down and leaned his head wearily on his hand. It was clearly time to bring in the big guns.

Judith knocked on the cottage door and Will called out to her from his chair in the parlor. She came inside carrying a parcel. "I've brought you some of the latest woolens . . . they're using a wonderful new dye, a sort of silvery blue. It looks especially nice woven into a lady's shawl."

She spread the samples out across his sofa. "Such a lovely color . . . rather reminds me of Lady Roarke's eyes."

"Oh, blast," Will said as he threw the book he'd been reading onto the floor. "No one ever faulted you for subtlety, Judith. So my caring brother has sicced you on me to prod at me about Ursula."

She puffed up dramatically. "I would never have the effrontery to do such a thing. I was merely making an observation." She held up one of the shawls and dangled it enticingly before his face, like Salome of the Single Veil. He snatched it away from her with a curse.

"Oh, come on," she said as she settled on his footstool. "*I* miss her. You must miss her dreadfully."

He glared at her as he reached down for his book. "I am not going to discuss it."

"No, you will sit here like a great festering lump, while some merry-faced Irishman comes courting her."

"Stop it, Judith. I will not be baited."

She rose again and began to waltz around the room, singing softly, "A dozen roguish, rakish silver-tongued Irish lords . . ."

"Enough!" This time the book bounced as it hit the carpet.

Her brows rose. "You sounded just like Ardsley. Or at least the way he used to sound. See, Will, you can do it if you try. It's not so bad . . . and if you hate being a duke, you can just hole up in one of your many ancestral homes and become an eccentric." She grinned at him. "I could give you lessons."

He grinned back at her in spite of himself. She was in tormenting-sister mode, which always coaxed him out of his black moods. "You don't look very eccentric in that elegant bonnet."

She preened a little. "It's tiresome, but Damien seems to prefer me a bit fashionable." She poked him in the arm. "Anyway, wasn't it you who said, right in this very parlor, that I needed to go away from here and find myself a husband? I did it, Will, though I never had to leave to find Damien. And you didn't have to go anywhere to find Ursula. How could you have been so clever back then and so very dense right now?"

"You don't know what she said in that letter," he muttered darkly.

"Oh, and I suppose that means you just let go of her without a fight."

He raked one hand through his hair. "I believe she knew I was the real duke, just as the dowager hinted, that she gave herself to me only to cement her chance at the title."

She sank to her knees and clasped his hands. "You can't believe Ursula turned to you in an instant, once she realized Damien was no longer the catch of the county. There *are* such fickle, grasping women . . . but that is not how I would label someone who stayed by her gaming-mad husband for eight years and worked to keep his farm going."

He shook his head. "She claims she doesn't want me as I am . . . she wants me whole. Remembering my past for myself . . . not just taking everyone else's word for it. Gad, sheep are so much less complicated than people. Six weeks ago, I was happy and content. Now, everything is all turned about."

"Dreadful," she agreed. "You found your family, discovered you were a duke—and fell headlong in love with a beautiful, charming woman. Truly dreadful."

He laughed under his breath. "Gad, I am a pathetic specimen."

She nodded slowly. "Only when you are not thinking clearly. And it's love does that to a person, not any ducal titles. Let me share a secret with you, Will . . . I think it's time." She coughed once. "Ursula didn't write that letter . . . well, not by herself. She wrote most of it, but Barbara helped, and I added the bit about the widowed viscount. I was quite proud of—"

"Why are you telling me this now?" He'd leapt up from his chair. "Why did you wait? Good God, this changes everything!"

Judith gazed heavenward. "She was buying time for you, you great lummox. Time to get reacquainted with your family. She said that she'd already come between master and man. She didn't want to be the diversion that kept you from spending time with Damien and your mother. She thought if she turned away from you, you would have to turn to them . . . which you did."

He shot her a sideways glance. "Is this the sort of thing men are supposed to know about women . . . that they say one thing, while they are thinking the opposite?"

She gave him a toothy smile. "I see you're figuring it out nicely. It would be refreshing if you turned out to be one of those men who didn't need to be threatened with a stout club before your brain engaged with your heart."

Will cogitated for all of five seconds. "I think it's time I went to Ireland," he said. He swept up the silvery shawl from the sofa. "And I'll bring this to Ursula, shall I? To remind her of Myrmion and the Pride of Stratton Valley—in case she's forgotten."

She nodded enthusiastically. "Oh, yes. The Pride of Stratton Valley is exactly what she needs. And now, Anthony William, about this matter of the title . . ."

Chapter Seventeen

*D*amien had become determined to drag Will to every spot they'd ever shared as children, hoping to jog his memory. Two days before Will was to leave for Ireland, his brother took him to the waterfall, with Titan tagging along. He explained that this had been one of their favorite hiding places whenever they'd escaped from Rigger. Will was not impressed that he had rediscovered the dell as an adult; anyone would be enchanted by its magic.

Damien tugged off his boots, rolled up his breeches, and splashed into the water. It did recall a memory to Will— that of Ursula wading through the pool the day he'd first kissed her.

"You and I used to hunt here for tadpoles and killy fish," Damien said. "The water is so clear, you can see anything swimming past."

"Mmm," said Will as he drowsed in the warm sun. He recalled Ursula's skin that day—it had tasted of green grass and wild heather.

"And there was one time . . . we found the most amazing creature here. A two-headed turtle. You gave him some clever name . . . dashed if I can think of it."

"Cerberus," Will murmured, only a nod away from sleep. "Though Cerberus . . . had . . . three heads."

"That's exactly what you said the last ti—"

Will heard Damien give a great shout as he came splashing up from the pool. And then his brother's wet hands were dragging him to his feet, pummeling him on the back. "By God, Anthony William . . . you did it again!"

He blinked. "Did what?"

"You remembered!"

Will's face split into a wide grin of astonishment. He grasped Damien by the arms and sputtered out, "You wanted to bring the turtle home with you . . . but I warned you that Rigger would know then that we'd sneaked off from our lessons."

"Exactly!"

"I remembered! I *remembered!*" he shouted out, his face raised to the sun, while Damien stood there beaming and Titan danced around them barking wildly.

Damien cuffed his brother on the arm and said in a voice gone gruff with emotion, "Welcome back, Tony. Welcome home."

During the crossing to Ireland, Will continued to recollect more bits and pieces of his former life. Just as Damien had predicted, all it needed was for one tiny detail to be consciously recalled and the floodgates of memory opened wide. He felt again his mother's soft embrace and heard his father's wry laughter. He remembered the amber-eyed boy who'd viewed him as a hero.

They were not all happy memories. He knew again the pain of the spotted fever, and the subsequent nightmare of the recurring fits. He experienced anew the terror of being taken away in the dead of night by a man he'd trusted implicitly and left behind in a strange, frightening place. Every beating he'd endured, every punishment that had been dealt him, he lived again.

But in reliving those dark experiences, he'd been able to move past them . . . not by closing his mind to their horror as he'd done when he was eleven, but by accepting them. They'd made him tough and resilient, he knew, in a way that Damien would never be.

But tough or not, Will was still not certain he was equipped to be duke.

Rigger Gaines stood beside him now at the ship's rail. They'd begun to rebuild their relationship. In accepting his past, Will had also come to terms with his friend's betrayal. Will had been a servant of sorts, but he'd never served a master, not the way Rigger had.

As they will, so shall we do. Rigger had done as he'd been ordered by the duke—and then tried everything in his power to undo it. He had surely redeemed himself over the past fifteen years. It was enough for Will.

They hired a coach in Dublin and tooled along the dramatic, undulating coastline. Damien had told Will that Ursula was renting a farm in Howth, not far from Roarke Stud. When they got to the rugged track that led to the farm, Will signaled the driver to stop. He leaned from the window, pushing away the coach's third, intensely curious, occupant and read the hand-lettered sign that hung on the rickety gate. *Touchstone Stud.*

He was smiling as they continued on. This was a very good omen.

The stone farmhouse was small, barely more than a cottage, with a cobbled stable behind it. The grounds around the house were overgrown and weedy—Will mused to himself that she could have used a sheep or two—and the whole aspect was depressingly run-down. Still, the fences looked stout enough, and the turf inside them was an impossible blue-green that looked so rich, it might even put Devon grass to shame.

Barbara came to the door as they pulled up in front of the cottage. Her face broke into a smile as Will descended; she positively beamed when Rigger climbed out after him. The third passenger evoked little response from her, save a shake of the head, since he'd darted out of the vehicle and taken off over the nearest hill. Will sighed.

"It took you long enough," Barbara said as Will came up the flagged walk. "I warned her that letter was a mite harsh."

"It worked, though," Will said as he clasped her hands. "I am returned to the bosom of my family, just as she wished. And I must say, Miss Falkirk, Ireland has put a bloom in your cheeks."

She blushed. "That's more than I can say for my girl. Peaky doesn't begin to describe her."

Will leaned his head down to her. "I think I've got the cure for that, ma'am."

"Then away with you now," she said. "You'll find her beyond that hill . . . she's working the Magpie. That horse is the only thing that's kept her from fretting herself to flinders. Meantime, I'll have myself a comfortable cose with Mr. Gaines." She looked past Will and smiled at Rigger.

"You do that," Will said as he headed toward the path,

musing to himself that romance was so thick in the air, you could practically cut it with a knife.

Ursula had just finished lunging the Magpie. It helped to keep his lameness at bay and got her outside in the sun. As she latched the paddock gate, the horse came to rub his face against the weathered, splintery wood. It was not what he'd been used to at Roarke Stud, but then, they'd all had to make compromises.

She'd sold everything, her dresses, her books, even the Roarke diamonds, paste though they were, to afford the rent on this shabby little farm. But already horsemen were taking note. One of the Magpie's sons was the current favorite for the Derby and the St. Leger, and several others were being touted as serious contenders. The more often they won, the more word would spread of her crippled stallion and his amazing get.

She was leaning on the fence, stroking Maggie's nose, when she heard a sharp bark from the direction of the house. One of her neighbors raised wolfhounds, but they rarely ventured onto her land. She scanned the hillside, and was startled when a black-and-white collie came bounding into view.

Her heart began to hammer, even as she chided herself for her foolishness. This couldn't be one of Will's dogs careering toward her with an eager, delighted expression on his face. But as he drew closer, she recognized Titan. He flung himself at her, nearly becoming airborne in his excitement, and tried to lick her all over. She wrestled him down, scrubbing at his ears, her heart soaring. Only one person could have brought him here. The only person in the world she wanted to see.

Once Titan had gotten his fill of roughhousing, he slipped into the paddock and began to herd the horse, moving him incessantly from place to place. The Magpie seemed to think this was a capital game, and began to feint back at the dog, splaying his forelegs and snorting.

Ursula dragged her eyes away from their antics, but was afraid to look back toward the hill. What if Rigger was the one who had brought Titan here? What if Will was still back at Myrmion?

But then she caught sight of a tall man coming along the path. That graceful, long-legged stride was unmistakable. She saw that he was dressed like a top o' the trees Corinthian, the gem-bright topboots, the butter-soft buckskins, a low-crowned beaver angled over his blond hair. She caught a glimpse of a patterned waistcoat as the sides of his long driving coat swung open. He was polished and gleaming, and the sight of him was more than mortal woman should have to bear.

And here she stood, dressed like a tinker's wife, in a worn calico gown and Roary's tattered hunting jacket. She hadn't even done anything with her hair that morning, save tie it back with a bit of faded ribbon. She grumbled to Maggie, "Isn't it just like the man to outshine me?"

He was striding along the paddock fence now, his face stern. Her insides quaked a little, in fear that he had come only to task her over her letter. Then she realized he was frowning at the dog, who had slithered under the fence and was now capering around his boots.

"So much for the element of surprise," he drawled. "He just wouldn't wait . . . not that I blame him."

Before she could make any response, he closed in on her. Sweeping his hat off, he sent it spinning onto the grass, and then clasped her around the waist with both hands. He lifted her right off her feet, holding her there above him as though she were a featherweight.

"Will!" She was laughing, and then made nearly breathless when she saw the ardent hunger in his eyes.

"God, you are a tonic to me, Ursula."

He let go of her—she felt herself falling—but he caught her hard against him before her feet touched down. The next instant he'd swung around and thrust her back against a fence post. And, oh, Lord, when he leaned into her and kissed her, he took her mouth with such force that it wouldn't have mattered if the earth had been beneath her feet, because the heat of his onslaught would have swept her right off them.

She'd managed to get her arms around him and had crooked one leg half around his calf; she clung there, kissing him back . . . urgent, openly needy, and thrilled beyond anything.

"I'm sorry . . ." she gasped out between kisses. "Letter . . . idiotic idea . . . God, Will . . . I missed you . . ."

"No . . . I was . . . nitwit . . . dolt . . . dammit . . . where are your buttons?"

He had pushed her coat down off her shoulders and was fumbling at the back of her gown. She heard the ancient fabric tear, and then his mouth was on her throat and working its way over her breast to the edge of her chemise. She thought she would die right there in that scrubby field.

But then his face suddenly tensed, and he lowered her gently to the ground.

"*A-h-h* . . ." He threw his head back, drawing in a ragged breath. "This is not the way I had planned it. Not taking you up against a paddock fence."

"Not the welcome you had in mind for Lady Roarke, hmm?"

He laughed down at her. "Don't quote my brother at me, wench. I was thinking more along the lines of a nice Irish featherbed." He laced his hand in her hair, and his voice softened to a caress. "How are you, Ursula?"

"Better now. Much better."

"You did a very wise thing, leaving when you did. You told me once that I rarely thank people . . . but I came to Ireland just so I could thank you—from the depths of my heart."

Her face fell. "And that's all you came for?"

"No," he said as he tidily tugged the front of her gown up and drew her coat around her shoulders. "Of course not." He leaned in close. "I've come to invite you to a wedding at Myrmion."

She managed an enthusiastic smile. "So, Damien and Judith have finally set the date?"

"No, they appear to be waiting for the return of Halley's comet or some such idiocy. That's not the wedding I mean."

She cocked her head. "Oh, has Rigger come with you? Is he going to ask Barbara to marry him?"

"Ursula," he said patiently, "who do you think is being the dolt now?"

She showed her teeth. "I have to say, even Ardsley did a better job of it than you are doing."

He gave her an odd, secretive look. "And which Ardsley would that be?"

Then he grinned widely, and she saw the answer in his face.

"Oh, Will!" she cried, leaping up like an eager puppy. "You didn't?"

He bowed with a flourish. "You have the honor to be addressing His Grace, the ninth Duke of Ardsley."

She curtsied elegantly, then grabbed for his hand. "What finally convinced you to take the title?"

"Several things. First of all, I had a conversation with Snap. No, don't goggle at me . . . I saw you talking to yon fine horse. You see, she reminded me about bloodlines. A herd dog is bred with the instinct to tend sheep. I realized that I had been bred with an instinct to improve things . . . I made Myrmion prosper, built up my flock to be the finest in Devon, helped Stratton back on its feet. It's what I do best . . . and being a duke doesn't mean I have to stop."

"Of course it doesn't. It just means you can work on a grander scale. But you said several things convinced you. What else?"

He leaned forward, set his mouth on her ear, and said jubilantly, "I remembered, little bear."

She threw her arms around him and hugged him with all her strength. "That is the best news of all, my sweetest, dearest Will."

"Damien calls me Anthony William. He still wants me to be his Tony."

He explained how he and his brother had gone to the waterfall, how her two-headed turtle had triggered his memory until every last detail of those missing years came back to him.

"Damien and your mother must be so happy. And Rigger? Have you forgiven him?"

"Water over the dam," he said. "He's about somewhere, sparking Miss Falkirk."

He took her arm and drew her to the gate. "Now show me the Maggie, Ursula. You are a fine-looking woman, but you know how I feel about blooded horses."

She huffed a little as she led him into the paddock. Magpie came over at once and started snuffling her pockets for a treat. Will ran his hands over the horse's shoulders, along his chest, and then down to his deformed foot.

"You can see there," she said as Will stood upright, "where the hoof is concave. He's never been able to put his full weight on it at a gallop, not the way racing demands, though he's sound most of the time. It helps to lunge him, and I restrict his sweet feed, so there's little chance of founder. I even ride him occasionally, whenever I—" She stopped short when she realized Will was leering at her comically. "What?"

He tsked. "And you used to mock me for going on about my sheep."

"He is rather special to me."

"I notice he's marked like a sheepdog—black with a white blaze and stockings. A real beauty," he said, gazing down at her. "Just like his mistress. Who, by the way, has not yet answered my question."

She scratched her chin. "I don't recall you actually *asking* me anything, Will Ridd."

"Shall I get down on one knee?"

"Mind the dung, if you do," she said impishly, and then danced back when he reached out for her.

"Gad, you are going to be such a trial to me. I thought facing the House of Lords would be my worst challenge. But to have a duchess who shows me no respect whatsoever . . ."

"Except in the dark," she reminded him. "Always in the dark."

"Then come here," he said, holding out his arms. She walked into them. "Now say you will marry me . . . because I love you and need you . . ." His gaze wandered off to the Magpie. "And because that is one extraordinary horse you own—"

"Will!"

He was almost falling down with giddy laughter. "Sorry, sweetheart, but you do get such an expression on your face when I tease you. It could pierce Toledo steel."

"I suppose I'd better marry you. *Someone* has to have a little dignity."

"Hang dignity." His voice lost some of its mirth. "I have no intention of becoming another dour duke. I lost six years of my life in Chenowyth, Ursula, and I've decided that the only way to ameliorate that is to grasp as much happiness as I can. And it begins and ends with you."

"There," she said as she nuzzled his throat, "that was very nicely said." Her voice lowered. "You know, Will, I've been thinking a lot about what your grandmother put you through. In spite of all that, you've got the stoutest spirit of anyone I've ever met . . . and the best nature. The dowager might not have *named* Anthony Danover the duke, Will, but I believe she made him one, all the same."

She could have sworn he blushed.

"Well, my first official duty as duke will be to have you painted—

Oh, here it comes, she thought wryly. *The stiff official portrait, the white gown, the glittering diamonds—*

"Exactly as you are right now," he continued, "with your hair all coming down, in that tatty coat . . . with the Magpie at your shoulder. My little bear and her touchstone."

And that's when she knew it was going to be all right. So very right.

She stroked her hand over his face—which had regained its look of winsome innocence—and whispered, "*You're* my touchstone, Anthony William."

"And you are mine. More than the sheep, more than Myrmion. You brought me back, Ursula, you made me remember what it felt like to be loved . . . what it felt like to have caring arms close about me, and someone's heart beating next to mine. That damned turtle might have triggered my memory, but the first stirrings began with you."

"And the things I said in that letter . . . you're sure you forgive me? No poisoned seeds floating around waiting to sprout?"

"Not a one. Judith explained it all to me. Oh, wait a bit . . . she sent you this." He drew a silvery blue shawl from the deep pocket of his coat. "The Pride of Stratton Valley."

She rubbed it against her face and grinned up at him. "That's what Judith calls you . . . God's truth."

"She's daft."

Ursula shook her head. "She might be the wisest woman I know."

His hands settled on her shoulders. "Damien said *you* called me a sheep dog. I was very flattered. And so I say the wisest woman is the one who trusts her sheep dog to come home. I came to you, Ursula . . ." His bright gaze was bluer than the Irish sky and brimming with love. "Because wherever you are is my home."

Hand in hand they left the paddock and made their way along the path toward the farmhouse. Titan brought up the rear, his tail waving like a banner, the new duke's elegant hat—slightly mauled—held tight between his teeth.

Will Ridd always said sheep dogs were the smartest breed on the planet.

That Falkirk woman was right, the dowager muttered as she pulled her shawl tight around her. It was plaguey cold in Scotland. Even now, in late spring, the daytime mist was chilling and the night air almost frosty.

She took a yellowed paper from her jewel box, then shifted her chair closer to the fire before settling there. For twelve years, since the day the letter arrived, she read it every night before retiring. It was her penance, leaving scourge marks on her soul far worse than those on Will Ridd's back. It never failed to chill her—even more than the mist that swirled outside the windows of the manor house where she was virtually incarcerated.

Her hooded eyes now scanned the note of condolence, even though the words had been long ago imprinted on her memory.

> *Most sorry for the loss of your son . . . I was attending physician at Chenowyth during the first few years of your grandson's stay . . . Anthony was a bright, winning child—though so troubled by his situation that he developed a severe stammer. He had no impairment of the mind, however, that I could detect, other than suffering an occasional falling-down fit. I have observed that these episodes sometimes occur less frequently as children mature, and I was happy to see noticeable improvement in his condition during my time there.*
>
> *I returned to Chenowyth five years later to ask after the boy with the stammer—you see, I had never quite forgotten him—and was told that he had been recently taken away by a kindly man and looked to be in good hands.*
>
> *. . . It was my understanding that Anthony was your*

*late son's heir . . . I take leave to wonder, ma'am,
if you have somehow lost track of him or had been
mistakenly informed that he died in the fire at
Chenowyth. If this is the case, and you wish to locate
your grandson, you must find the man who took
him, a spare, black-haired Devonshire man of middle
years. Perhaps someone with a connection to your
family . . .*

She lowered the letter with a sigh. For years after receiving it she'd waited for Rigger Gaines to come to her, to present her with her addled grandson, now recovered, and prove her despicable before the whole world. Even though he'd been paid plenty to keep quiet, she knew he wouldn't hesitate to attack her that way. She doubted he would ever forgive her for ordering him to betray Anthony.

But Rigger had never contacted her, except to occasionally keep her abreast of the doings at Myrmion. She eventually convinced herself that he was not the one who had taken the boy. And when none other came forward with the lost heir, she began to breathe easier.

Until the day Damien and that managing Coltrane woman came to fetch her to Myrmion.

There in the parlor she'd finally learned why Rigger had never confronted her—the boy he'd taken from the asylum had no memory of his past. The groom hadn't known for sure if it was Anthony he'd rescued or a stranger.

It was ironic that for all her suspicions of Rigger's involvement, she hadn't connected Will Ridd with her missing grandson, even though Gaines himself had sponsored his appointment as bailiff. It had never occurred to her that a duke's son would let himself fall so low.

Now the truth of what she'd done had come out . . . and she was a pariah to her family. Merely because she had tried to protect and preserve the Danover name. Did they think she was some kind of monster who had sent away her clever, golden-haired grandson without just cause? Did they think it had not been a torture for her to drug the boy with laudanum, then watch the groom bundle him in a blanket and carry him from the house in the dead of—

A sharp pain zigzagged through her chest. Her eyes opened wide with shock. She never got palpitations. *Never!*

But the lancing pain grew ever stronger. She groped for her water glass, fumbled and sent it spilling onto the carpet. *"N-o-o!"* she cried silently.

As the aged paper fell from her fingers and wafted to the hearth, a rasping sigh whispered through the room. "Anthony . . . forgive me."

And then all was still, save for the gentle crackling of the fire as the doctor's letter was consumed.

SIGNET
Regency Romances from

ANDREA PICKENS

"A classy addition to the ranks
of top Regency authors."
—Romantic Times

A Diamond in the Rough   0-451-20385-2
A young woman defies convention by posing as a
young male caddie on a golf course—only to fall for
an English lord and score in the game of love.

The Major's Mistake   0-451-20096-9
Major Julian Miranda accepts a long-term army
commission after catching his wife in what appears
to be a very compromising position. Seven years
later the couple meets again. But will it be pride—or
passion—that wins the day?

To order call: 1-800-788-6262